DEAD MAN'S JURY

ISBN-13: 978-1-63696-405-8

ISBN-10: 1-63696-405-2

Cover design by: Damonza

Printed in the United States of America

www.righthouse.com

www.instagram.com/righthousebooks

www.facebook.com/righthousebooks

twitter.com/righthousebooks

David
ARCHER

Oliver
BLACK

DEAD

A slain father.

MAN'S

An orphaned son.

JURY

Only a lawyer can help them both.

A **Ben Carter** LEGAL THRILLER

RIGHTHOUSE

1

HOW DIFFERENT WOULD THINGS HAVE BEEN IF I HADN'T stopped for the boy? From the moment I saw him, I knew I had to, as any normal person would have. And yet, something was building inside me, a weird kind of apprehension the moment I pulled over. Call it intuition, sixth sense, or maybe just nerves, but the second our eyes met, I knew my life would never be the same.

The funny thing is, I shouldn't have been on that specific stretch of road in the first place. A dark room and a bottle of bourbon would have been just fine after my latest client ended up with a fifteen-year stretch down in Belmont Correctional. That's a different story entirely and one I know the prosecutor will be telling his grandchildren for a long time to come, but it hurt nonetheless and not one I want to be telling anytime soon.

Camping had never really been my thing, but my assistant, Grace, had suggested it would do me good after the loss, and before I knew it, there I was, setting up a tent on the side of Lake Erie. I was booked in for five nights, made it through the first, and immediately knew I wouldn't get through a second. And so, like any non-camper anxious to get back to their apartment to save what was left of a dreary weekend, I hit the road as early as humanly possible, and that's where my life turned on a dime.

The kid looked no more than seven or eight from a distance, but as I got closer, things took a turn—and I mean the kind that sends your head spinning. You see, shortly before I pulled up beside him, recognition began to set in, and by the time I actually stopped the car, I knew exactly who he was, right down to his name.

When you're a criminal lawyer, you tend to notice things, and by things, I mean cases from right across the country. News bulletins, front-page newspaper stories, website links, you name 'em. I loved reading headline-grabbing cases as much as some people loved watching true crime stories, and at times, it provided insights into my own cases. Call it *off*-the-job training, if you will, some free pointers from attorneys who I most likely would never meet.

The second I pulled up next to the kid, chills ran down my spine as I immediately recognized him. The chills didn't exactly come from identifying him but rather because the kid had already been on my mind in a round-about way. It wasn't so much him that I knew but rather his father, a man named Harold Dunning, a name I'd been hearing on the news for the better part of a week.

Up until just a few days before, I'd never heard the name Harold Dunning before, not until his arrest made headline news around the state. Dunning had been taken in for drug trafficking and murder and should have remained in a holding cell, but somehow he'd managed to escape custody during the night and ended up dead in some random warehouse. The twist came when Dunning's son and the child's temporary caregiver also went missing during the night. Security footage from the woman's home showed a man abducting the pair of them just an hour after the escape, and it definitely wasn't the escapee. The news bulletins had been talking about the execution-style murder all morning, and having recognized the name, I'd been following them myself. So how did I recognize the kid?

The first time I ever laid eyes on Dunning was via footage shot for a Pittsburgh news outlet that had filmed him at the time of his initial capture. What made the vision so much more gut-wrenching was the child hiding behind Dunning, little Max, too scared to cry as he clung to his father's leg. Police eventually convinced the father to hand his son over before they proceeded to arrest him. From what I understood through subsequent news reports was that with no mother and no other family, the seven-year-old had ended up in the care of Child Services while his father faced some serious allegations. Imagine my surprise when I found him standing on the side of a road inside Evangola State Park.

I could barely contain the hundreds of questions racing through my head as I pulled over and climbed out of my Mustang. The kid stood his ground as he stared at me wide-eyed. The fear in his face was something I'll never forget, his entire body frozen in place as I slowly approached him. I expected him to run, but thankfully, he didn't.

"Hey, there, fella," I said, ensuring I lowered both my voice and my stance while trying to get close to him. He didn't answer. "Your name's Max, isn't it?" With his eyes fixed on me, he didn't move a muscle as he watched me slowly approach.

That was when I remembered one final detail about the kid and the reason why he was so quiet during his father's very public arrest. He'd been classified deaf and mute, and according to one report I'd read, he had never spent a single day in school. What little he *had* learned was taught to him by his grandmother, but she'd passed the previous year.

"I'm not going to hurt you, OK?" I reached the point where I knew I should stop to try and maintain a bit of distance until he got used to me. With crazy thoughts still running through my head, answers weren't coming quickly enough, and to top off the current situation, I noticed an uncomfortable dark patch on the front of his pants that tracked about halfway down his left leg.

Looking up and down the road, I couldn't see any signs of life, probably one of the reasons the kid had been dumped there, the only logical conclusion I could come up with. I tried to remember what I knew about the kid's situation once I knelt down, but other than the arrest, there wasn't much to go on. My only real question was how he managed to end up on the side of the road a hundred miles from his previous known location after being abducted from Child Services.

Two things suddenly occurred to me, and neither eased my mind. The first was that I needed to get him out of sight. If whoever dumped him came back and saw me with him, then things might take a decidedly dark turn. The second was that he needed a change of pants and sooner rather than later. But first, I needed him to trust me.

Yes, I should have called the cops right then and there, but my instincts overpowered common sense as something told me there was more to this than met the eye. If I didn't report finding him, then I'd be up for any number of charges myself, including some that had the potential to put me behind bars, and yet...something told me not to do it.

Remembering I had a candy bar stashed inside my coat pocket, I pulled it out and showed it to him, essentially going against every bit of legal advice my logical side was telling me.

"You hungry?" Kids and candy, right? He didn't move immediately, but he did shift his gaze from me to the candy bar and back again. I slowly shook it a couple of times, hoping I didn't appear too creepy, and then opened the top of it to show him the actual chocolate. If anybody *had* driven by at that very moment, I can't say the scene would have appeared favorable, but what choice did I have?

Finally, I saw his foot inch forward, pull back once,

and then take a step toward me. I reached out a little farther, and that's when he finally snatched it from my fingers. A second later, he hungrily bit into it and dropped his defenses.

"My name is Ben," I said after ensuring that he was watching me. I didn't know if he knew how to lip-read, but it was all I had. He watched me as he chewed, the Snickers bar slowly disappearing. I waited until he finished the last bite before pointing to my car. "We need to go," I said. "Go get help."

When he shoved the last bit into his mouth, I held out my hand for the trash, and he surprised me by stepping forward and dropping the wrapper into it. To try and build some more rapport, I smiled and made a fist that I held out. He looked at it and after a few seconds, made his own and bumped it against mine. Fist-bumps...one of the world's great ice-breakers.

"We need to go," I said, again pointing at my car, and this time he gave me a nod. It was a shy one that barely registered, but it was enough for me. I walked to my car, opened the passenger door, and waved him inside.

I can't say that getting him into the car changed anything for me as millions of questions continued to circle around my head. How could a kid linked to a crime scene a hundred miles away be standing all alone on the side of a random road in Upstate New York? The biggest question of all was what to do next.

The problem with being a lawyer was that I viewed the world very differently from the regular person on the street. Call it a suspicious mind or maybe just a professional side effect, but something had changed in me since taking up the law. How an LA boy ended up in Upstate New York is another intriguing tale and one I may share with you a little further along. For now, though, I had some serious issues to contend with.

Max grabbed a seat in the back and buckled up the moment I closed the door. He even managed a reserved smile once I climbed back in, and after another fist-bump, we got underway. Where to, I still didn't know. What I did consider a priority was to get the kid a change of pants. I couldn't imagine it being very comfortable sitting in his own urine for God knew how long, and I figured it might go some way to building a bit more trust between us.

Something that did cross my mind during the first part of that drive was the notion of keeping the boy's whereabouts secret, or at least low-key until I could figure out the situation. Call it instinct, intuition, or even just a feeling in my gut, but something definitely told me to keep my find to myself. Or at least within my circle of trusted associates, one of whom I would call the moment I had the first couple of issues dealt with.

Rather than pull into a Walmart, I spotted a Goodwill store just outside of Warren, Pennsylvania. Even with a couple of old-school cameras, I figured the quality of the footage would resemble something from the mid-90s and not give me away if someone did happen to take an interest, something I still couldn't fully discount. For all I knew, we could have been under surveillance since the second I pulled over to talk to the kid.

I ended up finding some fresh underwear and a pair of

jeans as well as a Steelers baseball cap, just enough not to attract unwanted attention. I also paid cash to avoid any electronic trail. Next, I pulled into a nearby Wendy's, grabbed a couple of breakfast sandwiches and drinks, and then continued on down Route 62. My investigator once told me that there was no such thing as too much caution, and she knew her stuff. It was also Linda who I phoned an hour after our stop once Max nodded off in the back seat.

"Don't tell me you're already bored of the lake," Linda Chi asked the second she answered my call.

"Bored and packed up," I said with a grin. I heard her chuckle and imagined the eyes rolling. "Don't judge me."

"What the hell, Ben?" There was no missing the frustration in her voice. "Don't you know the meaning of taking a break?"

"I wish I did," I said and was about to turn the conversation to more pressing issues when something else crossed my mind. What if they were already listening?

Looking into the rearview mirror, I tried to think back to before our previous stop and whether I had seen the yellow F-150 that was sitting about a hundred yards back. I didn't *think* I had, but I suddenly doubted my own memory.

"Ben, is everything OK?" I pulled the phone away from my ear suddenly, way too aware of the ramifications if I was wrong. With the murder of his father already confirmed, what if Max was next on their hit list? What if whoever dumped him was just moments ahead of the real threat? "Ben?"

"Is this line secure?" I shook my head at the stupid question.

"Secure? It's as secure as any, I guess. Why? What's the matter?"

"Have you seen the news this morning?"

"If by news you mean the Dunning thing, then yes, why?" I hesitated again, feeling uneasy about talking over the phone but figured I didn't have much of a choice.

"Because I have Dunning's son in the back seat of my car right now," I whispered, lowering my voice as if those I was trying to avoid were already in the car.

Now it was her turn to go silent as I nervously watched the road ahead. Behind me, the F-150 had disappeared, turning down some random side street and leaving me alone to continue on.

"Dunning's son? Are you sure?"

"Positive," I said as I looked over my shoulder at the sleeping child.

"But how..." Her voice trailed off as she faced the same questions I had initially asked myself, questions I still hadn't come any closer to answering.

"How did he happen to end up a hundred miles from where his father was executed?" I finished the question for her. "I have no idea, but it's him, Linda, I guarantee it."

"What are you going to do?"

"Honestly?" Despite having that very question floating around my head for more than an hour, I still hadn't come up with an answer. "I have no idea," I finally managed. "All I know is that this kid is scared out of his wits, and I need to think fast if I'm going to keep him out of harm's way."

"Are you coming back to Pittsburgh?"

"As we speak. Do you think I should go to the authorities?" It seemed like the most logical option, but again, my instincts weren't reacting the way I had hoped. Something was telling me to steer clear of cops for the time being.

"How far are you from the city?"

"A couple of hours," I said, figuring normal speed would get me home by eleven.

"Let me know when you are half an hour away so I can prepare. In the meantime, I'll start doing some checks."

"Thanks, Linda," I said, once again grateful to have someone as switched on as her on my side. She really did add a huge amount of weight to my team, something any lawyer would scream for.

Linda didn't answer, probably already mentally working out her next course of action. I imagined her walking straight into her office and jumping on to the laptop to begin whatever checks she felt needed looking into. For me, the concern was getting my precious cargo somewhere safe, somewhere where I could join in the hunt for answers and hopefully ensure that Max could be kept out of sight.

2

It felt odd not to head straight to the police station with Max, even more so when the first news reports broke about authorities searching for Dunning's missing son for whom they held grave fears. Not only had I committed a crime by not reporting his find immediately, but I had also effectively signed myself up for the case as more than just a simple bystander.

By the time we made it back to my apartment, Linda was already waiting for us, sitting on the front steps of the building while scrolling through something on her phone. We had ended up speaking briefly during the call a half hour out as we had arranged, and she told me to just head to my apartment, perhaps the best place for us. I parked in my usual spot and ushered Max out of the car. Surprisingly, he grabbed my hand as we approached my investigator. He kind of cowered behind me in the same manner I had seen him do with his father on the news footage.

"Hey there, Max," she said with a warm smile as she knelt down and offered him a fist bump. The second she did, he grinned, looked up at me for confirmation, and then bumped fists with her. "All right," Linda said and led us inside.

The great thing about my building was the lack of people. Being just three levels and half empty due to renovations meant not many people to avoid. We also took the stairs due to the elevator being out of service with just a single flight up to my apartment. It wasn't much, but I didn't mind. I had chosen it for a reason, and it had served me well for the previous few years.

Given that it was almost lunchtime, I dropped a couple of Pop-Tarts into the toaster once everyone had taken care of their bathroom needs, and after assuring Max he'd be fine on the living room couch, I set him up with the Pop-Tarts and remote control. First, of course, I found him something suitable to watch in the form of Barney, an old children's program about a purple dinosaur. I'm not sure whether my adding the subtitles helped him, but the smile and the first couple of bites of his snack seemed to indicate that he was good.

Linda and I sat out in the kitchen to talk business, of course, and after opening the folder she'd brought with her, she slid a couple of sheets toward me.

"This is what I found on Dunning," she said. "Looks like he was small time until just a few weeks ago."

"What do you mean?" I asked as I picked up the sheets and began to read.

"From what I can tell, he'd been into some small-time stuff before getting into the drug trade. Got himself picked up with three kilos of cocaine which he insisted he found on the side of the road."

"Is anybody buying that story?"

"Not even close," Linda said as she got up to grab some water.

"And what about the murder?"

"Michael Lozano...found shot to death on the side of the road in Northern Michigan. Prints found in the victim's car matched Dunning's, and police found security footage from a nearby gas station showing the two men talking just a couple of hours before the body was found."

She was right. According to his record, Harold Dunning had gotten himself arrested half a dozen times in the seven years since he was seventeen and all for low-level stuff. Each arrest resulted in no more than community service and just one week in jail for a burglary from his boss. On that occasion, the judge bought his reason that the boss refused to pay him a couple of weeks' worth of wages for which he broke into the office and stole a laptop.

The year of his first arrest also happened to be the same year his partner would have been pregnant with Max, and I didn't think that was any coincidence. Given the nature of his crimes, I wondered whether the man just wanted to provide for his family the only way he could. Dropping out of high school at fifteen wouldn't have given him too many opportunities, and from what I could tell, he appeared to be trying to earn a buck for his troubles.

"So for seven years, it's nothing but a bunch of burglaries and some random low-paying jobs he couldn't hold down, and all of a sudden he's running a substantial quantity of high-grade cocaine across state lines worth around a hundred grand," I said as I finished reading before looking over at Linda.

"The guy didn't have two nickels to rub together."

"And had his kid in the truck with him," I added.

"Who ended up with Child Services before being found by you in Upstate New York," Linda said as she sipped her water.

"Do we know where Max was being held?" I asked as I looked past Linda into the living room. The kid was sitting on the floor in front of the couch while watching a new episode of Bluey and chomping on the last bit of the Pop-Tart. From where I was sitting, he looked a world away from the scared child he had been just a few hours before.

"Not yet, but I'm working on it," Linda said when I suddenly remembered Christy, who I might be able to question about it.

"I think I might have a way of finding out," I said.

It was during a case the previous year that I happened upon a witness who had agreed to testify in a domestic abuse case I was involved in. The father had been accused by his ex-wife of assaulting their son, and after spending some time with Child Services, it became clear that the person doing the assaulting happened to be none other than the accuser herself. Christy Yang ended up spending considerable time with the boy and agreed to testify for the defense. It was her testimony that ended up helping us win the case after the mother broke down on the stand in a Perry-Mason-style interrogation.

"I think I've got someone on the inside," I said and pulled out my cell phone but stopped when I saw the look on Linda's face. "What?"

"Christy Yang, huh?" The grin was enough to tell me what she was thinking.

"What if it is?" I asked, probably sounding more than a little defensive. Linda chuckled a bit as she shook her head.

"You're a glutton for punishment, Mr. Carter, you know that, right?"

Christy didn't just take the stand for my client but ended up asking me out on a date. Despite going against my better judgment and while also enduring a rather dark time of the year, I agreed, and let's just say it didn't go as planned. What followed were six weeks of shameful evasion tactics I employed to avoid a repeat. The woman pursued me in ways I never expected, and it took one hell of an effort to get her to quit. Our paths eventually crossed again, and while Christy still dropped hints about another date, I continued to decline them.

"She's the best chance we have at real inside information," I said, hoping that I wasn't seeing her role as anything else.

There's probably something else you need to know

about me before we continue down this path, and it has to do with how I ended up in Pittsburgh in the first place. I was actually born and raised in one of the poorer suburbs of LA, often dreaming of a way out of the life I had been handed. Raised by an overzealous aunt with a taste for red wine, it wasn't the kind of upbringing a person would go out of their way for. Education felt like my best chance of escape, and I eventually turned my full attention to the law.

I graduated with honors in November of 2013 and landed a job with one of the city's firms, although it wasn't exactly a great place to hang my hat. The pay sucked almost as much as the partners, and to try and build myself a little financial buffer, I took on a part-time job in a nearby café. Not exactly glamorous, I know, but it was while working as a barista that I made enough to keep my head above water and pay my bills through college, and it was that experience that led me to the job at Leslie's on Venice, the café where I eventually met the woman of my dreams.

Maybe a sidewalk near Venice Beach on an overcast Sunday morning doesn't sound like the kind of setting where a person might meet their soul mate, but that's how it happened, or at least in my eyes it did. Naomi had been backpacking her way around the country and was in her final week in California when she decided to take a random Sunday morning stroll down a street near the beach to check out the culture. *Skinny weak cappuccino...* that's what she ordered, the words rolling off her tongue like seasoned friends.

Right from the moment our eyes first met, I knew my life was going to change. Something in my gut tightened with a kind of excited nervousness I couldn't ignore. One thing led to another, and Naomi ended up extending her stay for an extra three months. When that came to an end, I happily accepted her invitation to check out her own hometown. A few months later and after several courses to bring me up to speed, I ended up with a job at a Pittsburgh firm where her father knew the senior partner, and a year later, I took the bar exam.

Life was great. No...life felt *perfect*. I was in love with a great woman, had a great job in a great city, we had friends like I'd never had before, we were financially secure, we'd bought our first house and a car for each of us, we were trying for a baby...life couldn't get any better, except for a little addition to our clan, something we hoped to expand several times over. By 2017, my life had turned on an absolute dime, feeling more like a dream than reality. I remember waking some days and needing to pinch myself to make sure it was real.

Naomi once saw me doing the pinching thing and laughed, promising me that every bit of our life was real. That was another one of those mornings similar to the one where we'd first met and a date forever etched into my brain. May 14, 2017. She'd still been asleep, and feeling nostalgic, I headed out and bought breakfast for us, including one large skinny weak cappuccino which I held under her nose until the scent woke her up. Breakfast in bed on a Sunday morning used to be her favorite, and that was perhaps one of the most memorable. That was the day I pinched myself the hardest, and when she finished laughing at me, I told her that it felt like life couldn't get any better.

"I bet I can make it better," she whispered to me as she lay in my arms.

"Not possible," I whispered back with my eyes closed, letting my senses focus on nothing else but the touch of her head on my chest. That and the smell of her hair. When she didn't answer me back, I curiously opened my eyes, and there it was, her promise in living color right before my eyes.

I remember a kind of buzzing in my body, this numbness of electricity building in my stomach before reaching out to every fiber of my being. Goosebumps...I remember them as well, my arms rippling with their tingles as I stared at the positive line of the pregnancy test. While I knew we'd been trying, I could never imagine myself as a father, and now that it had happened, the magic felt to be continuing, the magic that had already taken me out of my former life.

"You're pregnant?" I could barely push the words out, the threat of tears sitting right on the edge.

"No, my love," she whispered back to me as she looked deep into my eyes. "*We're* pregnant."

That was when the first tear did break free, slowly rolling down my cheek as the rest of the goosebumps rolled across my body. I pulled Naomi into my arms, and we held each other, me mostly in stunned silence. In my eyes, surprising me had always been her superpower, something she did time and again and always in a good way. That was until just three weeks later, one day before we were to have our first scan. June 1, 2017 is the other date firmly etched into my brain.

One of the things I'd come to know about Naomi was how fiercely punctual she was. Her fear of keeping someone waiting drove her to meticulously plan her day around any appointments she had with almost obsessive conviction. Nothing could stand in her way, and I mean nothing. So when she didn't turn up to our scan-eve dinner date that Thursday evening, I knew I had reason to worry.

We'd agreed to meet at Alessandro's at six, an Italian restaurant just a couple of blocks over from our house. We're not talking 5-star mega fancy here but more of a family place serving delicious food worthy of a night out. It was also one of Naomi's favorites and the first she introduced me to when I arrived in the city.

I left work around five and managed to drop by home first, enough time to leave my briefcase and make a quick bathroom stop. Being a relatively warm night, I opted to walk since Naomi would drive to the restaurant and then we could come home together in her car. I remember she texted me just as I was walking down our front steps, saying that she was leaving work and would see me shortly. *Just left. See you soon. We love you, Daddy*, was how she worded the text, that last part something she'd begun just a couple of weeks earlier.

In the months and years since that day, I've often

wondered about that text. I even took a screenshot of it later that night while sitting in a hospital room next to where Naomi was fighting for the lives of her and our baby. They say the car came out of nowhere as she crossed the street, the driver neither slowing nor stopping once he hit her at speed. Only a single security camera caught what one of the newsreaders described as a tragic accident the following morning while announcing her death. The driver never came forward, the Dodge Charger only seen from the side and giving the cops no distinguishing features to work with.

June 1, 2017. That was the date my life took another turn and one I could neither avoid nor forget, a date that would claim the lives of both my wife and our unborn child. She died at precisely 11:59 that night as I held her hand, waiting until the last possible minute to take her last breath and sending the monitors into a screeching mass of alarms and flashing lights. I remember nurses running in, but I knew their attempts to revive her would be in vain.

What I remember most about that moment was feeling her fingers tighten around mine for just a second, tight enough to get my attention. When I looked over at her, a single tear had broken free and was slowly trekking down the side of her face. She never opened her eyes again, my beautiful wife slipping off into the darkness after that final goodbye, our baby held close as they crossed over together. I still think her fingers squeezing mine was her farewell to me, the only one her body was capable of.

I came to stare at that screenshot a lot over the coming weeks and months, a million possibilities running through my head. What if I had called her back the moment I received it? What if I had sent back a text of my own? Could I have changed her course that day, maybe delayed her by just a split second, long enough for that car to pass harmlessly by? The what-ifs became a nightmare for me, questions that plagued me every waking moment and refused to leave me alone.

During the next few months, I found myself sitting by Naomi's final resting place often, usually in silence as I stared at the photo on her gravestone. Grief is a curious emotion and not something I handled well although I know things could have taken a dark turn if I had given in to the alcoholic cravings. I did spend one night with Mr. Jack Daniels, staring into the bottom of an empty bottle around sun-up and feeling like absolute crap. That was the last time I drank alcohol, fearing that if I gave in again, it might pull me in boots and all, and I would end up nothing more than a broken fool.

Christy Yang asked me to go on that date with her on June 1, a date I would have normally spent home alone and staring at a screenshot. I did spend the morning with Naomi and Bub, of course, sitting beside the grave and telling them about my life and how things had been going. And while instinct told me to pass on the date, I could hear Naomi's voice the loudest among those telling me not to give up the rest of my life for her. I gave in and went on the date, and well, you already know how that went.

"It'll be fine," I told Linda as I took out my cell phone and began typing the text. "We're just friends." I could feel Linda's eyes watching me with that grin of hers, the one telling me that I was probably kidding myself, but I ignored it.

Less than two minutes after sending the text, Christy sent her reply, saying that she'd meet with me in a couple of hours down at her local Starbucks. I didn't want to bring her to my apartment until I could work out how she would react to me having Max. I needed to feel my way through a few questions first to make sure I was doing the right thing.

I'd barely finished reading her message when the chair next to me rocked sideways, and I suddenly felt something tightening itself around one of my legs.

"What the..." I began as Linda slid off the side of her chair and knelt on the floor.

It was Max, looking more scared than when I'd first found him on the side of that country road. He kept pulling his face back behind my leg before peering out and into the living room. Both Linda and I followed his gaze and found Bluey no longer on the TV. Instead, a news bulletin had broken in, the red ticker at the bottom flashing *News Alert* multiple times. The detective onscreen was in the middle of giving the latest update, and it was him Max kept staring at.

It took quite an effort, but I eventually managed to get Max to let go of my leg, not an easy task with a kid who couldn't hear my pleas. Both Linda and I watched as he took another look at the screen and then squeezed his eyes shut to keep the television screen out. All it took was one look from me for Linda to know what I wanted her to do next. If the news alert scared the shit out of a seven-year-old kid whose father had just been executed, then I needed to know the reason why.

3

IT TOOK A BIT OF AN EFFORT, BUT I FINALLY MANAGED TO convince Max to remain with Linda while I headed out to meet up with Christy. I couldn't take him with me, and I definitely didn't want Christy in on my secret until I could be sure that she wouldn't turn me in. There were too many emotions rolling through me indicating that something wasn't quite right, and Max's very life could depend on my actions.

"I'll be as quick as I can," I told Linda after setting Max up with some Netflix so no further news bulletins would interrupt him. She assured me she would guard him with her life. I knew she meant it.

I had the radio on the entire drive to Starbucks, listening out for any new updates about the case that seemed to have gripped the city. The biggest question of all? The whereabouts of the missing child and his caregiver. Believe me when I say that my insides just about churned each time I heard the newsreader mention Max's name, the guilt almost enough to completely overwhelm me.

Christy waved at me as I walked through the door and held up two cups to show that she had already ordered for me. I gave her a nod and walked toward the booth, immediately second-guessing my decision to call her. Perhaps I should have listened to Linda and resisted the temptation to get some inside information. It wasn't as if Christy was the only source we could have gotten our news from.

"How are you?" I said as I sat opposite her. She smiled coyly as she slid one of the cups over to me.

"Confused," she said.

"Why?"

"I don't hear from you in ages and then you message me out of the blue? Are you lonely?" I suddenly remembered her straightforward nature. Christy was not one to beat around the bush. She was the kind of person who spoke her mind without a filter safely sitting between her brain and mouth.

"Actually, I just wanted to make sure there were no hard feelings between us after that Peter Mitchell thing."

"Why would there be? The guy was an asshole. It wasn't as if you could have ever won that case given his guilt."

SHE WAS RIGHT, of course. Mitchell had beaten his nine-year-old son to within an inch of his life after the kid walked in on his parents arguing over something. Both mother and son ended up in the hospital, and Mitchell was charged with multiple offenses including breaching court orders to keep away from his ex-wife.

"Yes, he was," I admitted. Judging by the curious look in her eyes, I could tell that she knew I hadn't brought her to the café to talk about Mitchell, but I wasn't about to admit it. Or at least not at that point.

"So why?"

I grinned back and waved my hand in the air. "Can't a guy ask a lady out for coffee without needing a specific reason?"

"In your case, yes, but I'm still curious." I knew I had to tread carefully. Thankfully, it was Christy who brought up my real reason for being there when another news bulletin appeared on a TV up on the wall. "Can you believe that?"

I turned slightly in my seat and pretended to watch along with her as the silent screen showed several police cruisers parked outside a warehouse earlier in the day.

"Imagine that poor kid," she murmured when the news anchor turned to other stories.

"Wasn't he in the care of your department?"

"He'd been put into temporary accommodation, yes," she said as I sipped my coffee and turned back around.

"And the woman looking after him is also missing, isn't she?"

"They showed footage of someone going to her house and abducting the pair."

"Think it's linked to the father's killing?"

She looked up at the TV again shaking her head. "If it isn't then it's one hell of a coincidence."

I tried to continue acting nonchalant, slowly sipping my coffee while watching an old man being served at the counter. What I was really doing was trying to work out what I needed from Christy and how to get information without raising suspicions.

"The woman that was looking after him, the kid I mean. Who was she?" Christy looked at me with that same mischievous grin.

"Why do you want to know?"

"Just curious," I said. "Maybe it's the defense lawyer in me looking for answers."

"Think she was involved? The police have footage of a man walking out of her house with a gun trained on her. It didn't look like she'd be involved."

"And yet he somehow knew where the boy would be?" I took another sip, hoping not to look too serious. "I mean, don't you keep those kinds of things secret?"

"You think it was an inside job?"

"Why not? It just seems odd that someone comes and abducts the boy and his caregiver, and an hour later, the father is executed in some nearby warehouse."

That was when Christy straightened up and looked directly at me, her eyes narrowing down to slits as she tried to see into my head.

"Ben Carter, what aren't you telling me?"

"What do you mean?" I said, doing my best to hold a poker face. She didn't answer immediately, continuing to watch me with intrigue.

"The out-of-the-blue text message, the coffee date, the questions about the boy. Ben, what is going on?"

I should have retreated. Again, I questioned turning up at all for limited information that would have little impact on things going forward. Christy wasn't exactly a part of the hierarchy in her profession, but she did have access to the kind of information I could use. And then there was the way she interacted with children. It was probably that part that drove my need more than anything else. Christy just had a kind of empathic nature, a real matronly energy about her that I had seen firsthand around children.

Instead of answering her, I looked around nervously, not really sure of how to word what I was about to say. I also wanted to make sure nobody was close enough to listen in on a reaction I knew would quickly follow once I revealed my secret. I closed my eyes in anticipation of opening a massive shitstorm if Christy went rogue on me, but I knew I had already said too much to change my mind. When I opened my eyes again, Christy was staring at me with a look of confusion. After a deep breath, I waved her closer.

"I know where he is," I whispered, trying my hardest to keep the words just a single decibel above silence.

"I'm sorry, I didn't hear you," Christy said, and I gestured to her to lean in closer. "Ben, you're kind of scaring me."

"I need you to come closer, and I *really* need you not to flip out," I whispered, watching a young mother walk past pushing her stroller. I waited until she was a safe distance away before looking back at Christy and repeating myself. "I know where he is."

Christy tilted her head slightly as she looked at me with that same puzzled expression, unable to comprehend who I was talking about. And then it clicked. First, she clapped a hand over her mouth as her eyes widened enough for the balls to pop out of their sockets with a swift enough slap to the back of the head.

"No way," I heard her mutter between her fingers before she looked nervously around. "Ben, stop kidding around," she finally managed when she leaned forward again.

"I'm not kidding, Christy. Look at me. Do I appear like someone trying to use the kid for a punchline?" She eyed me suspiciously for a few extra moments before she found a few more words.

"OK, where is he then?"

"I don't want to talk about it here. But I do need you, and if you're willing to keep this quiet until I can work things out, then I'll be happy to share what I know."

I wasn't sure how she would react when she found out, but after the initial shock passed, I think she controlled her emotions quite well.

"Where can we talk?" she asked after agreeing.

"Let's jump in my car." I grabbed my cup and slid out of the booth. Five minutes later, I slammed the passenger door shut once Christy had climbed into my car, and a minute after that, I pulled out into the mid-afternoon Pittsburgh traffic.

"So where is he?" Christy asked once she'd had enough time to properly process the information.

"Maybe I need to tell you the whole story," I said and began telling her everything that had happened since I drove out of the campsite early that morning.

While my plan was to bring Christy back to the apartment so she could verify Max's identity for herself, I didn't head straight there, instead driving the long way around, so to speak. I needed time to share the moment I'd first found him, the initial interaction, and the reasons behind me believing the boy to be Max Dunning. I even went as far as to tell her my instincts telling me we needed to keep his current whereabouts a secret until we could figure out the danger surrounding him. At first, Christy didn't agree with me, but I reminded her how somebody had already managed to find his location and abduct him once, and there was a real danger of history repeating itself.

"You're just going to have to trust me on this one," I said when we pulled up in front of my apartment building. She didn't answer, and when I turned to look at her after switching the engine off, Christy sat in the passenger seat wide-eyed.

"We're talking about a felony here, Ben. If the cops find out, it could mean a lot more than just both our careers."

"I'm aware of that," I said. "But right now, this kid's life matters a whole lot more to me. I have no idea what I've gotten us involved in, but I know we need to keep him safe for now. Can you help me with that? Can you help me keep Max Dunning a secret?"

She didn't answer immediately, perhaps weighing up the risks of what I was asking. There was definitely a lot going on inside her head, and it took almost a full minute of silence before she gave me an answer.

"I don't know why I'm risking everything, but OK, I'll do it."

"Then you'd better come in and meet Max," I said and jumped out of the car.

Max had fallen asleep on the couch during my time away, but it was Linda who met us at the door when I walked in. She eyed me with surprise, the kind that didn't need words, but I knew exactly what she was thinking. So did Christy.

"It's OK," she said as she walked in with her hands up in a kind of surrender. "Ben swore me to secrecy."

"He's fast asleep," Linda said and pointed to where the little guy had stretched himself out with his back to the TV. "Hasn't stirred since he nodded off like a half hour ago." Christy walked closer and peered down at the child before looking up at me again.

"It's him all right," she said before shaking her head. "What the hell have you gotten us involved in?"

"I wish I knew," I said. "But right now we need to make sure we keep his whereabouts a secret. Just until we can figure out..." That was when Linda tapped me on the shoulder. "Huh?"

She was pointing to the television, and when I looked over, I saw that she had switched it back from Netflix to the regular channels. A fresh news alert was showing, the ticker along the bottom scrolling *Early Morning Execution*

Update on repeat. On the screen, a news chopper's view showed several police cars that looked to have descended in front of a house on some random street. I could see multiple officers circling around the yard with their pistols targeted at the front door. Seconds later, four more came out of the house with a suspect in handcuffs walking between two of them.

"That the guy who killed Dunning, you think?" Christy asked, but I was already somewhere else entirely.

"Guys, I have to go out," I said as I looked down at Max before turning to Linda. "I know you didn't sign up for this, but do you think you could watch him for just a little longer?"

"Yes, of course," Linda said. "Whatcha got in mind?" I pointed to the TV as the suspect was pushed into one of the police cruisers, the rest of the cops trying to keep the onlookers at bay.

"I'm sure he's going to need representation," I said. "Something tells me I'm probably the right man for the job."

4

I ENDED UP GIVING CHRISTY A RIDE BACK TO HER CAR BUT not before making her swear to keep our secret a second time. Seeing the man in police custody probably brought the reality of the situation a little closer to home for her, and when I pulled up beside her BMW, she shook my hand.

"Just let me know if you need anything," she said before climbing out. "Anything at all, Ben. Looking after a seven-year-old isn't exactly a cakewalk and definitely not a traumatized one."

"I understand," I said. "And thank you, I will for sure."

I waited until she was safely in her car before pulling back out into traffic. It wasn't the police station I was headed to but somewhere where I hoped the suspect would be guaranteed to me as a client...my office. My boss was perhaps one of the best I'd ever worked for, a man willing to listen to those he employed. I know a lot of people in those positions like to exert dominance over employees but not Dwight Tanner. Not only a fellow Californian who made the move to Pittsburgh in his teens but also someone I'd grown to admire after the way he supported me after Naomi's passing. And then there was Grace.

Imagine my surprise when I wasn't only given the job at Tanner and Dunn but also entrusted with an assistant who also happened to be married to the senior partner. Most law firms would have never allowed such a thing, but one point the firm promoted above all else was their family values. It was Dwight himself who introduced Grace to me and then surprised me when he said that she would be my assistant.

Something I had never gotten used to was the homey atmosphere of the office. The moment I walked through the door, people greeted me like a returned brother, some calling out when I walked past their open offices. Sylvia, the firm's receptionist, shot me a huge grin when I first entered.

"Thought you were camping," she said as I shot her a wave.

"Definitely not my thing," I said with a grin and continued on.

With me supposedly off for a week, Grace had reassigned herself to helping out around the office doing odd jobs and looked over at me with a look of curiosity when I popped my head into the open boardroom.

"Ben? What are you doing here?"

"Couldn't stay away," I said before pointing toward Dwight's office. "Big guy in?"

"He is," Grace said. "Think he's eating lunch." Before I could say anything else, a voice called out to me from farther up the hallway.

"I don't think you quite understand the meaning of the word *vacation*, Mr. Carter."

"I don't think I do," I called back as I gave Grace a wave before heading to meet my boss, who was already walking toward me with an outstretched hand. When I said *big guy*, I meant it, and when we shook, his hand completely encapsulated mine as if to prove my point. Standing at six-foot-eight and almost as wide across the shoulders, Dwight Tanner dwarfed most of the people in his life, including me, who stood a respectable six-two.

"Couldn't stay away, huh? How was the lake?" Dwight asked as he let go of my hand.

"The lake was OK, I guess, but I've got more important things to deal with right now. I need your help."

"Sounds serious," Dwight said as he studied my face. "We'd better go to my office."

When Dwight Tanner said that his firm was one big happy family, he meant it. No matter the issue, he would take the person into his office, close the door, and listen intently to whatever their troubles were. If he found that help was within his power, he didn't hesitate to offer the person whatever they needed to fight their battle.

"Have you heard of a man named Harold Dunning?" I asked the second we sat down and I declined the offer of a drink.

"Dunning as in the guy executed this morning?"

"That's the one," I said as I watched Dwight grab a cigar out of the box he kept on his desk. He leaned back in his seat and kind of rolled it underneath his nostrils to take in the aroma. He never smoked in his office but did like to hold it close when the urge came up, and I could see him studying me while using it as a kind of shield.

"Why the interest in a suspected drug trafficker?"

"Someone linked to the case has just been arrested over in Bridgeville."

"Someone linked to Dunning?"

"Actually, the guy suspected of kidnapping both Dunning's son and his caregiver," I said. "Both are still currently missing." Dwight continued studying me before reaching for his television remote and flicking on the screen set up on the opposing wall. I didn't bother turning to watch, already more than aware of the hype surrounding the arrest.

I think I saw the actual moment Dwight understood why I had brought the proposal to him, his left eyebrow rising just enough to break the stare. It reminded me a little of The Rock, and I half expected my boss to suddenly rise from his chair and beckon to me with his fingers while smelling the air.

"You want to represent this Mario Perez?"

"I think the exposure alone would be amazing for the firm," I said, hoping I didn't sound too anxious despite having never heard the name before. It appeared as if the reporters had done good for once by delivering me something new to work with.

That was when Dwight returned to studying me as he continued slowly rubbing the length of the cigar under his nose. I knew that was the moment he would try and see through me to find the reason for my bringing the proposal to him. It wasn't unusual for one of his lawyers to bring in a case such as this one, and so I held my poker face as best I could until he finally did what he always did.

"OK, run with it," he finally said as he leaned forward in his seat, transferred the cigar from his right hand to the left, and hit the intercom button on his phone. "Pam, would you please get me Chief Atkins on the line?"

"Right away," I heard Dwight's assistant answer back before a distinct click cut the connection.

"Sure you want to take this? You still have a few vacation days left, don't you?"

"Camping's never been my thing," I said.

"I can put Patterson on it."

"No, no, I want this," I said, and that was when he did see something, a kind of twinkle in his eye setting off the curiosity scanner he ran 24/7. "If that's OK with you."

"Fine by me," Dwight said with an approving dip of the head. "Just be ready for the media pack waiting for you when they get wind of your client."

"I'm ready," I said and stood before shaking my boss's hand again, effectively closing the deal between us.

Once back out in the hallway, I turned in the direction of my office, spotting Grace along the way. She gave me a wave before excusing herself from the current conversation she was having.

"I wondered how long you'd last in a tent," she

mocked the second she walked into my office. "I thought you men were all born campers."

"Not all of us," I said with a smirk. "Some just aren't cut out for the country life. Hey, listen," I added, needing to change course, "I'm possibly taking on a rather public client if I can get down to the police station in time. Dwight's phoning the station chief as we speak. Can you please do me a favor?"

"Of course," Grace said, her demeanor instantly changing back to work mode.

"Can you find me anything you can on a Mario Perez?"

"A new client?"

"I hope so," I said as I grabbed an emergency suit and shirt I always kept in the office closet. "He's the one connected to the Dunning murder that's been all over the news today."

"On it," Grace said with a thumbs-up and immediately headed for her desk.

I don't think I had ever gotten changed faster than I did at that moment, climbing out of my jeans and T-shirt and into my professional kit in under thirty seconds. Time was of the essence, and the last thing I wanted was for some underpaid public defender to snatch what could potentially be a career-changing client.

Grace had already managed to print out a couple of initial reports on Perez for me, and I dropped them into my briefcase after a brief thanks. I barely made it out the door before my phone began ringing. It was Linda.

"Hey," I said, answering the call after pushing my way out through the front doors of the building. "How's Max?"

"He's still sleeping. Christy said she'd watch him for us when we need while we worked the case. Are you sure she'll be OK with keeping our secret?" It was a question I'd asked myself many times over.

"She'll be fine," I assured her.

"Anyway, I've got the police report on this morning's killing," Linda said as she subtly changed the course of the conversation in her own special way. I felt the phone vibrate against my ear. "Email should be waiting for you."

"It just landed," I said as I hit the unlock button on the key fob. "Anything of interest?"

"Just that whoever killed Dunning really wanted to make a statement."

"What do you mean?" I asked as I climbed into the Mustang.

"Well, let's just say that a bullet to the face is usually one hell of a message. Hands and feet bound, forced to kneel and then shot at point-blank range."

"He knew his attacker, that's for sure," I said as I hit the start button and felt the engine come to life. "Dunning either double-crossed someone or—"

"Or someone wanted to shut him up permanently to make sure he didn't blab," Linda said, finishing my train of thought.

"That's my thinking," I said as I pulled out into traffic. "The question is who?"

"How did you go with your mission?"

"Got the approval from my boss," I said as I slowed for the first red traffic light, one of what I hoped would be just a couple on my way to the police station. "Did you get the name?"

"Mario Perez," Linda said, proving again how she loved to stay ahead of the curve. "Already checking into his background."

"Let me know what you come up with," I said as the light changed to green. A cab tore through the intersection at a high speed as he ran the red, forcing the car in front of me to hit their brakes. I did likewise as his horn sent a proverbial middle finger after the driver. "Damn it," I cried out as I came to a stop with just inches to spare.

"You OK?"

"Just an idiot in a hurry," I muttered. "Listen, I know you're busy, but is there any way you can shift your workstation to my place for a bit? I know it's asking a lot, but I don't want to be relying on Christy, if you know what I mean."

It wasn't that I didn't trust Christy, but considering her position, I knew she would risk a lot more than me or Linda if she was caught. I also wanted to take advantage of having an insider down at Child Services. With Max effectively snatched while in the custody of one of their qualified caregivers, I had a feeling that her office would be a hive of activity trying to deal with the aftermath.

"Already working on it," Linda said. "Will set myself up in your spare room later this afternoon."

"Perfect," I said, and after thanking her, I hung up. With the police station just a few minutes up the road, I wanted to get myself into the right headspace.

5

THE MEDIA PACK SITTING OUTSIDE THE STATION LOOKED TO be setting themselves up for the long run when I pulled up. Because of the sheer volume of extra vehicles, I ended up parking a block down the road and had to hustle it back to the building. None of the reporters gave me a second look, something I knew would change the second they caught wind of who I had come to represent.

Once inside, I went straight to the desk and asked for the only person I knew who would simplify the process for me. Dwight Tanner and Warrel Atkins had been friends for the better part of forty years, having been neighbors since childhood. The phone call my boss made had given me the keys to the proverbial door. What I did once on the other side of it depended on me.

"Follow me," Atkins said when he saw me walking up the hallway, excusing himself from the officer he'd been talking to. "He hasn't been exactly cooperative with us as yet, but I'm sure you'll work your magic on him."

"I'll do what's necessary, Chief," I said and left it at that. Two minutes later, I finally came face to face with Perez himself.

To be honest, I didn't think much of the man when I first laid eyes on him. He looked somewhat dejected, something to be expected given the situation he now found himself in, but he also appeared a lot younger than I was expecting. His file put him at just twenty-four, but initial observations put him closer to his teens, barely old enough to drive.

The other thing I found curious was how he reacted when he first saw me. I'd met plenty of new clients in my time, many in a similar position, but I don't think any of them had ever looked totally surprised to see me standing there.

"Hello, Mr. Perez, my name is Ben Carter," I said as I sat down before him at the small interview table. The suspect's eyes followed my every step as if I were some kind of apparition. Once seated, I paused to look back at him, in a way mirroring his expression.

"H-how—" he began but then squeezed his lips shut as he looked away.

"I'm not a public defender, if that's what you think. I represent a firm called Tanner and Dunn, and I've been given permission to take your case completely free. Pro bono, so to speak." He looked back at me with an expression of confusion, but something about it just didn't feel right for me.

"I-I'm not sure what..." He lacked the mental stability to finish sentences, and while I first thought it might have been because of the place he now found himself in, I quickly deduced that it was fear of something else entirely.

To try and get the conversation turned in the direction where I could extract some information from him, I opened my briefcase and pulled out my notepad as Perez stared at his hands.

"Can you tell me what happened, Mario? Why did the police arrest you?"

He looked over at me but didn't speak. That was when I noticed his fingers shaking as they wrestled each other on the tabletop. The nervousness coursed through him as he studied me, but he kept his mouth shut. Whatever was worrying him, it didn't look like he was ready to share.

"If I'm going to help you, Mario, then I need to know what happened. Now the police think you abducted a boy named Max Dunning early this morning, along with his caregiver, Hillary Warner. Can you just tell me if that's true?" No response. Just the same distant stare as he fought to keep his mental wall up. "What about the boy's father? Did you kill him?"

Before continuing with the questions, I pulled out the contract of engagement for him to sign. Without it, I would be nothing more than dead weight to him, and he needed me to represent him. I also needed to remain close to him if I was going to get the answers I needed about Max and the danger the kid was in, and so I worked on the signature first. Surprisingly, Perez didn't hesitate to sign the form.

I must have spent another twenty minutes working on him, but no matter how much I tried, Perez refused to speak with me about the kidnapping charges he faced. The only thing he kept saying was that he'd never meant to hurt the kid.

Time eventually ran out, and I ended up sitting next to Perez as a couple of detectives came in to question him. Dan Oakland and Rusty Malovic questioned Perez for close to two hours with no results. The hardest part for me was knowing where the child actually was. Yes, I know I was effectively hindering an investigation, but my instincts proved too great in this case. Something definitely didn't feel right, hence why I kept Max's whereabouts quiet.

It was around five o'clock when the detectives began talking of taking a break when a third officer came into the room. He asked to speak with his colleagues, and they left, leaving me alone with Perez once more. The second they closed the door, he turned to me and began begging for me to do something.

"Please, you have to get me out of here."

"Then tell me what I need to know," I said, watching as the kid's walls crumbled before my eyes.

"They'll kill me just like they did Harry."

"Who? Who killed Harold?"

He wanted to tell me, that much was certain, but when he looked past me toward the mirrored wall where we were no doubt being watched or filmed or perhaps both, I knew he wouldn't talk. His shoulders slumped as the reality of his predicament returned.

Both detectives returned a couple of minutes later, and I could tell from their expressions that things were about to go from bad to worse for my client.

"Well, counselor, it looks like your client is about to get himself elevated to first-degree murder," Malovic said as he sat down before turning his full attention back to Perez. "After our initial checks of your car, Mr. Perez, officers located a .38 revolver hidden under the driver's seat. It also happens to match the caliber of the weapon used to shoot Harold Dunning early this morning. What can you tell me about that?"

What followed were another two hours of endless questions from both detectives as I did my best to support a client still not forthcoming with information. Once done, the officers gave me another twenty minutes alone with Perez before suspending their interview until they could get the ballistics report for the bullet retrieved from Harold Dunning's skull. I figured I had less than twenty-four hours before that matter handed them enough to formally charge my client.

"You have to work with me if you want to see the outside world again, Mario," I told Perez once we were alone again. He didn't show the slightest interest in speaking with me. "If that gun matches the one used to murder Harold Dunning, then you're going to be charged with his murder. The detectives will show you on film abducting Dunning's son and his caregiver. They will then comb through every security camera within the city to track your car, and when they find you turning up to that warehouse, it will provide enough evidence to convict you." He didn't even look at me. "Mario, you will face life in jail, do you understand that?"

I began to feel my frustration rise as Perez continued ignoring me, and I figured that he might need a bit of time to let his new reality sink in. It wasn't as if he was going anywhere. After a good night's sleep in a prison cell, maybe he would wake up with a new perspective. It was the only play I had, given the circumstances.

"OK, I'm going to come back tomorrow, and hopefully you will have changed your mind about talking to me," I said, finally giving in. "Maybe then we can talk about trying to get you bail." Again, he didn't move, and so I packed up my things and headed for the door. Just as I banged on it to be let out, Perez called out to me.

"He told me he likes chocolate milk" was what he said, but before I could answer him, the door opened.

I didn't walk out immediately, standing my ground as I looked back at the kid still sitting in his seat. His fingers continued wrestling with each other, the fear visibly eating him from the inside out. I don't know why, but seeing him that way, I felt sorry for him, something I had never felt for a suspect before. There was just something about Mario Perez that didn't make sense to me. From the acne on his cheeks to the unkempt hair, he looked years younger, *too* young to be dealing with the kind of shitstorm now facing him.

Once outside the station, I expected the media pack to charge at me with a thousand questions flying all at once, each trying to get the scoop for their front page ambitions. I thought every camera would turn on me, the reporters thrusting their microphones in my face to try and get something for their next news alert.

Nobody moved. The only person who paid me the slightest attention was a lone guy leaning against one of the posts with a vape in one hand and a cell phone in the other. He looked up at me as I stood a few feet away but didn't seem to see anything of interest.

"Nobody knows yet, dumbass," I muttered under my breath and proceeded through the parking lot before turning down the street and weaving my way through a dozen reporters, feeling a little like a stealth fighter as I cruised through the enemy undetected.

It wasn't until I got back to my car that I checked my phone and found half a dozen missed calls, all of them from the same number, a number I immediately recognized. It wasn't one I had seen in quite some time, but it took just a split second for the face of its owner to rush back into my head.

Gabby Chapman had lived next to Naomi and me back when we'd first moved into the house on Roy Street. She and her then-husband welcomed us with a cheese platter and bottle of wine the day we moved in, and during the course of the next few months, we got to listen to their fights most nights until she finally managed to kick his drunken ass out for good.

It was also Gabby who stood beside me when Naomi passed, offering the kind of support that really helped me through those traumatic weeks. The funny thing is, I never sensed why she was doing it, not until almost a year later when she tried to kiss me over an innocent pizza and beer while watching the Steelers on television. She didn't take the rejection well, but the truth was, that had been a tough day for me. Actually, it had been a tough few months, but I wasn't one to advertise the current state of my mental health.

Gabby eventually ended up drifting out of my life and focusing on the new job she'd gotten after her divorce. Reporting had been something she had dreamed about since childhood, and it wasn't long before she hit the ground running. I imagined her talent taking her on a wild ride around the country as she propelled from one great publication to another, each time moving up in the ranks and spreading her wings further with each leap. Imagine my surprise when she suddenly quit the media world shortly after a popular social media app took off and turned her attention solely to TikTok.

Yes, I followed her account and watched this shy woman grow from humble beginnings into one of the biggest influencers on the platform, all through sharing daily news articles. Her account grew to almost two million subscribers the last time I checked, and it seemed like she had found her place in the world.

I waited until I was sitting in my car before looking at the screen of my cell phone again, contemplating whether to make the call. The last time I had spoken to Gabby was three years earlier, and it hadn't ended well for either of us. The tension that had slowly been building between us somehow came to a head when I declined an invitation to go to the movies with her. I never got the chance to explain the reason why, and at the time, I didn't think it really mattered.

Instead of hitting the call back button, I dropped the phone into the center console and pressed the start button, feeling the engine come to life through the steering wheel. I wasn't sure whether I was ready for another confrontation with Gabby, not with everything else currently going on in my life. With Max in my apartment, the time was definitely ticking down to whatever climax was fast approaching.

I'd barely gotten a mile down the road when the cell phone came to life again, the ringtone blasting through the Mustang's speakers. One look at the screen and I could see the same number staring back at me. I couldn't help but grin, remembering how Gabby's persistence was what got her that big break into media in the first place.

"This could be classed as stalking, you know," I said with a grin after hitting the answer button on the steering wheel.

"I call it following leads, Mr. Carter," Gabby said with a hint of amusement.

"Leads? What makes you think I have a story worth sharing?"

I felt a sudden surge of panic as I pictured some hidden camera lying concealed in my apartment for years just waiting to be put to good use. Did she know about Max? Was that why she was calling me after years of no contact?

"Because I saw you on PCNC walking into the Zone 1 Police Station looking like a man on a mission."

I chuckled, the smile breaking through my defenses as I remembered how she wasn't the kind of person to miss a thing.

"Of course you did," I said. "And what makes you think I was there for anything newsworthy, huh? I might have just been there to catch up with a friend."

"A man catching up with a friend doesn't run into a police station parking lot, Ben."

"I was late."

"You were running to beat the public defender."

That was when I laughed, unable to hold the amusement in any longer. Damn, she was good. No wonder her previous employer offered to double her wages when she first approached them with a resignation letter.

"I was late for a meeting with a friend," I said as I slowed for a red light. She refused to ease off.

"Oh, yeah? Who goes to a random meeting with a friend at 3:25 on a Wednesday afternoon?"

"We had coffee," I said, watching as several pedestrians crossed in front of me.

"Lying has never been your strong suit, Ben. Not a good trait for a lawyer." Again, I had to laugh. She'd always had that uncanny ability, a kind of power she held over me.

"Oh, Gabby," I said, still chuckling.

"So what did he say?"

"What did who say?"

"Mario Perez."

"I wasn't there for Perez," I tried again as the lights changed. "And even if I was, you know I couldn't share what went on."

"Perez is the hottest story going around, Ben. I need something. I know he was involved in that kid's kidnapping, and they still haven't found the woman looking after him. What's her name...Hillary Warner? You know some people are speculating she might have been in on it."

"Let them speculate all they want," I said as I wondered how deep this rabbit hole would go. Hillary Warner's name wasn't exactly a secret but Gabby made it sound like it was. It appeared as if her call had backfired in a way, helping me a lot more than she had planned. That was when she said something that caught me off guard, something that immediately sent a shiver through me.

"You know, once the media find out you're representing him, you're going to be famous. I mean, every reporter within a hundred miles is going to want to talk with you."

She was right, and it was definitely not something I had considered. What if they caught wind of who was representing Perez and found out where I lived? My apartment would be staked out, and all the while hiding a little boy whose life remained in danger I still couldn't fully explain.

"Did Perez tell you he took the boy?" And that's when it happened, my stupid mind too distracted by the previous thought to fully comprehend her question before answering.

"Perez didn't say anything, Gabby, " I said while thinking about the consequences of reporters watching my building.

"Oh, so you did talk to him? Then that means you represent him."

"Gabby, I—"

"That's all I need for now."

"Gabby—"

"Thanks."

The click of the line disconnecting sounded more like a hammer blow as chills ran through me. Within the blink of an eye, I had managed to blurt out all she needed in order to build a story, something I knew she wouldn't waste time on. What I'd learned from spending time with her was that timing was everything to a reporter, a job where seconds could mean the difference between front-page glory and yesterday's news. Little did she know that she had just stolen time from a little boy I was trying to protect.

6

Twenty-seven minutes. That's how long it took Gabby to turn my world upside down by breaking the news about Perez's attorney. By the time I walked back into my apartment, the first news alert popped up on the cell phone screen, and when I clicked into the feed, the news anchor was almost bursting with energy at the revelation. An hour later, the rest of the networks joined in.

"Wow, she's really thrown you under the bus," Linda said as she showed me the video on Gabby's TikTok app, the views already climbing beyond the 200K mark.

"She didn't know," I said, shaking my head in frustration as I watched Max eating a bologna sandwich on the couch.

"You didn't tell her?"

"I...she caught me off guard and then hung up before I could tell her."

"Why didn't you call her back? I mean, geez, if

reporters start coming around, how are we going to keep this secret?"

"I know," I said. "We're going to have to move him." I looked at the window. "After nightfall."

"Move him where?"

It was a fair question and now one that I knew I needed to find an answer for sooner rather than later. Time suddenly took on a whole new meaning as I felt the very seconds ticking away, each one bringing me closer to getting found out.

"Naomi's aunt has a house out in Freeport we can use," I finally said. "She's offered it to me numerous times, and I know she won't bother us."

"OK, guess I'll grab my stuff and set up there then," Linda said as she set her cup down on the table and stood. "Think you can handle the little guy for an hour while I go grab my gear?"

"I'm sure I'll be fine," I said. "The question is, will you be OK to watch him while I try and work this case? I mean, who knows how long this might take."

Linda chuckled. "You pay me by the hour, remember?" She patted me on the shoulder as she walked closer to the couch and waved to Max. He looked up at her and gave her a nod when she promised to return soon.

I don't know why, but it was right then that Perez's words came back to me, the ones he'd spoken just as I was about to leave.

"Max, would you like some chocolate milk?" He looked over at me without hesitation and smiled while nodding his head. Linda took a step back in surprise as I realized we'd been wrong.

"But I thought..." she began but didn't finish the sentence as I went to the fridge and grabbed a bottle. After pouring some into a glass, I took it to Max, who reached for it before I'd even gotten to him.

"You can hear me, can't you?"

He didn't answer but did take the glass when I got close enough and immediately began drinking. Linda watched from behind me.

"Was that just an assumption about him being deaf-mute?"

I shook my head. "I don't know, but Perez told me he liked chocolate milk." I shook my head. "No, that's not what he said. What he said was that he *told* him he liked chocolate milk."

"Well, that at least confirms that he was the one who took him from that house."

"Yeah, but what else don't we know?"

Once Linda left, I left Max to his own devices as I turned my attention to the laptop sitting on my kitchen table. I did take it into the living room so Max wouldn't feel alone and immediately went to work looking into Mario Perez while he searched for something new to watch.

Linda had already started her investigation and had built a folder for me to start my research. From what I could see, Mario Perez didn't seem like the kind of guy who would randomly kidnap a child and the woman looking after him, but more than that, he didn't appear to have any connections to the woman at all. While Gabby might have concocted that line about people suspecting him of being in cahoots with the caregiver, I couldn't find any possible link or motive for the rumor. What I did find was the man's criminal record.

Small time is the best way to describe what I found in that file with none of his previous convictions even leading to jail time. Nothing but misdemeanors, from what I could see, except for one incident from the previous year where Perez was charged with breaking and entering into a murder victim's house a day after the owner was killed in a drive-by shooting. Strangely, the charges ended up getting withdrawn the very next day.

To try and get a better picture of the entire case, I pivoted my attention over to Harold Dunning, clicking on the second folder that Linda had emailed me. Given that the two men shared *some* sort of connection, I figured that *it* might prove to be the missing piece I needed in order to start answering some of my questions. The biggest one I had was why a small-time crook would suddenly wake up one day and go and kidnap a kid and his caregiver on the very same night that the father managed to escape from jail only to end up dead in some backstreet warehouse.

Like Perez, Dunning was small time but also didn't appear to commit crimes just for the thrill of it. I had already established that Dunning seemed to be trying to survive by any means necessary, and that meant crossing the line here and there. The other thing I quickly came to realize about the man was just how dedicated to his son he was. Most might have assumed he was like most other dads whose partners had either died or simply run off, leaving them with the child. Max spent his time with his grandmother, but I could see from limited financial records that it was the boy's father who paid for a lot of the family's expenses. He was a man doing his best with the situation put before him.

Laughter suddenly broke out, and I looked over to see Max watching the first *Home Alone* movie where the two gangsters did their best to try and break into the house. The sound of his laughter was something that truly touched me, and I couldn't help but wonder just how little must have been in his life if people thought him a mute.

I closed the lid of the laptop and just watched him for a bit. Soon, I got into the movie as much as he did, and before I knew it, I could barely keep it together as Joe Pesci and Daniel Stern just about split my sides with their unfortunate misgivings. Talk about bad luck. At one point, I got up off the single seater and scooted over to the couch for a better angle of the television, and that was where I remained for the rest of the movie. By the time the final credits began to roll, Linda walked back into the apartment carrying a well-stuffed backpack.

"Well, you two look like you're having a great time," she said after depositing her bag on one of the kitchen chairs. "*Home Alone*, huh?"

"Nothing like a great Christmas movie in August to liven the place up," I said before turning my attention to Max. "Did you like that movie?" He didn't answer, but he did look at me. "It's OK, Max, nobody here will hurt you."

At first, I didn't think he was going to respond, his

shyness clearly evident as he seemed to withdraw back into his shell. But with me not shifting my attention away from him, Max only had two choices: to either turn away from me completely in the hope that I would move on or respond to my question.

"I liked the movie," he suddenly whispered without any hint of accent whatsoever. Linda and I exchanged a look before I leaned slightly forward.

"Max, can I ask you something?" He hesitated but eventually nodded ever so slightly as he cast his eyes down. "Do you know what happened to Hillary?"

I knew that asking a kid in such a fragile state to relive a possible traumatic event might be just enough to push them over the edge into lifelong therapy, but with the woman still missing and him being perhaps the only person able to shed some light on the matter, I had to try. And...I didn't actually think Max would answer me anyway. A part of me figured he would have been kept in a car away from the horror, although I couldn't for the life of me picture why he'd be taken when the father was going to be killed anyway.

He didn't look at me, but he did slowly nod his head, surprising me yet again. Linda and I exchanged yet another look before I tried to delve a little deeper, carefully treading a tightrope of emotion.

"Did someone hurt Hillary?" My instincts told me that given the severity of the situation, the fewer witnesses the better, although I still couldn't make sense of how Max fit in with the rest of the scheme, nor why he'd been found more than a hundred miles from the crime scene.

Again he nodded, his eyes still downcast as I felt my stomach tighten. Had he seen her being murdered as well? That was when the kid surprised me again, this time by looking at me.

"The bad man shot her," he whispered, his voice sounding frighteningly fragile. I didn't want to dig for information, but I knew chances wouldn't come by often and figured it best to continue while I was on a roll.

"Did you see the man shoot her?" Again, he nodded. "Was it the man you saw on the television earlier?" I didn't think the detective would be involved, but given Max's earlier reaction, it was worth asking. This time he shook his head. "Do you think you could recognize him if you saw him again?"

He nodded, and I looked up at Linda, who knew exactly what I wanted without needing to ask. She opened her cell phone, and after a few seconds of scrolling, she handed it to me. Once I saw the photo of Mario Perez on the screen, I showed it to Max, sure that he would either nod or try and hide behind the couch or something. He did neither, instead shaking his head.

"That's not him," he whispered, surprising me again. I was so sure that he would confirm Perez as being the shooter, I was already trying to plan my eventual meeting with the prosecutor. "That's Mario," Max continued. "He's the nice one."

Hearing those words confused me. "The nice one?"

"He's the one that bought me the chocolate milk when we went driving."

"Driving?"

That's when it hit me. Perez wasn't just the one to take Max and Hillary from the house in the early hours of the morning but also the one to drop Max off on the side of the road where I would eventually find him.

"Max, did someone tell Mario to take you to the place where I found you?"

"I don't know."

"What do you remember?"

I thought I was on a roll, nudging my way closer to the answers I needed in order to crack the case. I could feel it in my bones, but then a hand squeezed my shoulder, and I knew I needed to take a step back.

"It's OK, kiddo. You don't have to answer that if you don't want to."

"Can I please have some more chocolate milk?"

"Yes, of course," Linda said and shot me a wink as she headed to the fridge.

My cell phone dinged as Max followed Linda out to the kitchen, and after pulling it from my pocket, I saw a message from Christy telling me that Hillary Warner had been on the job for more than five years with glowing references. If she did have anything to do with the kidnapping, it would have been completely out of character.

I showed the text to Linda once Max was set with his drink and back in the living room watching another movie.

"Looks like she checks out" was her response, and I agreed, which meant we were basically back to square one with our investigation. "I did manage to find something that might interest you," she continued. "Perez faced a breaking-and-entering charge last year."

"Yes, I saw that. Any clue why it would have been withdrawn?"

"No, but I did find that the detective in the investigation was the same one who got Dunning off a similar charge two years ago."

"Similar how?"

"Drive-by shooting victim's house broken into."

"Really," I said as she showed me the report on her cell phone. I slowly scrolled through it, scanning the information as one name stood out to me. "Detective Dwayne Cook?"

"That's him. Seems both men ended up walking free despite plenty of evidence proving their crimes."

"Let's add his name to the list of things to follow up," I said as I looked outside and saw the sky begin to fade. "We should get things ready for the move."

We ended up filling a couple of bags with essentials including basic groceries, toiletries, clothes, and whatever else I could think of. I also threw in a couple of board games I had lying around and a deck of cards just in case the boredom got too great. Better to have them and not need them than...well, you get the idea. Anyway, once we were packed and had everything ready, we waited another hour before finally heading out into the night.

The drive up to Freeport took almost an hour thanks to me taking the long way around in case we had already picked up possible tails. Thankfully, the house sat on almost an acre of land, giving us enough isolation from nosy neighbors who remained on the other side of thick vegetation. Once inside, I set Max up in one of the three bedrooms before Linda helped him with his bathroom needs.

He seemed OK, and by the time his head hit the pillow, it took just minutes for him to fall asleep. I couldn't imagine the mental state of his poor mind after everything he'd been through, but I knew that for the time being, there wasn't a whole lot I could do to help him. Other than keeping him safe, I needed to find the source of the threat to his life. If I didn't, then the fate of a little boy would already be sealed.

7

RATHER THAN STAY AT THE HOUSE IN FREEPORT, I ENDED UP returning back to my own apartment a couple of hours after Max nodded off to sleep. With Linda watching over him, I knew he'd be safe as long as she was around, and that would free me up to continue following through with the Perez case.

My first port of call the next morning was the police station, where I hoped my new client had had enough time to think about how he was going to communicate with his attorney. Trust was an important factor in my line of work and something I needed to build with Perez if he was going to start opening up.

The second the officer led Perez into the interview room, I knew we still hadn't turned the corner when he could barely make eye contact with me. The officer sat him down and uncuffed him before heading back out again. I waited until we were left alone before trying to get through to Perez, who looked even more disheveled than the previous time I'd laid eyes on him.

"How are they treating you?" I asked to open the meeting. He shrugged his shoulders ever so slightly, and I took it as the smallest step forward. A tiny reaction was better than none at all. "Mario, I need to ask you how you came to be at Hillary Warner's home. You did take the boy and his caregiver, did you not?" No response. "I'm walking into a bail hearing in less than three hours from now, and you have to give me something if you expect me to be able to get you out of here today."

I wasn't expecting much from him, but that was when he did look up, his bloodshot eyes like those of a man who'd drunk himself into oblivion the previous night or cried himself to sleep. Something told me it was the latter.

"You don't know anything," he said as he looked down at the table again.

"Then tell me," I snapped back, my patience growing thinner by the second. "You want me to help you, then speak to me."

"Listen, Mr. Carter, I get that you have a job to do, but I'm safer in here than I am out there."

Finally, a sentence and a sense of direction. I seriously felt like applauding, but my mind began to take off again, wondering why he would think prison to be safer than the real world.

"I can protect you out there." I leaned forward to amplify my point. "If that's what it takes, Mario, I'll make sure you're protected, but to get that protection, you're going to have to give me something."

He looked at me again and studied my face.

"You don't know these people. They will kill me the first chance they can."

"Did you kill Harold Dunning? Tell me that much."

"No, I didn't," he said, shaking his head as he tried to convince me. "I tried to save him, but…"

"But what? Who killed him? Mario, who shot Harold Dunning?"

I think he wanted to tell me, but the fear got to him.

"I can't tell you."

"OK, then don't," I said. "But believe me when I tell you that they have a lot more chance of getting to you in here than they will out there. I can't protect you in here and certainly not once they transfer you to prison. But out there, Mario…out there, I can keep you safe. You just have to believe me."

"What makes you think you can even get me bail, Mr. Carter? Damn fool if you think you can dictate to these people."

"The one thing I know is that you *will* go to jail if we don't try. This way, we at least have a chance."

I didn't think he was going to come around, but I saw him slowly begin to come out of his shell. Being defensive, angry, and unsupportive…it all added up to engagement, and that was exactly what I needed in order to build rapport. What I needed was for him to trust me. Once I had that, anything was possible.

"You don't want to get involved in this, Mr. Carter. Honest. These guys don't play around."

"I'm already involved," I said, thinking about the little

orphaned boy with an uncertain future sitting up in Freeport. "And whether you like it or not, I'm in this until the end."

When he looked over at me again, I could see his defenses dropping, the walls finally coming down enough for him to consider my proposal. I don't know what part got to him, but when he spoke next, I felt our differences finally falling away.

"If something happens to you or your people, just remember that I tried to warn you."

"I'll remember," I said. "Now tell me who it is that you're so afraid of."

Before answering, he looked past me toward the door and then behind him to make sure we weren't in one of those rooms where one wall was made of glass. "There's nobody listening to us," I said. "Of that, I'm positive."

"That doesn't make me feel any better. You have no idea who you're dealing with."

"Then tell me."

"I wish I could," he said as he pulled back ever so slightly.

"If I'm going to help you—"

"They're cops, all right?" He hissed the words, pushing each of them through his clenched teeth in the hope of silencing them a little more.

"Cops? Do you mean actual police officers? Which ones? How many?"

"Yes, real cops, and I don't know how many."

"Name them." I was starting to blunt my words, hoping to give him just enough of a shove to open up.

"I can't." He looked past me again. "If they find out I've talked to you—"

"They already think that anyway," I said, cutting him off. "Mario, they saw you getting picked up on TV, saw me walk into the police station on two occasions. They're not thinking that you're sitting silently in a cell. They're picturing you sitting with your attorney spilling your guts." He looked at me wide-eyed. "I'm sorry, but that's the fact."

"Then I'm a dead man."

"A dead man with choices." He sat back in his seat and looked up at the ceiling as I felt the fear radiate out from him like a furnace. That's when I thought I'd try a little more fishing. "Is one of them Dwayne Cook?"

He snapped his eyes back on me as his jaw dropped open. Whack a mole this wasn't, but I could see that I'd nailed one on my first try.

"How did..."

"How did I know it might be him? Call it instinct," I said. "It's kind of what I do."

A knock on the door suddenly interrupted us, loud enough for Perez to just about jump out of his seat. When I called out, the door opened, and one of the detectives poked his head through.

"Sorry to interrupt, but we have an update regarding your client," Dan Oakland said to me before turning his attention to Perez. "Well, Mario, looks like we have an update for you. We've just found Hillary Warner."

"You found her?" Oakland nodded but didn't look at me as he kept his gaze fixed on Perez.

"We also found blood on the side of your truck which we're having tested as we speak. So are you ready to talk with us?" Malkovic came in behind his partner, and together, the detectives stared at Perez.

"My client will cooperate," I said, taking the initiative.

"That's awesome," Oakland said as he dropped into one of the chairs. His partner did likewise after closing the door. He pulled out a recorder while Oakland switched on the camera to film the interview. After making sure they had set everything up, Oakland took the helm and began asking questions.

Perez answered some of the questions, but his answers were far from helpful, most of them vague while others he deflected with a standard *I don't know*. I could feel the tension in the room rise with each passing second as the detectives took turns trying to get any sort of lead out of my client but to no avail.

"Mario, we found Hillary Warner with a bullet to the face." I felt adrenaline hit my system as I recalled what Linda had told me about Dunning's fate. "We found a blood spatter on the side of your truck that we believe will match the victim, and we have a firearm found inside your vehicle. You're in a world of trouble right now. Make it easy on yourself and tell us where the boy is. Tell us where Max is so we can call off the search."

Perez kept his head lowered, his jaw clenching and relaxing as he felt the world closing in around him. At one point, he looked over at me, but there wasn't much I could do for him, not unless he helped himself.

"I didn't kill her," he whispered. "I didn't kill Dunning, and I didn't kill the woman."

"Then how did the blood end up on your truck?"

"I don't know."

"What about the gun? It was found under your seat, Mario. Under your seat. I mean, guns don't just turn up randomly under people's seats."

"I don't know."

"What about Dunning? Was it he who asked you to go and get his son?" That was when Malovic joined in.

"I think Hillary Warner got in the way," he said, hoping for an outburst. "Your friend asks you to go and grab his boy, and what do you know, some broad gets in the way and you pop her."

Oakland took over again. "Did you think she was going to identify you? Is that it?"

"No," Perez said as his fingers began trembling in earnest.

"THEN WHERE IS THE KID?" Malovic roared as he slammed a fist down onto the table. Perez jumped, as did I. "DAMN IT, YOU PIECE OF—"

"Cool it, Detective," I said, cutting in. "My client is trying to answer as best he can."

"Your client is hiding the location of a seven-year-old child," Oakland snapped at me. "Maybe you can help us convince him to tell us what he knows."

Talk about guilt. I could feel the heat rising in my cheeks faster than the cop's fingers tapping on the table as he continued berating Perez. I felt like my own conscience would get the better of me and I would jump and spill the beans at any moment. I imagined the stunned silence as both detectives stared at me before arresting me right there and then. Maybe that's what I should have done: shared the news that Max was safe and not lying in some ditch like they were expecting. But I couldn't. I just couldn't.

With Perez revealing that cops were involved, I knew that Max's safety remained firmly in my hands and I had to continue hiding him until I had all the answers. For all I knew, the two detectives sitting in front of me could have been working for Cook. No, I needed to continue holding my cards close to my chest if I was going to ensure Max's safety.

"Gentlemen, we're going in circles," I said, cutting off the needless questions. Malovic stopped immediately while Oakland continued for a few more seconds before finally giving it a rest.

"I'm charging you with the murders of Harold Dunning and Hillary Warner, Mario," Oakland said as he slid his paperwork back into the folder. "Also kidnapping, breaking and entering, and obstruction. And that's just for starters."

By the time I walked out of the station an hour later, Mario Perez had become the lead story on every news network in the state, if not the country. He was the hottest news going, and this time when I walked out through the doors of Zone 1 Police Station, what met me almost immediately was a crowd of reporters all vying for an exclusive they could use to lead their six o'clock bulletins.

I spent another twenty minutes or so standing in the

middle of that crowd answering as many questions as possible while giving away very little information. It could have been an hour and I don't think I would have satisfied their curiosity any more than I eventually did. Reporters weren't known for letting a source walk away without answering every last question, and I eventually had to force my way through their ranks in order to escape. A couple of the more enthusiastic ones ended up following me all the way back to my car, something that annoyed me due to the prospect of now having the world know what I drove.

Once back in the Mustang, I didn't hesitate to fire up the engine and get the hell out of there, and once on the road, I phoned Grace to see whether she was still at the office. Thankfully, she was, and I made it my mission to get there before she left so I could fill her in on the latest. As it turned out, she had news of her own the moment I walked through the door.

"You have a meeting with the district attorney at ten tomorrow morning. His secretary sent me the email confirmation while you were talking to the reporters." I noted the television on the back wall playing that very scene thanks to the Channel 2 news, although I couldn't hear anything due to it being muted. The screen was just one of Dwight's ideas for the office to keep up to date with current events.

I led Grace through to my office, where I dropped my briefcase on the desk before walking over to the window to check for stalkers. In all of my years working as a defense attorney, I had only ever had one case that turned into a kind of media circus, but not even that case came anywhere near this, and this was still just the beginning.

"Grace, can you please find me a car to drive for the next couple of months?"

"A car?" I turned back to see her looking at me curiously.

"Yes, I don't care what kind, just something cheap and reliable. I don't care if it's rented or an outright purchase, but I need something tomorrow."

"Of course, but why?"

"Call it intuition, but something is telling me that I'm about to spend a lot of time on the news networks, and I don't want to be constantly followed because people recognize my car. That and because I treasure this set of wheels." I walked back to my desk and sat on the edge of it. "Try and make it as inconspicuous as possible. A lot of people are going to be hating on me because of that little boy still being missing, and I can see the public coming for blood once they know I'm representing the defendant in the case."

"OK, I'll see what I can do. Any particular budget in mind?"

"Nothing extravagant," I said. "Maybe try and keep it under five grand."

"OK, under five grand it is," Grace said before changing the subject. "How was he? Perez, I mean. Did he tell you where the boy is?"

"No, he didn't," I said, and that was the very first time that I'd ever lied to my assistant. To say that I felt bad for doing so would be an understatement. Grace had been nothing but good to me, an honest woman with a heart of gold. I immediately loathed the day she found out the truth, and I knew it would come at some point or another. It was just a matter of when.

"So sad," Grace continued. "To think that poor little boy is now an orphan."

"Yes...yes, it is sad."

After handing me a couple of messages she'd taken on my behalf, Grace wished me a good night and left me alone as I dropped into my chair. Something about the way she mentioned Max just affected me in an unexpected way. I felt bad in so many ways, and to be honest, I again questioned whether it would all be worth it. I had taken steps to essentially alienate myself from friends and those I considered family, had broken the law, and I was now withholding evidence in an ongoing investigation. If caught, and I had no doubt that I eventually would be found out, I would face disbarment, risk losing my job, and potentially end up in prison myself. If this wasn't a risk then I didn't know what was.

8

LINDA AND I AGREED NOT TO CONTACT EACH OTHER UNLESS it was absolutely necessary, even with the burner phones she'd brought with her when she came to my apartment the previous afternoon. It was that phone I kept feeling in my pocket as I sat at my desk that early evening while listening to the rest of the staff slowly vacate the building. Staring back at me on the laptop was Perez, his mugshot from a previous charge making him look even younger than when I'd met him in that police interview room.

I must have worked my way through his criminal record no less than half a dozen times during that late afternoon, ending up right back to where I'd begun just as the final remnants of daylight left the ever-encroaching night sky. It was around six-thirty when I walked to the window and leaned against the frame, my brain working overtime trying to make sense of the hundreds of questions still floating around in there.

An electronic ding from my laptop brought me back into the moment, and when I went back to it, I found a new email from Linda waiting in my inbox. *More files on Perez* was in the subject line, and when I opened the email, I found a couple of links to our cloud server dropbox. I hit one and found several files on Perez's background, including school records and work history.

I clicked into the school records to begin with, working my way through the limited information on hand. I could see from the results that Mario Perez was never going to be a Harvard scholar based on his grades. In total, he had two suspensions in Grade 3, another one in Grade 4, and then an expulsion, after which he changed schools. Two years into high school, he faced another suspension, after which he turned his attention to the workforce.

After closing the school folder, I opened up his work history and began working my way through his many jobs, jobs that fell far short of providing an income capable of supporting a bachelor's lifestyle. In one year alone, Perez had held no less than seven jobs, each lasting just a few weeks before coming to an abrupt end. The longest position was as a laborer for a construction company back in 2019, a role he'd held for four months.

I was about to close the folder and head home when I spotted a name that felt very familiar to me. According to the report, Perez had worked for a company called Lassiter's Transport, a delivery service that employed a vast fleet of trucks to carry goods all over the country. Lassiter's worked with a vast number of clients and had been in business for a couple of decades, the owner a name well known around the greater Pittsburgh area. Klaus Weber owned several high-profile businesses, the most well-known being Pinkman Coffee. Not surprisingly, the coffee in my current cup just happened to be Pinkman's Dark Roast, my personal favorite.

I leaned back a little as I tried to remember where I had seen the reference to the transport company, but it didn't jump out at me. Frustrated, I got out of the chair again and took my near-empty cup back to the kitchen, where I rinsed it out before setting it down on the drying rack. The notion of not finding any answers to the hundreds of questions was beginning to not just frustrate me but also outright annoy me. I needed those questions answered if I was to have any chance of moving forward with the case, especially now that I also had an impending meeting with the district attorney. Dealing with a murder charge was hard enough, but with two and a missing person directly involved in the case?

That was when it hit me, the answer jumping out while I was thinking about the murder charge. I nearly ran back to my office and dropped into the chair a split second after my fingers had already begun working their way across the keyboard. Two seconds later, I began scanning the new folder I had opened, my eyes looking for the one keyword that would finally open up a new path.

I found it halfway down the page: Harold Dunning's work history, just a few entries smaller than Perez's. Like my client, he had held various jobs in his time, including a stint for Lassiter's Transport running Pinkman's Coffee across state lines. It also just happened to be one of the Lassiter's trucks that Dunning had been caught in with the cocaine.

Harold Dunning and Mario Perez both worked for Lassiter's Transport. That was the connection between the two men and a place where I could now turn my attention. I was about to punch the name into Google when a voice interrupted my concentration.

"You aiming to burn the midnight candle, Carter?"

I looked up to see Dwight staring at me through the doorway. He wasn't dressed in his usual suit but rather in a full-on tuxedo complete with an untied bowtie.

"Possibly," I said. "Got a meeting with the DA tomorrow and want to make sure I'm ready. You look like you're ready to party, though."

Dwight chortled as he shook his head. "I don't think bigwig fundraisers qualify as party central," he said. "You think you can handle this case? You know, to be honest, I wasn't sure how big this would get when I agreed to give it to you. A double homicide and a missing kid? This is primetime stuff. Gotta keep a level head on your shoulders if you're going to get through it. "

"What, no faith, boss?"

Again, he grinned at me. "I got faith in you, Ben. Just don't let me down."

"I won't," I said, feeling that familiar rumble of guilt as I thought of Max. When I'd stopped on the side of the road and picked him up, I had no idea that it would lead me down a path of lies and deceit to those I trusted most. It didn't just frighten me to think of how this might end. It just about killed me knowing that I would be breaking the trust of people I considered family.

"All right, I better run or Grace will yell at me. She's waiting for me in the car."

He left before I could answer, and I listened to his footfalls make their way down the corridor before eventually fading out into the night. Once I was sure he was gone, I turned my attention back to the emails and sent Linda a quick message with my findings, asking her to add the lead I had found to her own extensive list of things to do. It was the first connection found between the two men, and I could feel a lot more hiding in the background.

Once I hit send, I shut down the laptop as well as the rest of my office and headed out into the night. I still had a lot more questions than answers, but now that I had found my first breakthrough, my hopes grew exponentially of snowballing that one small bit of success into more. I was still trying to picture the two men working at the same place when halfway across the parking lot, I suddenly had the sensation of being watched, so much so that I stopped in my tracks to look around.

Our parking lot didn't have the best lighting, with one side joining the back end of a park and thick vegetation running the entire length. Lamp posts stood on opposite corners, but their light failed to stretch far enough into the lot, and the majority of the space sat in darkness, not really a problem for those who worked normal hours. With the sensation refusing to go away, I slowly continued toward my car, still carefully studying the tree line beyond the lot. As if feeling the urge to add to the atmosphere, the breeze suddenly picked up enough for a discarded soda can to start rolling along the ground, the sound giving me the absolute creeps.

If it hadn't been for a car pulling into the lot right at that moment, who knows how things would have turned out? Maybe a werewolf would have jumped out of the shadows or some mugger anxious to make a quick buck. Thankfully it was neither who jumped out, and after giving Chelsea and her daughter Alison a quick wave as the two cleaners parked their car, I continued on to my own.

When I walked into my apartment just twenty minutes later, I had every intention of leaving my briefcase next to the door, grabbing a beer from the fridge and then dropping into my recliner to watch whatever ballgame I could find on the television. That plan lasted all of two seconds when I kept my briefcase in hand, went to the fridge for the beer, and then dropped onto the couch, where I took the laptop out for some more detective work.

At some point during my drive home, Linda had sent me a brief email with just the word *Thanks*. I opened it while muting the television, and after dropping the remote onto the couch, I fell headfirst into some more detective work. I say headfirst because I don't think I looked up again until well after ten, by which time I'd completely skipped dinner and felt my eyelids ready to drop at any moment.

But while it might have felt like nothing more than me chasing my tail for the most part, I did happen to find a name that I thought warranted some further investigating.

It was the name of an accountant not only linked to Lassiter's Transport but also to the two men currently on the top of my list. That name was Matthew Foster.

Just before making the decision to call it a day, I sent Linda a final email, adding yet another name for her to add to our current list of witnesses we needed to investigate. I could see her face when she opened it and couldn't help but grin. It wasn't all bad, though. She once told me that she appreciated my wanting to get involved in the investigation side of things. Before me, she used to work for a lawyer up in Wexford who spent more time trying to date her than actually giving her work.

It felt good to finally close the laptop after another long day, and I don't think I spent more than a few minutes staring up at the darkened ceiling once I fell into bed. Sleep took me with little effort but not before I thought of a little boy no doubt already sleeping several suburbs over. Everything I was doing I did for him, and my only hope was that we'd all come out relatively unscathed on the other side. If we didn't, I wasn't sure if I could handle the repercussions, not when people like Linda and Christy were also relying on me to see this through. If I failed and they fell with me? It was a question that frightened me to the core.

9

I WOKE UP EARLY THE FOLLOWING MORNING WITH AN EXTRA bounce in my step and not because I'd had a relatively good sleep. What gave me that extra boost of emotional energy was the fact that it was what I saw as the first day of the case where I would officially take a step forward with an actual direction. Thanks to some early investigation, we had some names to follow up on, and I knew that Linda did her best work while in front of a keyboard with an active Internet connection.

While my meeting with the DA wasn't until ten, I wanted to drop into the office first to catch Grace up on the latest developments. I'd found out early on in our professional relationship just how switched on she was, which was why she was such a great assistant. Just like I knew she would be, I found her already sitting at her desk by the time I arrived.

"How was the party last night?" I asked as I shot her a wave.

"Don't remind me," she said with a roll of the eyes. "I ended up leaving Dwight there and went home early."

"That good, huh?"

"Not really my scene, if you know what I mean."

"I do know," I said as I gestured for her to follow me. "Got a few minutes to catch up?"

"Of course."

It took me a few moments to set myself up, during which time Grace grabbed each of us a cup of coffee. When she returned, I had my laptop open, along with the folders Linda and I had set up for the case.

"Can't believe they still haven't found that little boy yet," Grace said as she sat down. "It's been all over the news."

"Yes, I know," I said, wishing we could have avoided speaking about Max. Guilt is a horrible thing to hide. "I'm sure they'll find answers soon. In the meantime, I've managed to come up with a few things we need to check up on before we go to trial with Mario Perez. He's now been charged with two counts of murder and various other things, so we need to make sure we've got everything ready."

"Has he given you no indication about the boy at all?"

I could see she couldn't let it go, and like any parent, I guess her maternal side just wanted to help in any way she could.

"If I tell you something, can you promise me you'll keep it to yourself?" Her eyes lit up in an instant.

"About the boy?"

"Grace, promise me."

"I promise. Tell me. What is it?"

"There's every chance that Max Dunning is alive and well."

"Then where is he?" Her knuckles turned white as she gripped her iPad tightly.

"Perez assured me that he's OK." Lies. More lies. I hated them, knowing they would all come back to bite me in the ass sooner or later.

"But how do you know?"

"He gave me his word that the boy is OK. Now please," I said as I looked at her with hope. "If we're going to see this through, we have to find out the truth, OK?"

"OK, I'm sorry. It's just heartbreaking to think of what he's already been through and now..."

"And now we can make sure that we help bring him home by proving our case." I looked at my laptop screen, deflecting Grace's emotions as I turned her attention to matters at hand. "I found a link between Perez and Dunning that we need to investigate further. As it turns out, they both worked for Lassiter's Transport, and through that company, they both had contact with an accountant named Matthew Foster."

"Matty?" I looked up at her, surprised.

"You know him?"

"Yes, of course. He went to school with Dwight's sister. Dated her at one point, if I remember correctly."

"Oh wow, small world."

"It is," Grace said. "He's been to our home a couple of times. His wife, Anne, runs a florist business."

"We need to speak with him," I said. "Find out what he knows about Perez and Dunning. How big is his accountancy firm?"

"Not huge. I think he employs three or four accountants throughout the year, a couple of extras around April to deal with all the W-2s."

"Can you set up a meeting for us? Sooner rather than later."

"Of course. How's this afternoon, if I can get us in?"

"This afternoon works fine," I said. "I'll let Linda know so she can turn her focus elsewhere."

"Where *is* Linda?" Grace suddenly asked, catching me off guard. "I haven't seen her in a while."

"Staying with her aunt," I said, the words rolling out of my mouth before I had a chance to audit them. "She's kind of old and just came out of the hospital."

"Oh, OK. Give her my best."

"I will," I said, checking the time. "We'd better wrap this up soon. Don't want to be late for the DA."

"No, Arthur is not one to let tardiness slide. He's kind of a stickler for punctuality."

"Yes, I've seen it firsthand," I said before changing the subject. "And please don't forget about the car. I really don't want to be driving the Mustang right now. Too many angry people looking for someone to throw their wrath at."

"Can you blame them?"

"No, of course not. I just wish they'd understand that everyone has a right to defend themselves."

"They do, although many of them don't care. They just want someone to yell at so they don't have to think about their own lives." She typed something on her iPad. "I'll find you something."

"Thank you, Grace."

We finished our brief meeting a few minutes later, and after repacking the laptop into my briefcase, I headed back out into the morning. The sun was just breaking through the clouds as I walked through the doors, and it kind of felt like a welcoming to the next phase of the case. With one name now on my list, who knew where Foster would lead us?

Once back out on the road, I couldn't resist the urge to call Linda on the burner phone. I needed to know how the little guy was doing, and she answered on the very first ring.

"Geez, that was quick," I said when she answered it with a *Good morning, Ben.*

"Call it a woman's intuition," she said with that amused tone of hers.

"How is Max?"

"Still sleeping, if you can believe it. We stayed up late playing Monopoly."

"Who won?"

"He did, and I wasn't even trying to let him win. He's a smart kid."

"Listen, if Grace calls you, I told her you were staying with your aunt who's just come out of the hospital."

"I have an aunt?"

"You do now," I said. "She kind of caught me off guard. Any updates on your end?"

"Just one about Matthew Foster. He ran an importing business with a partner named Enrique Porter."

"Doesn't surprise me. Most rich guys have multiple businesses."

"Yes, but Porter is currently serving time. His rap sheet is quite the read. We're talking blackmail, bank fraud, deception, assault."

"Why would a man like Matthew Foster get into bed with a guy like Porter?"

"I'm still trying to work that out, but one thing's for sure. Police reports indicate that they believe Porter was taking the fall for someone else."

"You mean Foster?"

"It doesn't say, but there's a possibility."

"OK, keep me updated," I said. "Turns out that Grace knows him and is trying to set up a meeting for this afternoon."

"Grace knows Foster?"

"Aha. Dwight's sister dated him back in college. There's definitely history here, so we'll have to tread carefully."

"OK, on it," Linda said and just like that, ended the call. Five minutes later, I parked my car outside the DA's office building and prepared to walk into enemy territory.

While I had met and worked with multiple prosecutors, I could count on one hand the number of times I'd met with the district attorney. Arthur Clements wasn't known for his social skills but was a dedicated servant to the people of Pittsburgh with a mission to clean up the city. He'd held the position for a good number of years, and the number of prosecuted criminals spoke for themselves.

I grabbed a seat in the waiting room after letting the receptionist know I'd arrived and watched the limited view of the common office area behind her. The place was buzzing with people actively working their cases. Some stood by their desks while talking on phones while others sat behind computer screens as their fingers danced across keyboards. Less than two minutes after taking a seat, my number was called.

"Mr. Clements will see you now," the receptionist called out to me and gestured toward the only door at the end of a very short corridor. It stood open, and I could see someone's side profile as they stood just out of full view.

The first thing I noticed when I walked into the office was the tension hanging in the air, most of it coming from one of the three men in the room. I didn't recognize him, and as it turned out, I didn't need to as he gave me a half head nod before passing me on his way out.

"See you next week, George," Clements called after him from behind his desk before turning his attention to me. "Ah, Carter, so good of you to come. Sit down." He pointed to one of the two chairs facing him. Standing behind him and a little to the right was Xavier Bartell, the man prosecuting the Mario Perez case and my direct opponent.

"Thank you," I said as I took a seat. It didn't come as a

surprise to me when I felt that familiar tightening in my stomach after Max came to mind. I was beginning to get used to the kid showing up every time I had to lie about him.

"Quite a mess we have on our hands," Clements said as he leaned back in his seat. The guy weighed upwards of three hundred pounds, and the protesting screech from the back of his chair confirmed its struggle. "This department doesn't want to waste weeks bringing your client to trial in this matter. We feel a sense of urgency to move things along considering the missing boy still hasn't been found."

"What has your client said about Max Dunning?" Bartell asked as he leaned against the wall and folded his arms. "Is he willing to cooperate?"

"He wants to help any way he can, but unfortunately, he doesn't know where the boy is."

"How is that even possible?" Clements said as he looked at his prosecutor. I could see unspoken words passing between them but kept my own silent as Clements turned back to me. "Look, Carter, there isn't a whole lot of negotiation to be had here. Your client is facing a double murder charge, and while I might not be able to push through a death penalty with the current moratorium, Perez will still face life regardless. If he tells us where the boy is and we find him unharmed, we'd be willing to offer thirty years, plus he may even be able to persuade the judge for bail."

Talk about an offer to tear at the heartstrings. Mine, not Perez's. Thirty years *and* the possibility of bail.

Imagine how tough it was for me to sit there knowing not only where Max was at that moment in time, but also knowing that he was completely unharmed. I could have come clean right then and there, perhaps saved countless hours of pointless searching, and yet...I couldn't.

"I honestly wish I could give you the information, Mr. Clements, but I've spoken with my client, and he's adamant he doesn't know anything."

"Tell him the deal in any case," Clements continued. "He knows something. We all know he does. He kidnapped the kid and saw the two people get shot. Appeal to his humanity if you have to; maybe that will work. But remember this, counselor." Clements leaned forward to make his point as he stared at me with his red cheeks and bloodshot eyes. "If he doesn't cooperate and we prove his guilt in a court of law, I'll see to it that your client serves the hardest time there is."

He held my gaze as Bartell looked on from his side of the room. I let the threat blow over my head, figuring it best not to react. I knew that my day would come, and when it did, I hoped to have the answers that would ensure all of us would come out of this ordeal relatively unscathed. If I didn't, the repercussions would end more lives than I was willing to consider.

10

Checking my cell phone as I walked out of the DA's office, I found a text from Grace advising me that the earliest she could get us in to see Foster was the following Monday. Using the delay to my advantage, I immediately sent a reply asking her to try and get me in down at the courthouse for a bail hearing. I knew the chances of the judge granting Perez temporary freedom while facing a double murder charge with a third victim effectively missing was virtually zero, but I still had to give it a try.

I barely got out on the road before her reply came through with confirmation that the bail hearing had been set for three that afternoon. Feeling a need to speak to someone in on the secret, I pulled out the burner phone and called Linda. Call it a momentary weakness, but I think what I needed was to hear someone else tell me that what we were doing was the right thing.

When she didn't answer after the first few rings and

the system ended the attempt, panic immediately set in as visions of police storming the home suddenly filled my head. My fingers even gripped the steering wheel tightly enough for the knuckles to pop, my arms preparing to swing the car into a U-turn so I could race up to Freeport. Thankfully the phone began to ring just a couple of seconds later.

"Linda?"

"Sorry, I was out in the backyard with Max. We needed some fresh air."

"Had me worried," I said. "I had no idea it was going to be this hard talking to people about him knowing where he is."

"You met with the DA?"

"I did, and they don't know anything. As far as they're concerned, Perez is holding out on them, and they want nothing more than to give him the death penalty and hope for the governor to end the current moratorium on executions."

"I bet they do," Linda said. "How did Grace go with Foster?"

"Seeing him Monday. In the meantime, I have a bail hearing in a few hours after which I'm hoping to pick up a new car and come up to see you guys."

"No, don't," she suddenly said, surprising me.

"Don't as in don't come up and see you guys?"

"Better to stay where you are. If one of the reporters or detectives decides to wise up and put a tracker on you or your car, then we're going to be screwed. Don't risk it for the sake of a visit. We're fine."

"You sure? I could bring some Papa Dom's pizza." I knew how much she loved the place. "Pepperoni with chili flakes."

"Hey, don't tease, Ben, that's not fair." I could hear the pain in her voice as I recanted.

"OK, OK, I'll stop," I said with a slight chuckle. "Sorry. Just feeling a bit alone in facing this."

"I get it, but you have to stay strong. We all do, at least until we can figure this out."

"There are people still out searching for him, you know? I feel so bad knowing that we could end it with just a single phone call."

"Yes, and then we put Max right back in the firing line." Of course, she was right. "We're doing the right thing, Ben. Just stay strong and work the case."

Linda didn't see herself as a girly girl, if you know what I mean. She'd told me plenty of times that she had never been into dolls and dressing up and the things her friends used to be into. While she didn't quite adopt the whole tomboy persona, she told me that she just preferred shooting guns and driving fast cars, doing things that had always been considered *boy things*. She had a '73 Mustang in her garage that she had been restoring for years while every bookshelf in her house held all manner of automotive memorabilia. And yet there was no denying that distinctive maternal energy I felt come off her whenever someone needed some sort of reassurance.

"Thanks, Lin," I said and hung up, feeling a whole lot better about the obstacles still lying ahead of us.

I ended up heading back to the office. Grace followed

me into my office, where she handed me a Post-It note with an address on it.

"Found you some wheels," she said. "Got you a deal on a superseded rental car that Hertz was advertising for half price. Two months long enough?"

"Two months will be perfect," I said as I slipped the piece of paper into my pocket. "Listen, can you do me a favor?"

"Of course."

"Can you follow me home in a couple of hours and then drop me off at the rental place? Think I'll pick it up before heading to court."

"Worried about stalkers, huh?"

"I've been listening to the news, and I'm not getting great vibes from the general public."

"Did you know that the governor has been inundated with requests to turn over the moratorium on—"

"Executions, yes I heard," I said. "Even had the DA in my ear offering Perez a deal if he gave up little Max's location."

"I heard that Clements is one of the people calling for the executions to resume."

"Yeah, with my client in mind." I dropped into the chair and closed my eyes, feeling the weight of the world on my shoulders.

"Can I ask you something?" I opened my eyes again and watched Grace sit in one of the spare chairs. "You brought this case to Dwight. You didn't have to take it on; it wasn't even on our radar." I knew what she was about to ask long before I heard the words. "Why did you take it on? I mean, I can see it from a publicity point of view. Geez, it might even give your career one hell of a boost. But even knowing that you would be representing someone who the public would lynch in a heartbeat, you still took it on."

I didn't respond immediately, the answer not coming as freely as I had hoped. The truth is, I didn't know what to tell her. The real reason was something reserved for another day, one far into our future, or so I believed.

"Call it intuition" was all I could come up with, a response without any real substance. Grace accepted it just like I knew she would.

We each spent the next couple of hours at our respective desks researching the current case. It was also during this time that the prosecutor sent through his evidence for me to go through, evidence I would need to fully understand if I was to have any chance of saving my client. The first part I went through was the folder containing most of the photographs, and boy did some of them hit me hard.

Topping the list were the crime scene photos of both Dunning and Warner, each of them shot brutally in the face. Dunning lay on his side, his hands tied behind his back. He'd been executed by a cold-blooded killer, someone lacking any shred of human decency who didn't care about his actions in the least. Staring at those photos, I couldn't help but wonder whether we'd been wrong thinking the method used to kill them was meant as a kind of message, that the killer must have really hated their victims.

It was seeing the similarity between the crime scenes

that got me thinking, namely about how both the bodies looked like discarded trash. If anything, it felt as if the killer just didn't care about how they died just as long as they did, thereby freeing him or her of their presence. What I saw beyond those photos was someone who viewed the victims as nothing but an inconvenience who needed to be silenced and disposed of.

The worst part about Hillary Warner's death was that she would have never seen her fate coming. The poor woman had been shot through a blindfold. It looked like someone had popped a pillowcase over her head and then simply shot her in the face without any sort of hint of what was to come. I wondered whether she expected to walk away, perhaps to be left alone to remove the hood once her abductors made their escape.

Next, I moved on to the photos of the weapon found in Perez's vehicle. The revolver was nothing exceptional. There were a couple of pictures of the seat it had been found under before showing the vehicle from the front. The instant I saw the truck, my blood turned cold with a shiver running down my spine. The yellow F-150 shouldn't have been anything remarkable to look at, and yet it changed everything for me in a split second. Visions of seeing the truck in my rearview mirror suddenly filled my mind.

It was the rusty hood that I immediately recognized, the shape of it looking like a weird kind of owl face. I remember thinking that perhaps the owner might have manipulated the rust to look like that when I saw it following me along that lonely stretch of Route 62 just after getting Max his change of clothes and some food.

To try and get a better look at the photo, I imported it into one of my editing apps and tried to play with the settings a bit. Once done, I left it open on my screen and stared at it for several minutes. Was it really the same truck? Sadly, I didn't have a rear-facing dash camera in the Mustang, although now I cursed the day I'd refused it when I bought the car. The salesperson even tried to convince me, although at the time, it felt too much like an upsell, and I had politely declined.

"Dumbass," I whispered to myself as I stared at the truck, imagining me staring at it through the rearview mirror.

The moment I realized the truck before me and the truck following me the morning I picked up Max were one and the same, two things hit at practically the same time. The first was that Mario Perez had been at the wheel of the vehicle that morning, my now client following me for God knows how long. The second thing I realized was that he knew the whereabouts of Max Dunning.

I leaned back in my chair, too stunned to do anything but stare at the photo of the truck. The rest of the items still open faded from my mind as that one thought struck me dead center. I felt my jaw drop open, hanging in utter shock as I felt powerless to close it. If Mario Perez knew about Max, how many others did? Had he told someone?

"Are you OK, Ben? You look like you've seen a ghost."

I looked up to see Grace walking into the office and staring at me with concern. Despite trying to answer, nothing came out, the words somehow stalled in my throat. She managed to walk all the way around to my side of the desk and saw some of the other photos still open.

"You know, dead bodies creep me out too," she said as she turned the laptop screen away from me. I wanted to correct her, to say that those didn't bother me, but my attempts proved fruitless.

"Just stomach cramps," I finally managed as I closed the laptop the rest of the way.

"Oh, really? What did you have for lunch?"

"Just a Wendy's burger. I probably should have opted for something else."

"Think you'll be OK for court?" She checked her watch. "Not long to go."

"I'll be fine," I said although I wasn't too confident. The stomach cramps weren't a lie, but they certainly weren't caused by bad chow. The thought of telling her again crossed my mind, but I ended up pushing it aside just as fast. "Maybe we should get going," I suggested, hoping for the shock to pass enough for me to refocus my attention elsewhere.

"Yeah, sure, we can go."

After shutting everything down and dropping the laptop into my briefcase, I followed Grace out to the parking lot, where we parted ways toward our respective cars. She gestured me ahead of her when we reached the exit a few minutes later, and I took the lead, heading back to my place. Traffic wasn't too bad, and I only lost sight of Grace a couple of blocks from my building thanks to an ill-timed light, but it did give me a few moments to stow my car and walk back to the entrance.

The car the rental place had waiting for me turned out to be a Toyota Camry, some hybrid thing that could do like a gazillion miles on a single tank of gas. The thing looked almost brand new, but that wasn't what surprised me. The power it had when I first took off just about floored me, getting up to speed effortlessly in just a couple of seconds. OK, so I have a heavy foot when it comes to driving, which is obvious given the car I normally drive, but wow, this thing put a smile on my face when I had been anticipating a lackluster couple of months ahead of me.

With more pressing matters in my very near future, the car's performance faded the closer I got to the courthouse with the bail hearing quickly taking center stage. It wasn't the court hearing itself that I was thinking of but rather the repercussions for Perez if I failed. He would remain in prison and effectively out of my control. With him holding my secret, it didn't fill me with a whole lot of confidence moving forward. I needed him out here with me where I could keep an eye on him and make sure he didn't spill the beans.

What made me smile just a couple of blocks from my destination was not wanting to take the Camry all the way to the courthouse parking lot in case it would be attacked by some unscrupulous people feeling a need to vent their rage at the defendant's lawyer. Within just a twenty-minute drive, the car had grown on me enough to feel a need to protect it. It was a little ironic since I'd gotten it in the first place to protect my Mustang. Trying not to laugh, I ended up parking a couple of blocks over from the courthouse and walking the rest of the way.

When I rounded the next corner and saw the building directly ahead of me, I was surprised by the lack of reporters waiting on the front steps. I took it as a kind of win and only stopped for a couple of minutes to answer some of their questions before pushing through the half-dozen or so on my way inside where I breathed a little easier. I knew the chances of the same thing happening during the actual trial were almost zero.

I continued through the foyer and onto the allocated courtroom where I found both Bartell and Clements already sitting on their side of the room. Neither man paid me the slightest attention when I took my seat, but I didn't much care. I knew that this would be nothing more than a formality, not unless some divine intervention would help me get my client out of custody so I could whisk him away to some secret location until the trial.

Less than five minutes after I took my seat, the bailiff called the room to order, and a few seconds later, Judge Melissa Coltrane came out of her chambers to deal with the bail hearing. She gave the room a cursory glance on her way to the bench but didn't offer anybody so much as a head nod before taking her seat. The bailiff gave the all-clear for us to take ours, and it was time for proceedings to begin.

The judge began with the usual summary of the hearing before looking out to where both counsels sat waiting to plead their respective arguments on the matter.

I had a feeling that Bartell wanted to get the jump on me, and while I might have normally steamrolled him, this case proved a bit different.

"Your Honor," Bartell said, jumping in almost immediately. "We strongly oppose any notion of bail in this matter given that we still have a missing child somewhere out there, as well as two confirmed murder victims, both of whom have been directly linked to the defendant."

"Mr. Carter, I tend to agree with the prosecution on this matter," Coltrane said as she turned her attention in my direction. "Unless you have some truly exceptional revelation you want to share with the court."

Yes, Your Honor, was what I wanted to say. *In fact, I know exactly where Max Dunning is at this very moment, and I'm only too willing to take you there myself to prove that the child is actually fine and well.* That's what I wanted to say, but of course, I couldn't, not unless I wanted to throw away the only ace I held and subsequently risk the child's life even more. No, I couldn't reveal the truth without signing Max's death certificate myself. I had to continue the illusion until Linda and I had the answers we needed in order to confirm Max's safety.

"Your Honor, the prosecution's evidence in this matter is circumstantial at best, and given the lack of—"

"Your Honor, we have the murder weapon found in the defendant's truck, blood from one of the victims on the side of the defendant's truck, and video evidence showing the defendant in the company of not only one of the murder victims but also the missing child shortly before one of the murders. We strongly oppose—"

"OK, OK, Mr. Bartell," Coltrane said as she held a hand up to ease the prosecutor's emotions. "I hear you loud and clear." She turned her attention to me with a look of conviction that I knew to mean only one thing. "Mr. Carter, unless you can show me anything to prove your client not being linked to this matter, I have no choice but to deny bail and remand your client in custody until the trial."

"I have nothing further to share," I said as I pictured Max and Linda playing Monopoly at a kitchen table some forty miles from the courthouse, a place we could reach in less than an hour and subsequently help ease the minds of countless people. Again, I pushed the opportunity aside.

"Then bail is denied," Coltrane said as she slammed her gavel down onto the soundblock for the only time that afternoon. The echo of it punching the air hit me a couple of times over as I felt Bartell's brief look in my direction. He might have seen it as a win, but I knew that it had never been a real contest. The real battle still lay ahead of us, and that was one I had no intention of handing over so easily. The next time we met in open court, it would be a fight to the bitter end.

11

I'M NOT SURE WHAT THE REST OF THE COURT ATTENDEES thought when I practically ran from the courtroom, but the truth is, I didn't care. Yes, I'd lost, and maybe that's the part most of them, namely the DA and his prosecutor, saw when they watched me hustle it out of there, but there were far more urgent matters I needed to deal with. I barely took notice of anybody else, not when I left the courtroom and not when I walked out of the courthouse. I don't think the reporters waiting outside expected me to start running the second I hit the pavement, but again, they weren't my concern.

I ran the two blocks back to my car at speed, one because I was in a hurry to get to the prison to speak with my client and two because I wanted to avoid anybody following me. I knew people seeing my car would just be a matter of time, but I guess I wanted to try and protect myself for as long as possible. Who knew how crazy things would get during the next few weeks, especially when the authorities still wouldn't find any trace of the missing Dunning boy?

Hoping to avoid a ticket, I skirted the very edge of the speed limit on the drive to the station, weaving in and out of traffic like a seasoned racecar driver. I did get honked at a couple of times but didn't hang around long enough to endure any serious repercussions. Thankfully, the lights turned in my favor with just a single red briefly pausing my anxious drive.

I knew that the moment bail was denied, someone watching the proceedings at the courthouse would phone the police station and inform them of the result. Someone would then phone the nearest jail to transfer my client as soon as possible to clear the holding cells at the police station. I wanted to avoid having to go through the prison's admission process given that most halted visiting around four most days.

While some jails used a correctional bus to scoop up all the latest inmates in one go from all the local police stations, I knew that some inmates earned themselves a more personal ride courtesy of the local sheriff's department. If that was the case for Perez, then I knew my time would be extremely limited given his notoriety. I also expected the DA to make the call himself to ensure that Perez got to jail sooner rather than later.

I pulled into the station's parking lot in under twenty minutes of leaving the courthouse and immediately continued my running streak the second I slammed the door shut. I locked the car by holding the key fob over my shoulder but wasn't sure I heard the digital beep-beep before I reached the station entrance and pushed my way inside.

"One second, I'll see if he's still here," the cop manning the front counter told me, and it was only once she left to find out that I began to suck in some serious breaths. I'm not exactly the fittest guy around, and short sharp bursts of speed had a way of draining my energy... and oxygen.

"Come on through, Mr. Carter," the same cop called to me a few seconds later, and I followed her down to where the interview rooms sat lined up along a narrow corridor.

Once inside, I took a seat and waited patiently. I hadn't bothered to bring my briefcase as there wasn't really anything I needed to share with him, other than the outcome of the bail hearing...and the secret we shared. It was that secret which had driven the urgency that afternoon and nothing else. What I needed...the *real* purpose of this meeting, or the only reason for this meeting as far as I was concerned was to weigh up the risk of Perez blowing the secret wide open. If he did, then I and the rest of those I had already involved would be screwed. Finished. Our careers would essentially be over, and who knew how far the authorities would go with punishing us. To me, this was perhaps the most important meeting with a client ever.

Despite my breathing returning to normal, the beating in my chest did no such thing, continuing to thrum with conviction as a reflective beat continued pulsing in my temples. I could feel sweat begin to bead on my brow and wondered if it would be noticeable. Recalling how easily Grace had picked up on my nerves, I hoped to mask it enough to keep Perez from seeing the same.

Not only did my heart refuse to slow down and calm itself, but the second I heard footsteps coming down the hallway, it picked up again as I listened to my client approaching. I closed my eyes and took a deep breath, almost forcing my brain to take control of the traitorous blood pump. Only when I heard the door handle twist did I open my eyes again and turn my attention to the two men walking in.

The escort walked in behind Perez and waited until my client had taken his seat before speaking.

"We have the sheriff's department en route to take Mr. Perez to his new accommodation."

"Thank you, Officer," I said. "We won't be too long."

The cop gave me a nod before he turned around and walked out, closing the door quietly behind him. I could tell he was new due to his mannerisms. I went to the door to peer through the narrow slit of glass.

"He's gone," Perez said. "They don't tend to hang around."

"Yeah, well, I need to be sure," I said with a low tone, and only when I was absolutely sure there was nobody left behind to eavesdrop did I return to my chair.

"How was the bail hearing?"

"A complete failure," I said, returning to my usual tone as I dropped into the chair and stared at Perez. "But we both already knew that was going to happen," I finished before falling into silence.

For the next few seconds, I did nothing but stare at Perez while behind the scenes, my mind began racing with multiple ways of approaching the subject. The problem was that I suddenly had a bad feeling of letting the cat out of the bag, not just to Perez but also to the rest of the world. What if there were listening devices in the room I didn't know about? I knew the chances would be minimal but not zero. Any secrets picked up on those listening devices wouldn't be admissible in a court of law, but that wouldn't stop the secret from getting out.

Perez knew. That much was clear. He had this curious look as he watched me, maybe wondering whether I was searching for some kind of apology for losing the bail hearing. I needed a way of letting him know I knew his secret without using the words. I needed to let him know that I knew he knew about me finding Max.

"Route 62," I suddenly blurted out before having a chance to consider the words. While Perez did maintain eye contact with me, I did see him shift his hands ever so slightly as I watched the connection between us solidify. What's more, I think I saw the exact moment when he finally understood the clue as his eyes briefly dropped away. That was when I decided to throw caution to the wind and just deal with the problem at hand. I couldn't leave the station without knowing whether the secret was safe. What if something happened to Perez on the way to the prison and he'd told someone before walking into the room to speak with me?

"I know that you know," I whispered, lowering my voice enough for it to barely reach his ears.

He didn't answer immediately, but I could see that it rattled him somewhat. I didn't know how he would react, but I did understand that like me, he was a man of caution, someone who got used to watching their own back.

"Tell me he's safe," Perez finally said, his voice even lower than my own.

"He's safe," I said. "But for how long? Who have you told?"

"I've told nobody," he said. When I didn't respond, he reiterated his comment. "I swear to you, nobody knows."

"Why? Why would you leave him there?"

"Because it was either that or go through with my orders."

"Which were?" Rather than answer, he ran a finger across his throat. I narrowed my eyes as I watched him. "Why?"

"Loose ends."

"Who ordered you to kill him? Was it the same person who murdered his father?"

"Look, I was told to get rid of the kid and then go back to clean up the scene. They left before I did, and I panicked."

"They? There was more than one?"

"Yes. Like I said, I panicked and fled that place with the kid in my backseat. When I thought we'd gone far enough, I let him out."

"You didn't go back to the warehouse?"

"I did initially but then backtracked." Perez shuffled in his seat uncomfortably as he looked over his shoulder toward the door. "I knew the chances of getting back in time to clean up the scene was almost impossible, and I felt bad for leaving the kid on the side of the road. It was still dark, and part of me was scared he might get hit by a car."

"You saw me pick him up, didn't you? You followed us for who knows how long and still didn't tell me you knew when I first saw you."

"Seeing you walk through that door just about knocked me out of my seat. Who would have guessed the odds of that happening." Surprisingly, that was when he turned the tables on me. "Why didn't you head to the nearest cop shop and turn him in? There are people still out there searching for him."

"Because I had a suspicion that someone wanted the kid silenced, and you're going to tell me who so we can put this matter to rest."

"I wish I could, but the truth is, I don't know."

"What? How? You already confirmed that Dwayne Cook is involved. Is he the one who pulled the trigger?"

"That's the thing," Perez said as he again looked over his shoulder as if expecting to find a detective's face pressed against the narrow glass panel in the door. "There's someone else, someone who Cook takes orders from."

"Who?"

"I don't know, but he's the one pulling the strings. He's also the one who pulled the trigger."

"Can you identify him? You saw him, right?"

Perez shook his head. "Nope, the guy mostly stood in the shadows."

"Shadows? Surely you must remember *something*. Hair color, eye color, weight, height."

"Just an average dude who wore a baseball cap."

"Baseball cap? What sort? Which team?"

"Wasn't any team," Perez said. "It was this weird green cap with a logo on it."

"What kind of logo?" I asked. "Give me something."

"I don't know. I'd never seen it before. I could see the word *Bitter* running along the bottom of it, but that's about it."

Before he could say anything else, fresh footsteps suddenly echoed from the other side of the door, and a few seconds later, someone tapped on the window. I waved the cop in, and he opened the door.

"Sorry, the deputy is here for your client."

"We're done anyway," I said as I gave Perez a final look. I think he understood, but I needed to make sure. "Remember what I said about opening your mouth." He gave me a final nod before leading the cop out into the hallway. I followed them down as far as the next junction where I wished my client all the best. The next I would see him would be in prison, by which time we would both know whether he'd keep our secret.

12

Mario Perez

PRISON WASN'T A NEW EXPERIENCE FOR PEREZ. WITH HIS kind of lifestyle, it was always going to include stints behind bars, a place where people like him lived the other side of their lives. He'd never gone out of his way to end up in there. It had always just kind of come with the territory, a man trying to make a quick buck always at risk of getting caught, especially when drugs were involved.

This time was different, though, that much was obvious. Murder had a way of escalating any situation, and given that he now faced not one but two charges in the first degree, he knew his very life depended on how well his lawyer could fight for him. With two life sentences hanging over his head, Perez understood that this time, prison would look a whole lot different from what he'd been used to, and that difference showed up the second he stepped into the processing area of the jail.

A kind of heaviness hung in the air, and as the sheriff's deputy handed him over to the prison authorities, the mood turned south fast. There'd been some conversation between a couple of the guards when they first walked in, with someone even whistling somewhere in the background. Like a scene straight out of an old Hollywood Western where the hero walks into a saloon and the crowd falls into immediate silence, the same silence fell over the processing area when Perez walked through the doors.

Eyes turned to watch him as the deputy walked the new arrival to the admission window. The guard manning the station froze in place, and the deputy had to wave a hand to prod him into gear again. Behind him, another guard working on a computer turned in his chair to watch, while a second guard standing near the back door of the reception desk stopped sorting handcuffs.

The only ones who didn't stop what they were doing beforehand were the inmates already housed in a bunch of holding cells running along the back wall. A couple continued banging on their cell doors while a third kept calling out for a phone call he insisted was his legal right. Someone else had caught sight of the star's arrival and began calling out for him to be brought to his holding cell so he could take care of the child killer.

Perez watched all of this unfold without so much as a blink, his face that of an experienced poker player. It wasn't the first time he'd been the center of attention, and while it might have felt somewhat intimidating, he knew he wasn't about to share that emotion publicly. Prison was an entirely different kettle of fish, a place where the laws of the jungle ruled the masses and only the strong survived. Wolves and sheep was a common analogy used to describe the majority of inmates, and Perez knew which he needed to be if he was going to make it through the approaching nightmare.

Once the handover was complete, the deputy bid his counterpart farewell and left Perez standing alone at the counter while the guard prepared to finalize his admission. Since most of his credentials were already in the system, it was just a matter of updating anything that was out of date. It took the guard just over ten minutes to update the files with the inmate's current information.

It wasn't long before Perez found himself led to a holding cell. He felt his heartbeat reach near fever pitch as he followed the guard over to where several of them stood along the far wall. Faces gazed out at him from narrow windows, and he was sure his day was about to go from bad to worse.

Thankfully, the cell the guard stopped at appeared empty. Perez briefly stopped in front of the door to make sure, but his escort wasn't about to ease up on him. He gave him a significant shove in the back that sent him skittering inside.

"I ain't got all day, inmate," the guard mumbled under his breath before slamming the door shut.

The stink of stale piss immediately invaded Perez's

nostrils as the banging from other cells restarted in earnest. Some of the inmates called out to him by name, promising to make the new fish pay for his crimes, while others simply yelled obscenities. It took Perez a moment to regain his balance, and for the first few seconds, he stood almost frozen in the middle of the cell. Eventually, the stench of urine seemed to subside slightly as his body acclimatized itself to its new surroundings and the initial shock began to wear off.

Once he was a little sure of himself, Perez took a seat on the edge of a questionable metal bench that appeared to be wearing a few permanent stains. His insides remained in a tightened state, and only the beating in his chest subsiding slightly indicated that he was getting used to his surroundings. The part that he couldn't ignore was what would come next once he got through the rest of the induction process.

The one thing Perez feared most about being in prison wasn't the fact that he might spend the rest of his life there. It wasn't the guards who had already shown their severe disdain for him. It wasn't even the other inmates to a certain degree, although they would prove to be the greatest challenge for him. What Perez feared most was the classification he received the instant he walked through the doors.

Mario Perez now found himself to be an inmate under the state's protection. Other inmates sharing the same classification would be anybody who had committed a crime against a child from abusers, to rapists, to murderers. There were other crimes, of course, like standard rapists, terrorists, snitches, inmates with huge drug debts, and various other crimes. Most of these could be ignored, but not somebody accused of hurting a child. When it came to finding his spot on the ladder of respect, Perez had just dropped to the lowest rung possible.

Being a protected prisoner meant the complete opposite of those serving time within the general population, or Gen Pop. If any of those inmates wanted a protected prisoner dealt with, it took very little effort to slip a note to one of the orderlies or even a bribed guard to action a hit. With Perez currently the state's, if not the country's, most talked about prisoner at that moment, the chances of someone taking a contract out on him were high. He had told his lawyer that prison might be the safest place, but as he sat on that metal bench listening to the torrent of abuse aimed at him, he wondered just how true that idea really was.

It took almost an hour of waiting before a guard opened the door and escorted the new arrival down a couple of narrow corridors to a small office. The woman sitting inside thanked the guard and waited for him to close the door before starting her interview. Perez had been through these before and breezed through the questions in a matter of minutes. The only one he actually paused on was when she asked whether he had any feelings about hurting himself.

Normally, the question wouldn't have bothered him in the slightest. Perez knew he had a strong mind and an even stronger will to live. This was the kind of place where a survival instinct came in handy, and he wasn't about to crack under pressure. But the question brought back a moment from the previous year, a speck of time where he almost...*almost* thought about ending the cycle he'd grown tired of.

That had been the night he'd been tasked with robbing a courier who was expected to be carrying a couple of kilos of Colombia's finest. His boss had a habit of stealing from those who couldn't report the crime and making pure profits from the subsequent sale of the gear. After going through with the robbery, Perez found himself at the back of a parking lot beside an abandoned Wendy's with a near-empty bottle of Jack Daniels in one hand and a .38 snub nose in the other.

His boss had paid him on the spot, given him a clap on the back, and promised to call when more work came along. Perez took the money, found the nearest liquor store, and bought some much-needed alcohol to numb his frustrations. An hour into his parking lot drinking session was when he pulled the revolver out of his pocket and went to drop it into the glove compartment. The pause, the momentary hesitation only lasted a couple of seconds, the thought even less. Maybe a split-second of mental attention was all that thought ever received, but it was enough to give him a fright.

"No," Perez said with conviction, answering the nurse's question abruptly. Her pause told him that she suspected something more, but he wasn't about to add fuel to the fire by trying to convince her. He knew how the game was played and understood that even a hunch would bring with it restrictions.

The nurse ultimately ticked his file off and called to the waiting guard, and Perez found himself escorted back to the holding cell. She did give him a final glance just before he disappeared beyond the limit of her vision, but Perez made sure not to return her gaze. Halfway down the first corridor, a new smell had descended over the holding area, and given the near silence hanging over the place, Perez knew exactly the reason why...dinner.

One aspect he had learned early on in life was that inmates felt the strongest about two specific areas of prison life: food and medication. Nothing else in their day mattered as much as those two things, and getting between a prisoner and his food or medication meant instant revolt. The cells where previously he'd seen rabid faces staring out at him now stood empty as the occupants focused on their food.

Not surprisingly, he didn't see a waiting meal for him in his own cell, and when he asked about it and the guard said he'd hunt one down, Perez knew better. Tonight, there would be no dinner, not in the holding cell and certainly not later when he would eventually make it to his pod. This was prison, and his reputation had preceded him. Even if some sort of food did show up, Perez knew that the chances of it being untouched would be virtually zero. Tampering with a protection prisoner's food was just one of the ways other inmates ensured a living hell for their targets.

For the next hour and a half, Perez sat quietly in his cell listening to the sounds of the admissions area. Shortly after finishing their food, the other inmates resumed their previous burning of him, with some only pausing when called out by a passing guard. Not even the threat of an ass-whoopin' dissuaded many of them from launching verbal attacks.

Perez took it in his stride, so to speak, occasionally closing his eyes in an attempt to disassociate himself from the toxic environment. It very nearly worked a couple of times when he also pressed both hands over his ears hard enough to block out the sounds. He imagined himself sitting in a hotel room down in Florida, one of the few places on the planet he ever felt at home.

"Let's go, inmate," he faintly heard someone call out to him at one point, and he opened his eyes to find a guard standing in the doorway of his cell. "Let's go, let's go, soldier. I ain't got all night," the hulk of a man hissed at him while waving his meaty hands for the prisoner to move.

"Sorry, boss," Perez managed and immediately got up and followed the man out.

Night had already fallen by the time they reached the pod, with Perez looking at the blackened sky through barred windows sitting high above him. He wondered how long it would be before he'd see the same view without bars to break it—or a sunset, something he suddenly realized he hadn't paid attention to in months.

Before he could react to the sinking feeling, the guard stopped beside a door marked with a giant D, the letter dominating the very center of the metallic surface. Beside it stood an orderly holding up a bed roll, another part of prison life Perez was only too familiar with.

"Grab your bedding, inmate," the guard ordered. The orderly didn't bother waiting for Perez to reach for the roll, instead raising one arm high enough for the mattress to roll from his grip. It struck Perez in the middle, and he briefly grappled with it to regain control. When he pushed it into one armpit and looked up at the orderly, the man was already gone.

"Nurse has got you down for meds. You'll get those at 8 a.m. sharp," the guard began. "Chow arrives shortly after, and anything else you need, you ask Wilkins. He's the answer man in here. Anything else?"

"No, sir," Perez said with a shake of the head.

"Good answer." The guard nodded. "Place is already locked down for the night. Got you in a single cell for now. Not sure for how long so make the most of it."

Before Perez could answer, the guard opened the door and waved him inside. The moment the newest inmate walked through the door, he felt dozens of sets of eyes on him, multiple faces looking out at him from behind windowed doors that ran along the entire back wall on two floors. With the lights out in the common area and on inside the cells, most of the faces looking out had to shield their eyes to try and get a glimpse of him, making Perez feel even more on show. Halfway to his new cell, he felt his insides tighten as a familiar noise began to grow as numerous voices began calling out to him.

The guard ignored the shouts, continuing to usher Perez to his new cell, and once inside, he slammed the door shut without hesitation. The voices calling out to him slowed as the guard headed back to the door but erupted the second the outer door closed, the pod effectively alone again.

For the first few seconds, Perez stood his ground in the darkness while still clutching the bed roll. The smell wasn't as bad as it had been in the holding cells, but he could still detect a certain aroma he remembered from previous stints inside. It smelled a little like misery, with undertones of rancid sweat and tobacco smoke. This was a place that held its population close enough to squeeze most joy from their lives, and Perez had just been dropped into the middle of it. He turned slightly to look back at the door where the common area remained eerily dark, allowing only the voices to invade his space.

"You're the kid killer, right?"

"Watch out, folks...we got a kiiiillllleeeerrr in our midst," someone else called out. Before long, a torrent of voices called out random comments, all meant for the sole purpose of intimidation.

Perez knew he'd have to face those people eventually. Protection didn't mean he'd be safely locked in the cell all the time, just segregated from the general population who lived just a wall or two away. Come morning, every cell door in the pod would open automatically, and he'd have to face the source of those voices alone.

Instead of flicking the light on, Perez lowered the mattress onto the bed and unrolled it. His eyes had adjusted enough to make out the pillow and bed sheet. It took him just a couple of seconds to fix the bed properly, and once done, he lay down on his back, propped one hand behind his head, and stared up into the darkness. As the voices continued trying to get a rise out of him with ever-increasing insults, Perez sighed as he closed his eyes, doing his best to block out the sounds. He knew he had no choice but to accept the fact that his entire future now lay in the hands of a single man, and if that man failed, this would be his fate until the bitter end.

13

It wasn't easy leaving the station without a solid answer, but I think I got more than I expected. For one, I now knew that Detective Dwayne Cook was one of the men I needed to focus on while also searching for whoever was giving him orders. Once back in the Camry, I headed home. During the drive, I phoned Grace to ask her to reconfirm our meeting with Foster for the following Monday. That was another name I didn't want to let slip between the cracks.

While I had every intention of heading up to see Linda and Max, I knew I couldn't risk picking up a tail if I ventured out during daytime hours. So I spent the night in with pizza and beer and a silent ice hockey game on the television. I sat on the couch with the laptop in front of me going over the evidence the prosecutor had emailed me. To add extra pressure to my ever-growing list of things to do, I also received an email from the courthouse informing me that the trial date for Mario Perez had been set for September 4, giving me just two weeks to prepare my case.

The thing is, I always knew the powers that be would push for a quick turnaround. They understood the need to get the case over with, especially with the kind of publicity surrounding it. A lot of the media had begun circulating reports that authorities didn't believe Max to be alive and that the police were set to charge Perez with a third murder. If it did indeed come to pass as they predicted, then it was perhaps the only charge I could confidently prove wrong beyond any reasonable doubt.

I ended up heading to bed around nine, but instead of not setting my alarm like I normally would on a Friday night, I set it for three in the morning. Thankfully, my fatigue pulled me down into sleep just a few minutes after my head touched the pillow, giving me just under six hours of uninterrupted slumber. I'm unsure whether I dreamed at all, but I did wake up to a damp pillow beneath my face as some faint recollection of Naomi faded back into the darkness.

Rather than follow my usual morning routine, I kept the lights off and headed to the bathroom in the darkness, where I took care of my needs with the door closed and nothing more than my cell phone's flashlight for illumination. I did take a quick shower but finished in less than half the time I normally took, aware of the time continuing to count down.

It might have looked like some cloak-and-dagger routine from the outside, but I couldn't risk being seen leaving my apartment so early by any overenthusiastic reporters. I knew how hungry some of them could get for an exclusive, and the last thing I needed was for one of them to follow me and find out about Max. It was the image of me picking up a newspaper and finding a picture of him and me plastered all over the front page that drove me to desperate measures.

When I first stepped out of my apartment around a half hour after waking, I briefly paused to listen to the early-morning silence hanging over the building. Only when I was absolutely sure I couldn't detect even the slightest hint of life did I carefully close my apartment door and head for the stairwell. Just like the building itself, people wanting to gain entry into the underground parking lot needed a security pass, but I still looked over my shoulder several times while I walked to my car.

Every little creak and shudder sent a burst of adrenaline into my system, giving the beating in my chest an extra kick as I stealthily made my way along the line of cars. Rather than use the remote and risk the beeping catching someone's attention, I used the key manually before closing the driver's door as quietly as possible.

The great thing about having a hybrid was that I could set the car to use just battery power, and after getting myself ready, I silently navigated the Camry to the exit. Then I lowered the window and took a deep breath as I swiped my fob across the reader. The gate immediately began to rattle as it slowly raised, sending metallic echoes bouncing off the nearby walls that could have woken the dead. I had little choice but to sit there and watch as my only way out opened before me. If anybody *had* been watching the building, the gate gave them a big enough cue that someone was trying to make their escape in the early morning hours.

I did breathe a little easier once I had managed to put a few blocks between the building and myself, but I still kept my eye on the rearview mirror. Remembering how Perez had followed me before, I didn't want to risk a second such scenario, and I took a possible tail serious enough to head down several detours along the way. At one point, I circled a four-block radius twice to ensure I wasn't being followed, just like Linda had taught me.

Despite the drive from my apartment building to the house being just over forty miles or so and hardly any significant traffic to speak of, it still took me just under two hours to reach the place because of the constant detours I took. I figured it was better to be safe than sorry, and with no real time restraints to speak of, it didn't much matter being a little over precautious.

I did feel somewhat apprehensive when I eventually turned into the driveway, but it was short-lived as I pulled the car around the back. With the sun only just breaking above the distant horizon, I thought I'd done pretty well considering.

"Well, look who it is," Linda said from the door as I grabbed my backpack from the passenger seat.

"Thought you'd be suffering from a severe case of cabin fever by now," I said as I closed the door.

"No chance," she said as I saw a little face peek around

the corner. Linda looked down at Max and grinned. "Not when I got such a great housemate for company."

"How are ya, kiddo?" I said as I swung the bag over my shoulder and walked to the back door. "Brought a few things for you guys."

We headed inside where I emptied the bag on the kitchen table. It wasn't much, but my stash did contain all the important things, such as peanut butter cups, chocolate milk, and of course Pop Tarts. Linda's eyes lit up when she saw the orange candy bag, and she snatched them up.

"Keep these coming," she said as she tore the bag open and stuffed a couple into her mouth.

"You know it's breakfast time," I said with a grin but quickly shut up when Max reached up and grabbed a few of his own. "OK, I'm outvoted."

I picked up a small box that had fallen out and called Max over to me after taking a seat. I held it up to show him the picture of the yellow robot on the front of the box.

"Meet Bumblebee," I said as I held it out for him. "He's a Transformer. Can change into a real cool car."

I watched him tear open the box and pull out the less than impressive Transformer and immediately begin to manipulate the small arms and legs. I wished I could have brought a larger-scale version of the toy, but with limited time, it was the best I could do. Max didn't seem to mind one bit as he took it and a teddy bear Linda had given him earlier into the living room where he let his imagination run wild. It also gave my investigator and me a chance to talk.

"Perez knows we have Max," I whispered while still watching the kid play with his new toy.

"What? How do you know?"

"I asked him, and he confirmed it. I spotted him briefly following me on the day I picked him up, but at the time, I didn't think much of it. His truck only sat behind me for barely a couple of minutes, and I dismissed it."

"What changed your mind?"

"Finding photos of it in the prosecutor's evidence pack he sent me. It was the yellow F-150. I confronted Perez about it late yesterday, and he finally admitted to me that he knew."

"Damn it, Ben," Linda said as she closed her eyes and pretended to look up at the ceiling. "If he tells anyone..."

"I know. Damn it, I know," I said, more than aware of the consequences of our secret getting out. "I spoke with him, and he assured me our secret is safe."

"What else did he tell you?"

"That he had orders to kill him," I said as I watched Max lie on his belly and drive the converted robot around the seated teddy bear. "That's why he panicked and drove out to that isolated road."

"And dumped him."

"And spared his life," I said, meeting Linda's gaze. "He's not innocent by any stretch of the imagination, but thankfully he's not guilty of killing a kid."

"And now whoever ordered him dead is going to be looking hard at Perez while he's sitting in a prison cell."

"I think someone will try and find out if he actually

went through with killing him, and when they do, I think they'll arrange for him to meet his maker."

"You mean he's alive because that mystery person doesn't know Max's current status."

"Exactly. Our secret is probably the only thing keeping him alive right now. If he blabs to *anybody* and his puppet-masters find out, he'll have effectively signed his own death warrant."

"So where to from here?"

"Perez confirmed that Detective Dwayne Cook is involved but doesn't know who the top guy is."

"Cook isn't the top guy?"

"No, there's someone else, someone who pulled the trigger on both Dunning and Warner."

"Who?"

"I wish I knew."

"Did he give you anything to work with?"

"Just that he's a guy wearing a baseball cap."

"A baseball cap? Ben, really?"

I shook my head. "I know it's not much, but that's all we have right now."

"Not much? It's nothing. Half the population wears baseball caps."

"We just need to start poking around."

"So we start looking into Cook's file and hopefully find whoever he's been playing with."

"Yes, but I also want to deep-dive into Lassiter's Transport. Have you had a chance to look into them yet?"

"I have, yes, and they run trucks all over the country.

None of the routes really stand out, but I'll give it another look."

"Maybe look into some of the individual drivers as well. Perhaps we'll find something among them."

"Any update on the trial?"

"We have two weeks to get our case sorted out."

"Two weeks?" I knew the number would surprise Linda considering we would normally have three or four times that. "They're really gunning for a quick result, huh?"

"The publicity alone is bringing pressure on the DA."

"Well then, we'd better get cracking," Linda said as she reached for her laptop and dragged it across the table.

I completely agreed with her, and with Max busy in the living room still keeping the Transformer occupied, Linda and I turned our attention to the case, each of us taking a different area to research. The thing that troubled me was the fact that it felt so different than the usual murder cases I'd defended and not just because of Max. The prosecutor had Perez pegged as the murderer of all three victims and considered the case a slamdunk. For me, this wasn't a matter of proving his innocence but rather someone else's guilt. He was at the scene of the murders, had kidnapped one of the victims and a boy, and had possession of what I knew to be the actual murder weapon. This wasn't a matter of trying to prove any of those things wrong.

For me, the hardest part of all was trying to figure out how I would work the case once the prosecutor had called his final witness. Who could I possibly call to the stand to help me prove that someone else had actually pulled the trigger? Not only that, but what evidence did I have to show that someone else called the shots?

As Linda and I sat around the table working the case, I couldn't help but again wonder whether I was out of my depth on this one, whether keeping Max a secret really had been the right move. But as I watched him lying on the floor with his face resting in his hands and watching an episode of Bluey, I couldn't help but see the sheer innocence before me. I shuddered at the thought of what would happen to him if the likes of Cook and his accomplice got their hands on him, and it was for that very reason I knew I needed to continue.

14

I ENDED UP SPENDING THE ENTIRE WEEKEND WITH LINDA and Max, the three of us giving the Monopoly board one hell of a workout during the Saturday evening pizza night. It wasn't until late Sunday night that I headed back to the apartment, figuring that *returning* home would be far less of a risk than leaving there to come to the hideout in the first place. Both Max and Linda walked me out to the car before I left, and the kid even gave me a hug, promising me that he would look after my investigator as best he could.

If it had been up to me, I would have brought them home with me and set Max up in my spare room, but the risks would have been too great. While my building didn't have that many people, there were a couple of elderly busybodies who spent most of the day with their faces pressed against their living room windows in search of the latest gossip. I didn't want to be the one to give them the opportunity to make me the following day's headline.

The worst part for me from that entire weekend happened just ten minutes after I walked through my front door, the silence of my apartment becoming way too noticeable for my liking. It reminded me of the days immediately following Naomi's death when the house felt more empty than I could ever have imagined. It took me weeks, if not months, to get used to that silence and to understand that this was my new norm. Being around Max and Linda had changed my perception again and all within just a matter of two short days.

To try and take my mind off things, I opened my laptop and began going through some of the case notes, in particular those concerning Matthew Foster. It was a name I still couldn't quite fit into the scheme of things, and I knew I needed to get to know it better if I was going to find out whether he had any direct involvement in the case whatsoever. For a man linked to three specific aspects of my investigation, I didn't think it was just a simple coincidence. There was a reason Foster had connections to so many details, and I needed to find it.

That Sunday night turned out not to be the moment where I cracked the case wide open by finding Foster's connection, and by ten o'clock, I knew it was just a matter of time before I gave in to my fatigue, closed the laptop, and went to bed. I ended up surprising myself by persisting for another half an hour or so, but by then, my eyes were just about falling out of my head, and I knew it was time to admit defeat.

The annoying thing was that despite feeling like I hadn't slept in days, I lay awake in the darkness for what felt like hours, tossing from one side to the other. While sleep rejected me entirely, my brain refused to shut down, with names and faces all continuing to roll around in there. Talk about frustrating. I don't actually know when I did eventually manage to lose consciousness, but it must have happened at some point because before I knew what was happening, my morning alarm began ringing.

It was with a groan that I forced myself to roll out of bed, the heavy eyelids almost warning me not to allow them to close again. If I did, there was every chance I would drift off to sleep a second time and possibly risk missing one of the most important meetings of recent days. It was thinking about that very meeting that convinced me to drag my butt out of bed and start my day.

After doing the shower thing and getting dressed in my usual business attire, I headed to the kitchen and fixed myself a coffee that resembled something more akin to tar. One sip was enough to send my toes into a curl with the bitterness rolling through me like a steam train. Talk about kicking my system into gear. Any hint of fatigue quickly faded out once the caffeine-loaded drink hit me.

The drive to the office turned out to be something of a surprise with the traffic barely registering during the twenty-minute commute. With no breakdowns or fender benders, I stared blankly at the back of the car in front of me as I thought about the weekend I'd just finished and how the upcoming meeting might go. During the usual drive to work, I would normally be more likely to be cursing the traffic for wasting so much of my time but not this morning.

Grace was already sitting at her desk by the time I walked into the office, and she shot me a smile and a wave when she saw me.

"Matty Foster sent me a message earlier," she said once I got close enough. "Asked if it would be possible to see him earlier than planned as he's had something pop up." Not wanting to risk delaying the meeting a second time, I immediately agreed.

"How soon? I'm happy to go now," I said.

"Sounds good to me," Grace said as she got up off the chair and grabbed her handbag. "One sec. I'll just let Dwight know we're off."

"Meet you out in the car," I said and ignored my office completely as I did an about-face and headed back out into the day.

I barely got the Camry started before Grace climbed into the passenger seat next to me, and once she had her seatbelt clicked in, I joined the morning Pittsburgh traffic for the second time. Things still ran smoothly enough for us to make it through the first two sets of traffic lights, but the third stopped us in our tracks.

"You haven't met Matty before, have you?" Grace asked as I stopped behind a cab.

"No, why? Is there anything I need to know ahead of time?"

"He's a nice enough guy but can come across as a bit... abrasive, maybe?"

"Abrasive in an arrogant sort of way?" Abrasiveness

wasn't something that tended to bother me much, not when nearly every witness for the prosecution tended to share the personality trait.

"No, not arrogance, so to speak. Just...abrasive. I think he's shy to a certain extent. At least that's how Annie describes it."

"A family man though, right?"

Grace nodded as the lights changed and the taxi turned down a side street, effectively giving me a clear run to the next set of lights.

"He and Annie have been sweet on each other since high school. Two kids, one of each, house in the suburbs, pretty standard sort of family, I guess."

Except Foster seems to have a taste for getting into bed with questionable business people was what I wanted to say, but I held my tongue. I didn't know just how much Grace knew about Foster's darker side and figured I'd keep the information in my back pocket in case I needed it.

"Well, let's hope he can steer us in the right direction" was what I did say, the last words we exchanged before pulling up out the front of a small office building located off the main street.

Foster's office appeared more like a converted home, sitting at the very top of a suburban street. It looked like the kind of place where regular people might go to visit their accountant for help sorting their W-2s. As I climbed out of the car, I looked around at the front yards of adjoining homes. *Peaceful* was the only word that came to mind.

"Annie fixed those flowerbeds running alongside the

path and fronting the building," Grace said as she walked around to my side. "Loves her gardening."

"Gardening is probably the main reason I sold my house," I said as I pressed the lock button on the key fob. It might have been a quiet community, but I had no doubt that thieves still lingered nearby.

"You're not a fan?"

"Almost as much as camping," I said with a grin and followed Grace down the driveway toward the front door.

Stepping into the reception area, the first thing I noticed was the smell, an aromatic mix of vanilla and woodsmoke hanging in the air. I saw a candle sitting on the side of the reception desk, the yellowish hue shining through the side of the glass container. An older woman sitting behind the desk looked over at us and smiled as we walked in before giving Grace a wave.

"Well, look at you all bright and early," she said as she rose out of her chair and walked around to our side of the barrier. Grace wished her a good morning before returning the embrace and kiss on the cheek. To be honest, I kind of felt out of place standing behind Grace, but with her being the thoughtful assistant, she immediately turned and introduced me.

"Ben, this is Maureen, Matty's mom." The revelation came as somewhat of a surprise. I'd had no idea I was walking into a family business when I first asked Grace to set up the meeting.

"Pleased to meet you," I said, forcing a smile of my own.

"Ben is also from California," Grace said as I finished shaking hands. She turned back to me.

"Maureen spent a good deal of her childhood in Playa Del Rey.".

"Oh, really? Right by the airport?"

"My father was a pilot during the mid-seventies," Maureen began but was cut off when the intercom on her desk suddenly came to life.

"Mom, has Grace shown up yet?" Maureen excused herself and answered the call by clicking the button.

"She just walked through the door, dear," she said with that same pleasant tone of hers, and I wondered whether what I had heard about Foster had been correct. From what I could see, he didn't appear to be the kind to get involved in shady stuff, not when he seemed to be surrounded by warm family and respectable friends.

I heard a door open up somewhere down the hallway before bootheels clapping on floorboards made their way to the reception area. A moment later, another friendly face joined us as Matthew Foster finally appeared with outstretched arms for my assistant.

"Grace, so good to see you," he said before turning his attention to me. "And you must be Ben Carter. I've heard so much about you."

"Likewise," I said as we shook hands.

"Mom, could you please let David Hunt know that I'll meet him at one when he calls," Foster said before beckoning Grace and me to follow him. He didn't wait for an answer from his mother, simply turning back down the hallway and assuming we would follow him.

Once in his office, Foster offered us chairs before taking his own on the other side of an impressively clean desk. The rest of the room looked equally tidy, and I couldn't help but wonder whether that was because of him or his mother.

"How's Dwight doing after the fundraiser?" Foster asked once we were seated. "I couldn't believe just how much they needed to raise."

"He's doing OK," Grace said with a smile, although I could sense some apprehension in her voice. Something about the question annoyed her.

"So, Ben," he said, finally turning his attention to me. "How can I be of service?"

"I was hoping you could help me with a case I'm currently working on," I said. "I understand you used to look after the financial affairs of Harold Dunning."

"Harold, yes, of course," Foster said almost immediately. Again, that warm smile lit up his face, and I was beginning to think he had it preprogrammed for most questions. "Such a tragedy to hear what happened to him."

"How long did you look after Dunning, Mr. Foster?"

"Matty, please, and not for long. He only came to me last year after a recommendation from his employer."

"Lassiter's Transport, yes, of course," I said. "And was it the same thing when it came to Mario Perez?"

That was when his demeanor did change somewhat but only for the briefest of moments. The smile wavered at the edges as I watched his eyes narrow down to slits for just a split second.

"My company was also recommended to Mario Perez by his employer."

"How long ago?"

"Around the same time." He leaned back in his seat. "I think they began working for Klaus sometime in June last year." His brow creased slightly as he tilted his head a little. "Is there something specific you're looking for?"

"I'm representing Mario Perez, and I'm investigating any links between him and Harold Dunning. So far, Lassiter's Transport seems to be the only connection, aside from you. I'm curious to know how well you know Klaus Weber. From what I can gather, you look after quite a number of his employees, is that correct?"

"We do offer financial services to Klaus and a number of his employees, yes."

"And would you say Dunning and Perez were regular clients?"

"Regular? I'm not sure I follow."

"I'm sure you would have helped them with their taxes, but was there anything else you helped them with?"

"Anything else? No, not that I can recall."

"What about their boss, Klaus Weber?"

"Klaus? He certainly is one of my wealthier clients, which means my office takes care of quite a few of his financial responsibilities."

"I'm curious to know why, though," I said as I looked around the room. "I mean, no offense, but I can think of at least half a dozen accountancy firms down in the city's financial district who could offer someone of Weber's stature solid financial services." Foster grinned at me.

"I know we look small in comparison, but I assure you, Ben, this office looks after significant clients."

"I'm sure it does. I'm just curious as to why." I looked at Grace. "Do you and Dwight use Matthew's services?" I felt bad for putting her on the spot, but I needed answers sooner rather than later.

"Dwight and Grace have been with their own accountant for many years." Foster cut in before Grace could answer. "And considering our friendship, I don't think it's my place to try and sway them over to my company."

"Tell me about your meetings with Dunning and Perez," I said. "I'm looking for any information about their dealings with Lassiter's."

"I'm not sure what you mean. Both men worked as drivers for Klaus, and that's as far as it went."

I didn't know why, but I sensed the lie as he resumed that plastic smile of his. For some reason, Foster was trying to hide whatever else he knew about the two men as he shut down any further questions by checking his watch.

"If there's nothing else, Ben, I have my next client probably already waiting for me."

"Actually, I have one more question, if I may," I said. "Do you ever still hear from your old partner, Enrique Porter?"

"No, I do not," Foster said, and the way he appeared to push the words through his gritted teeth told me everything I needed to know. Hearing the name definitely didn't win me any points.

"Grace, thank you again for stopping by," Foster said

as he rose from his chair, the smile returning as he pushed the frustration aside. He walked around to our side of the desk and gave Grace a hug before holding a hand out to me. "Ben." We shook but not without me meeting his gaze. I wanted him to know that I had my suspicions about him. It just annoyed me that I hadn't found out more.

Just as he had when we'd arrived, Foster walked us back out to the reception area where his mother was busy on a phone call. I was about to give her a wave on my way past when something else grabbed my attention: a man standing in the waiting room watching me. I recognized him almost immediately and noted his interest in me but refrained from acknowledging him.

"Thanks again for coming down, guys," Foster said, and before Grace and I could respond, he gave the man a wave and headed back toward his office. Detective Dwayne Cook waited until Grace and I had almost reached the door before he followed Foster down the hallway, but I did see him take a final look over his shoulder just before he walked into his office. It appeared as if the cop had some kind of interest in me. Little did he know that I felt the same for him.

15

"I'M SORRY IF HE APPEARED SOMEWHAT STANDOFFISH," Grace said once we were back on the road.

"I'm sorry for bringing you and Dwight into the conversation," I said, and I meant it. There was just something about Foster that rubbed me the wrong way, and I could sense him trying to use his connection to my boss against me.

"Do you really think he's involved in something shady?" Grace looked at me curiously as I stopped at a traffic light. "In all honesty, we're not as close to him as I might have made out."

"That's what I'm hoping to find out," I said, and that was when I had an idea. "Listen, can you do me a favor when we get back to the office?"

"Of course."

"Could you try and find any other businesses Foster might be involved in personally?"

"You mean like the kind he owns?"

"Yes," I said as the lights changed. "Maybe as a silent partner or just an investor. I need to know why a man running a small niche accountancy firm works for one of the state's wealthiest businessmen. It just doesn't make sense."

"Maybe there's a history we're not seeing," Grace suggested, but I didn't think that was it.

"Did you see the man waiting in reception?" Grace nodded. "Did you recognize him?"

"No, why? Should I have?"

"I recognized him because I saw him on TV. That was Detective Dwayne Cook," I said.

"And that's relevant because…"

I looked at Grace and smiled. "Because Cook also happens to be the detective leading the Dunning investigation." Grace's eyebrows rose. "Think it's just a coincidence that he shows up at the same time we did? And did you see the way he looked at me? He knew who I was, Grace."

"How can you be sure?"

"Call it instinct. I just do. That detective knew who I was, and if that's so, then he knows I'm the one representing Perez."

Grace did as I'd asked almost the second we got back to the office, dropping down into her seat and firing up her computer. I took a detour to the bathroom before heading to my desk and doing likewise. With everything that had been going on, I knew that time wasn't a resource I held in abundance, not when I still had a potential career-ending blip hidden from view. If someone like Cook took an interest in me, he could set up surveillance, bugs, or anything else. All he needed was suspicion, and if he found Max before I had a chance to prove our case, my life would be over, along with those close to me.

The problem for me was that I had two jobs to work, thanks to keeping Linda busy with Max. Normally, I would have had her do most of the investigation, leaving me and Grace to support her. But with Linda effectively limited to just her laptop, I had to step up and pick up her role as well and try to prepare for the start of the trial.

I don't think I looked up from my computer until my cell phone began to ring some two hours later. The caller ID came up as private, and I don't know why, but a part of me was sure that it would be the detective from earlier in the day. I hesitated to answer it but knew if I didn't, he would only grow more suspicious, and if he did, it would only make my life that much more difficult.

"Hello, this is Ben Carter," I said once I thumbed the call button. I could hear a background crackle but not much else, and after a couple of seconds of listening to the silence, I repeated my greeting. "Hello?"

The hum of the background itself confirmed that the call remained connected to whatever device had reached out to me. I could even make out some distant noises similar to traffic, but nothing confirmed the connection more than a sudden shuffle as someone shifted the hold on their phone.

"Hello," I repeated, this time with a lot more conviction, and I did get somewhat of a response. I could hear someone breathing and for a moment thought a voice would finally reply, but that was when the line went dead.

I pulled the cell phone away from my head and looked at the screen. The call had definitely ended, leaving me staring at nothing more than the lock screen image of my car. Curiously, I felt a slight twinge in my stomach, a kind of nervous tightening that had for whatever reason made its presence known.

"You OK?" I looked up to see Grace standing in the doorway.

"Yes, fine, just a wrong number, I think." Not fazed by my expression, Grace came closer and dropped a couple of pages onto my desk.

"Looks like your suspicions may have been right," she said as she sat down.

"About which part?" I asked, picking up the sheets and running my eyes across the top one.

"Looks like Matty has his fingers in several pies."

"Oh?"

"Turns out Matthew Foster is also known as Harrison Dunn, according to court documents from 2004 when he applied for his accounting license."

"He has an alias?"

"That he does, and it is under that alias I managed to find him linked to these other businesses."

While I had been busy putting together my opening statements, Grace had managed to find not just one but three different companies associated with our esteemed accountant. Two of them appeared to be nothing more than retail investments, stores that he had funded along with a partner who ran the place. The third one, however, ended up being a little more significant than the rest. According to some in-depth investigation by my assistant, it looked as if Matthew Foster shared part ownership in a transport company, one running just a single product across the southwestern United States...Pinkman Coffee.

"I thought Lassiter's Transport was the only business distributing Pinkman's," I said as I scanned the page. "Why would they need another company when they already own more than enough trucks?"

"I'm not sure, but according to what I could find, Howard's Haulage only owns two trucks."

"Grace, can you find out where these trucks run deliveries to and from?"

"Sure, but what about the two stores? Anything you want me to do with them?" I considered the options but figured I'd work on one thing at a time. If I really did need them looked into a little more, I'd do it myself.

"Let's focus on the trucks for now," I said and thanked her for the great work. I wasn't expecting much in such a short amount of time, but then again, Grace had surprised me more than a few times during our professional relationship.

While my assistant returned to her desk to continue searching through Matthew Foster's business dealings, I turned my attention to Dwayne Cook, the cop who I still felt uncomfortable about. At that point, just knowing that he had some involvement in the Dunning murder was enough for me to consider him my highest priority even though I knew someone else had pulled the trigger. I knew that Cook would be my best way of finding out who that person was.

The problem was, once Grace told me about the other businesses Foster was involved in, my brain refused to push them to the back of my head while I tried to focus on other things. No matter how hard I stared at the screen in front of me, those businesses kept creeping in until I finally gave up and began searching for the stores myself. With my assistant handling the transport company, I would turn my attention to the smaller fish and see what else I could find.

The first place was nothing more than a straightforward dry-cleaning business in nearby Carnegie. The place didn't have any form of Internet presence aside from a generic Facebook page probably put together by one of the owners. When I checked it, I found that the last post had been set some four years earlier and had managed to accumulate all of four likes.

Business number two turned out to be a pizza joint called Angelo's Pizza and Ribs which advertised itself as an *authentic Italian home-cooked food* kind of place. Located in San Diego, it sat just near the main transport hub of Sigsbee Row and had several hundred 5-star reviews on Google. The proprietor, a man named Angelo Traiforous, appeared to be the only contact for the place, and I guessed our friend Foster was just a silent partner in the operation.

From what I could tell from initial diggings, neither of the two businesses looked like anything out of the ordinary, especially to a suspicious mind like mine. Whatever

Foster was doing with them didn't appear to be anything illegal, and after a good hour or so of searching for anything I could find on them, I decided to turn my attention back to the transport company.

"Laredo to San Diego and Laredo to Pittsburgh," Grace said when she walked back into the room a short time later. "Twice a week, those two trucks drive the same route over and over. One drives back and forth from Texas to California, while the other one returns here before turning around and heading back."

"Filled with coffee, I'm assuming," I said as Grace retook her seat.

"Correct. It looks like one truck picks up the goods from a local warehouse, ships them to Laredo, and then meets up with the second truck, which then ships the packages out to San Diego."

"Wouldn't it be more beneficial to just have the one truck drive the shipment across to San Diego? And why Laredo? That doesn't sound like a major distribution point," I said as I brought up a map on my computer screen. I zoomed in a little closer to the city, and it immediately struck me at how small it was compared to the surrounding countryside. I shook my head at the screen. "Both Dunning and Perez were drivers for Lassiter's Transport, and both were sent to Foster for help with their taxes, only he ends up being involved in another transport company working alongside Lassiter's."

"Pinkman's coffee is pretty darn popular if you didn't know," Grace chimed in. "And I honestly can't see Matty getting involved in anything shady, Ben. He's a good guy, a family man."

"And yet he managed to get into bed with Enrique Porter."

"A bad choice which turned out to be his partner's doing," Grace said almost defensively.

I knew what Grace was saying, but my suspicious mind wouldn't let it go. What I knew above all else was that I needed to follow every possible lead, no matter how insignificant. The hard part, of course, was sharing my reasons for being so thorough in the matter with Grace. I knew that Grace would understand if she knew about the secrets I was keeping from her and the rest of the world.

"I'm sorry," I said. "I didn't mean to throw you into the middle of this."

"No, don't apologize, Ben. I know there's a reason why you're suspicious. If it was me, I would be doing the exact same thing, especially with that little boy still out there somewhere."

"Listen, I know this is probably going against everything you know about the man, but there's a reason he's involved in these businesses under an alias," I said. "And if it's linked to Dunning and Perez, then I have to find out so I know what I'm up against."

"I get it," Grace said. "I just want you to know that the man has family, and while I may not know every little thing Matty is involved in, I do know that his mother and Anne and the kids, they're the ones who will suffer the most if he has gotten himself mixed up in something dark."

"I promise to tread carefully," I said, and while I'm not sure if she believed me, Grace did give that acknowledging smile she always offered when trying to convince someone of her acceptance. What I didn't tell Grace was that I already had a plan to do a little digging of my own and not the kind she would want to come along on.

16

CALL IT A HUNCH OR JUST MY SUSPICIOUS MIND, BUT something in me refused to let go of my feelings about Foster. What I didn't tell Grace was that the second she returned to her desk, I probed a little deeper into the place where Howard's Haulage picked up their shipments from. The warehouse sat inside an industrial complex located a short twenty-minute drive from me, and while I would have normally given the job to Linda, I decided that considering her current assignment, I would step in to do a little poking around myself.

I didn't want to go in completely blind and so checked the place from as many different angles as possible using the resources available to me. It's amazing how much a person can find using tools such as Google, and the street view proved especially useful. Not only did I find out that the warehouse looked to be a distribution center for several different companies, but I could also gain entry via a hole cut into the chainlink fence near the bottom right corner of the property that backed onto a cemetery.

The good thing for me was that Howard's Haulage seemed to stick to a regular schedule with the Pittsburgh truck pulling into the depot at precisely 11 p.m. on both Mondays and Thursdays. Being a Monday, I had every intention of using the timing to my complete advantage by paying the warehouse a little after-hours visit.

Not wanting to take a field trip dressed in a business suit, I headed home after thanking Grace for her help but not before stopping by Dwight's office first. He'd sent me a message earlier that afternoon asking about the case, and I figured I'd give him a personal update. All it took was five minutes of my time and a shot of his current choice of single-malt whiskey for me to share the latest developments minus the secret parts as we sipped our drinks. He seemed happy with my update, and once we shook hands, I got the hell out of there.

Rather than sit around waiting for the time to wind down, I took my laptop to the couch and continued working on my opening statements that I would present in less than a couple of weeks. It was while finalizing the introduction to Perez that my second cell phone began to ring.

"Linda, hey," I said as I answered the call.

"How's life in the city?"

"Busy. Managed to meet with Foster this morning."

"Oh yeah? How did that go?" I could hear the television in the background as she spoke and imagined Max watching it while sitting on the couch.

"Well, let's just say I think he's hiding more than he was willing to share."

"Secrets, huh?"

"For sure. I'll tell you what I did see, though. When we left, Detective Dwayne Cook was standing in the waiting room. Gave me a decent stare as he walked into Foster's office."

"Funny you should mention Cook. He's the reason why I'm calling. Been doing a little digging of my own and found out he's been married before. Guess who his first wife was?"

"Tell me."

"Maria Lozano."

The second Linda said the name, I knew that I had heard it before. A sense of familiarity washed over me as I tried to remember where, but nothing came up.

"Why do I know that name?"

"Remember the guy Dunning was accused of murdering in Michigan?"

"Michael Lozano, of course. They're related?"

"Maria is his sister. And that's not all. I did a little further digging, and it looks like the biggest surprise is yet to come. Lozano wasn't just a regular drug runner. He worked directly for the Rojas Cartel and was their point man on this side of the border."

I sat quietly on the couch, stunned. Not only had Dunning been accused of murdering Michael Lozano and stealing his drugs, but now it appeared as if he'd ripped off one of the most dangerous Colombian drug cartels.

"Ben, you still there?"

"Yes, sorry, just trying to absorb the information. What the hell have we gotten ourselves involved in, Linda?"

"I don't know, but from what I can gather, killing Dunning may have been payback by the cartel for ripping them off."

"And if that's true, then they will want to do the same to Max."

"That's what I'm thinking too," Linda said as she lowered her voice. "Cartels have a way of not stopping until every member of a rival's family is dead."

"So you think we're dealing with a cartel hitman here? Perez did say there was someone else there that morning when Dunning bought it. Cook was there as well, of course, but according to my client, he wasn't the trigger man."

"A hitman might be the most likely explanation," Linda said as I finally recognized Pokemon playing on the TV. "Let me make some calls and see what I can find out. Cartels have been known to use local hitmen when needed, but I'm not so sure that's what happened in this case."

"Think they sent someone up to deal with Dunning specifically?"

"That's my guess."

"OK, let me know if you find anything," I said, and after thanking her, I ended the call.

Linda's revelation truly frightened me, and I'm not a guy that tends to scare easily. I've dealt with drug dealers before, even a hitman or two, but not one out to murder a child whom I was protecting. Not only that, but anybody linked to me was also now a prime target. I had the law to protect me, yes, but the law meant nothing to those who lived their life beyond it. Colombian hitmen weren't known for their compassion or respect of the law, and that meant I would be fighting for the lives of not only me but also Max and Linda. We had to get to the bottom of this... we *had* to.

With my focus effectively shot to pieces, I closed the laptop and set it on the coffee table while I contemplated our future. When that wasn't enough, I got up off the couch and began to pace around my living room while considering my next move. There were too many possibilities for me to work through, and with half my team on babysitting duties, I felt seriously out of my depth.

Before I had a chance to even think the idea properly through, I pulled out my regular cell phone and opened the messaging app. A few seconds later, I hit the send button on a small three-word text that I hoped would give me some extra help. Christy hadn't been my first choice when it came to looking after Max, but with things spiraling out of control, I knew I needed her. When the reply came through just a minute or so later, Christy's response contained just as many words as my own.

Me: Need your help.

Christy: Tell me what.

What I needed was for my investigator to be freed up so she could do what she did best. Linda also happened to be one of my most trusted friends, which made what I had planned so much more difficult. The only confidence I had in what I was about to do was the fact that Christy had known about Max for a while now, and with no authorities coming down on us, that meant she had managed to keep the secret to herself. If she had kept her mouth shut for this long, then maybe I could use her for a little babysitting.

I sent Christy a follow-up message asking if she'd be OK with meeting me at the same place as last time. Yes, I could have just gone to her apartment or even invited her to mine, but something told me we'd be much less noticeable if we just acted normal. As long as we kept our distance from other patrons, a Starbucks would be the perfect place to have the kind of conversation I needed to have.

Christy sent her reply almost immediately, agreeing to meet me in twenty minutes. After packing the laptop into my briefcase and stowing it in the office, I grabbed the rest of my things and headed out into the early evening. It wasn't until I was halfway to my car that I suddenly had the overwhelming sense of being watched.

Stopping in my tracks, it was perhaps the first time in several hours that my brain paused almost as much as the rest of my body. Clarity was what I felt as I began slowly looking around for whoever had set off my internal sensors. The final remnants of daylight continued to fade out above me as the street lights began to exert their power over the shadows.

The park across the street seemed like the most likely place for a person to sit and wait, but I couldn't see anybody from my vantage point. Just a single shape moved along the solitary track, and I could tell from the methodical up-and-down movement that the jogger wasn't in any way interested in me. I doubt they even knew I was there, the lonely figure going about their nightly run with headphones firmly attached to their head.

My phone suddenly began to ring, in the process scaring the living shit out of me. Anybody looking would have seen me flinch hard, perhaps even getting slightly airborne in the process. The beating in my chest felt like a hammer attack as I reached into my pocket and fumbled the phone out. Caught up in the moment, I thumbed the answer button before checking the number and pressed the device to my ear.

"Hello?"

Nothing. Just an unnerving familiar silence greeted me from the other end as I again began peering into the darkness, desperately trying to ascertain whether my previous suspicions and my current intruder were one and the same.

"Hello," I repeated while staring into the cabin of a passing cab, but the driver looked to be searching for his destination instead of paying attention to me.

I pulled the phone from my ear and checked the screen to see whether the call was still connected. Of course, I already knew it was due to that near-silent hum I could make out.

"Look, I don't know who you are," I began, suddenly feeling more angry than anything else. "But I'm going to—"

"Is this Ben Carter?"

The words came completely out of the blue, the male-sounding voice only vaguely curious, the question more matter-of-fact.

"Yes, it is," I said, doing my best to hide the nerves causing the hairs on the back of my neck to stand on end.

Before I had a chance to ask any questions of my own, the call suddenly ended as the connection dropped. I felt my lips relax as they backed away from the words I planned on speaking. I once again looked around the immediate area for somebody watching me. There was no one, or at least nobody that I could see, and after making sure I wasn't being followed, I continued to my car.

I won't lie, the phone call rattled me enough for me to take a couple of crazy detours in an attempt to throw anybody following me off track. With nothing but head-lights filling my rearview mirror, it was a bit hard trying to pinpoint any specific vehicles, and so I had two options: head back home and let Christy know I had changed my mind or continue on and take my chances.

I opted for the second choice, not because I wanted to live dangerously but because of the complete opposite. I needed my investigator's help, and getting Christy was perhaps the only logical card I had left to play. Without Christy, there would be nobody else to help me with Max, and so I pushed on.

Thankfully, the Starbucks ended up being fairly busy, and Christy had already arrived a few minutes ahead of me. I found her sitting halfway up the window aisle with two cups of coffee before her. When she spotted me walking through the door, she shot me a wave, which I returned and walked over to her. Both of the booths on either side of us were occupied, as were the half-dozen tables to our side, not a bad thing when wanting to converse in private. The volume of multiple groups interacting filled the air and meant Christy and I could have a normal conversation without fear of being overheard.

"I wasn't sure about asking you to come," I said as I sat down.

"I'm always here for you, Ben. You know that." She pushed one of the cups in my direction. "How is he?" Just the fact she asked about Max without using his name told me she was on the same wavelength as me.

"He's great and actually the reason I messaged you."

"I figured as much," Christy said. "I meant it when I said I wouldn't betray your trust."

"I know you did, but things have taken a decidedly dark turn." I tried to look around inconspicuously but couldn't see anybody paying us the slightest attention. "There are some serious people involved, Christy," I said as I leaned slightly forward and lowered my voice. "I mean *really* bad people."

"How bad?"

"Drug cartel bad."

"Are they the ones responsible for Hillary's murder?" I nodded. "Then I want to help. She never hurt anybody and only ever wanted to help children find a little sunshine in this world."

"These people don't care about sunshine, Christy. They don't care about anything except following orders, and right now Max is who they are after."

"But why, Ben? Why a little boy?"

"Because of something his father did." I looked around again, still too aware of the phone call and the sensation of being watched. Christy picked up on my insecurity.

"Were you followed?"

"No, I don't think so. I took measures Linda taught me, so I think we're good." I wanted to tell her about the phone calls as well, but I held back, figuring it best not to overwhelm her with too much at once. "Listen, I need your help with him," I continued, figuring it better not to use Max's name. "Do you think you could watch him for a few days? Or at least until Linda and I can follow up on some leads? I really need her in on this, and looking after a kid is really costing us."

"Of course," Christy said without a hint of hesitation. "Want to bring him to my place?"

"No, I'd rather not," I said. I paused to look at her as I continued weighing up my request. While I knew I trusted Christy, I still wasn't sure about handing over the lives of three people to her, one of them my own.

"Ben, you look like you have the world on your shoulders."

"I think in a way I do," I said, and I began to feel bad when it finally struck me how to proceed. "Listen, I know this is going to be weird, but I have to take you to a secret location, and the only way I know how is—" I paused again, but Christy knew exactly what I was leading to.

"You want to blindfold me or something?" She didn't sound pissed at all. "I get the risks you're taking, and I've already told you I'm happy to go along with whatever you need. If you have to take a few precautions, then so be it." She reached over and gave my hand a squeeze. "I get what you're trying to protect."

I checked my watch and saw that I still had some five hours up my sleeve before the truck would arrive at the depot, plenty of time for me to get Christy up to the house.

"OK, give me five," I said. "Bathroom needs."

"I'll be waiting," Christy said and picked up her coffee.

Although it wasn't exactly a bathroom kind of urgency for me, I did step into a cubicle and emptied my bladder. Coffee always had a way of rushing through my system, and I figured I'd take advantage. Once done, I pulled out the burner phone and sent Linda a message telling her about my plan to bring Christy so she could be free to help out in the field. Her response came less than a minute later consisting of nothing more than a thumbs-up emoji.

The drive up to the house didn't take anywhere near as long as I imagined with most of the evening traffic having already faded out. We first dropped Christy's car back to her house before heading north. Just a half hour later, we pulled into the driveway, where Linda was already sitting on the front steps in anticipation of heading out. Max took the change in caregivers a lot better than expected, having already met Christy before. Mind you, my investigator had already prepped him ahead of time, and this ensured there would be no unnecessary stress on the boy.

What I constantly had to remind myself of was the fact that the entire case revolved around a seven-year-old kid, a kid who'd already experienced way too much trauma in his short life. The scars this kid already bore ran deep, and the last thing I wanted was to add to them.

17

LINDA AND I DIDN'T WASTE TIME GETTING BACK ON THE road once we were sure Max and Christy were good. The clock continued ticking down to when the truck would roll into the distribution center. Rather than take Linda with me, I wanted her to begin following up with both Foster and Cook.

It was the cop who I wanted her to focus on, and in true Linda style, she had already prepared a list of people with whom she intended to meet. Street people. Hoods. Those with a history involving Dwayne Cook. One of them, a hooker named Denise Lord, wasn't a stranger to Linda and was propelled to the top of the list.

"According to Denise, Cook likes to think of her as his personal snitch" was how Linda put it.

"Any chance you can catch up with her?"

"Already planned, my friend," Linda said as I pulled

into her street. "She's meeting me down by the Smithfield Street bridge in an hour."

"OK, great. Keep me updated."

"What are you planning to do at the distribution center?"

"I'm not sure yet. Was thinking of just poking around and seeing if I can find out whether the coffee shipments are legit." That was when something else came to mind. "That reminds me, can you check into my cell phone records?"

"Why, what's wrong?"

"I'm not sure. Just been getting these random calls, and I don't have a good feeling about them." I gave her a brief rundown on the specifics, mainly about the person asking to confirm my identity.

"Leave it with me," she said as I pulled into her drive-way. "I'll see what I can find."

After giving each other a final rundown on our imme-diate plans, Linda climbed out and headed inside while I pulled back out onto the street and turned for my intended destination. With the clock continuing to tick, I wanted to make sure I was in position for whatever happened. I wasn't expecting much, just a truck with the right markings to pull into the distribution center and get loaded up. Once done, I assumed the load would get taken to its Texan destination, where it would repeat the process except in reverse.

The street running along the front of the place turned out to be almost a parking lot, both sides filled with endless rows of cars that curled around each subsequent corner. Some of the vehicles had even filled a small empty lot half a block down, and it was there I managed to find the narrowest of spaces which afforded me somewhat of a view. Just a primitive chainlink fence separated us, and I got a decent view of both the gate and the guardhouse managing the entrance.

After killing the engine, I sank deep into the seat and made myself comfortable. With still a good half hour to go before the expected arrival time, there was now plenty of time to watch the goings on of a place managing the distribution of around a dozen companies with the warehouses stretching back almost half a mile. Just to be sure I knew where I was going once inside, I opened Google Earth, zoomed in on the place, and studied an aerial view.

While checking out the Streetview earlier in the day, I'd noticed a couple of workers walking into the place and had seen that they wore nothing more than generic fluoro vests over their normal civilian clothing. So guess who went out and picked up a vest for the bargain price of $14.99 down at the local Walmart?

OK, so it may not have been the smartest move on my behalf, but damn it, I needed answers, and with nothing much happening with each passing day, I was beginning to wonder whether I was taking things seriously. It was time to ramp things up by taking some risks.

I kept a spare eye on the clock, and ten minutes before the expected arrival time, I grabbed a baseball cap and the vest and put both on while still sitting in the car. Once I was sure I at least *looked* the part of one of the workers, I locked the car and headed for the hole in the fence.

If there were cameras, I couldn't see them, and a few seconds after carefully climbing through the narrow hole, I made my way toward the side of the nearest warehouse. I figured it a good sign when nobody called out to me as I walked with purpose, and it appeared as if the security guards remained in their little office nestled between the opposing gates. Just as I reached the very edge of the warehouse, I heard a truck engine approaching, and a few seconds later, I watched the very one I hoped to find pull into view.

Pausing long enough to watch the truck first stop at the gate and then slowly move forward when the arm rose into the air, I felt my insides tighten as I pushed on. A couple of workers passed by the narrow walkway I was on, and after a few seconds, I took a deep breath and fell in behind them.

One thing I had always been taught was that if you ever needed to gain access to somewhere and make it appear as if you belonged there, just carry a piece of paper with you and walk with a sense of purpose. To add to the illusion, I also had a pen in one hand and pretended to be taking notes after random observations of the buildings I passed. I returned a couple of head nods from those passing me by, all the while keeping my attention on the truck continuing to slowly crawl in between the warehouses.

It wasn't until I reached my intended destination that I

faced my first real challenge when a worker waved hello at me and asked whether I needed help.

"Nah, brother, I'm good," I said, returning the wave. "Just getting numbers for Wayne at HQ." There was no Wayne, of course, and if there was, then I'd completely fluked it. Nevertheless, the guy seemed content with my answer and returned his attention to the phone he had in his hand.

I continued on as the truck pulled up halfway down the narrow loading strip and watched from a distance as the driver first climbed out and began opening the canvas sides of the trailer. Soon, an army of forklifts began delivering pallets of boxes, stacking two neat rows along the length of the trailer. The driver watched as he engaged in some brief conversation with a couple of random workers.

From what I could see, the boxes didn't appear to be anything special, just regular cargo grabbed from the hundreds I could see stacked up on the industrial shelving. Ten minutes after turning up, the first truck was joined by a second, albeit a different transport company but loaded up with the same product. The two drivers shared a brief chat before the first one, my guy, wished the other one a good night and returned to his rig.

I stayed in my vantage point near the mouth of an aisle for as long as possible, watching as the driver carefully resealed the trailer. Once done, one of the supervisors latched the locks with a couple of tamperproof metal security strips that would show if anybody tried to gain entry to the shipment.

From what I could see, there didn't appear to be

anything out of the ordinary about the pick-up. If it *was* some kind of smuggling operation as I had initially suspected, then I could only assume the drugs would already be packed into the boxes.

Continuing to try and look official, I made my way over to one of the stacks where the forklifts had taken several pallets. The workers continued to load the second truck as the first began to slowly roll out of the warehouse. I had to be quick if I was going to continue tracking my target. When I was sure I wasn't being watched, I took a quick look around for any cameras and only then ripped open the plastic wrapping of one of the pallets, pulled out a box, and carried it away from the crowd.

My heart just about stopped when a forklift suddenly turned down the very aisle I was walking along, rolling toward me fast enough to render any evasive action useless. I almost froze in place like a deer caught in head-lights. The driver's eyes and my own seemed to lock as he closed the distance between us in mere seconds, but I managed to keep my nerves under control. Along with a head nod, I also sent a wave his way, using the hand holding the box as if tempting fate. The driver couldn't have cared less about the box. He returned the wave and nod, throwing in an added grin on his way past.

I continued walking until I was sure the forklift had turned the corner. When I checked over my shoulder, the mouth of the aisle sat about thirty yards down with the back end of the trailer visible. That was when I set the box on a nearby pallet and tore the top open. The familiar pink foil wrapping of Pinkman's Coffee immediately appeared, eight packets making up the contents and sitting in two layers of four. One of these I picked out and shoved into the back of my pants, another I tore open.

Nothing but aromatic coffee beans spilled from the tear, running between my splayed fingers as they fell to the floor. Whatever I had been expecting to find wasn't there, and it quickly became obvious I was wasting my time. I watched half the packet empty itself onto the floor before tossing the remains into the darkness and quickly making my way to the exit.

Something still bugged me about the whole thing, and I wasn't quite ready to give up on my little field trip. Walking between the warehouses, I saw the Howard's Haulage truck pull up at the gatehouse, the entire rear end lit up in bright red taillights. I added an extra bounce to my step as I hurried up. If he pulled out before I managed to clear the fence, there was every chance I would lose him into the night.

The frontmost warehouse offered just enough cover for me to break into a sprint. I looked over my shoulder a couple of times to make sure I wasn't being watched, and once I was sure I had successfully made my way back to the fence line, I practically dived through the hole. I did roll along the grass for a bit, but once I caught my balance, I pushed myself off the ground and ran back to my car.

The truck had already disappeared by the time I climbed into the Camry, and I practically threw the coffee packet onto the passenger seat at the same time I started the engine and let off the emergency brake. It felt like I had four hands working at once, each completely independent of the others as I got the car moving. Once on the road, I headed toward the end of the street in the hope of catching up to my target.

Rounding the next bend, panic set in as the street ahead of me appeared empty. I hit the gas pedal harder, feeling the engine kick as the car sped up, then stomped on the break as I reached the T-intersection. Frantically looking left and right, another empty street greeted me with no sign of the truck. I had a choice to make and not one that came with a second chance.

I took another look in both directions, gripped the steering wheel tightly, and ripped it around to the right as I hit the gas. The front wheels spun ever so slightly before the traction control kicked in and the car took off. Another T-intersection faced me in the distance but not before I had to pass three cross-streets. Imagine my surprise when a split-second look down the second one showed the truck sitting at a set of lights. Instinct took over as I hit the brakes, performed the world's fastest U-turn, and cruised back to the intersection.

What followed after we pulled out onto the main street was me doing my best to fall back enough so that I could blend in with the limited amount of traffic on the road at that time. At one point, I found myself almost three blocks behind the truck due to the lack of cover. I knew it would have been unfeasible for the driver to recognize me from a distance but not completely impossible.

When he turned the truck onto I-79 a few miles farther along, I was beginning to think that my job was done. It wasn't like I was going to follow him all the way to Texas. I'd seen what I'd come to witness, and now that he was underway again, what purpose did it serve for me to follow him into the night? However, just two exits later and one before my intended departure, the truck's indicators suddenly came to life, and a couple of hundred yards farther along, the vehicle turned onto the exit.

With no other cars to hide behind, I had no choice but to show my card, so to speak, and I followed as best I could. Four blocks down, the truck took a left, a right, and then slowed until it eventually pulled into a service center, all as I was doing my best to keep my distance before flooring the shit out of the Camry trying to catch up again.

Laserback Truck Servicing Center appeared to be a kind of 24-hour mechanical place where trucks came for urgent repairs or around-the-clock servicing. *From engine to tires, we've got your back* was the tagline on the lit-up sign running along the front of the roof. He caught me off guard pulling into the place, and I had to drive past twice before I managed to find a suitable place to pull over so I could watch.

From what I could tell, and by *tell* I mean what little I could make out through the limited view through the binoculars, I watched a couple of guys remove the two spare tires sitting in a cage under the trailer. They were positioned about halfway along on the driver's side, and the area was probably all I could really see with the truck itself out of view. A few minutes later, a couple of fresh tires went back into the cage before I watched the men walk around to the other side of the truck and repeat the process with the spares over there.

Ten minutes was probably all it took, the brief visit reminding me somewhat of a Formula 1 pitstop, albeit in minutes instead of seconds. Not bad considering the size difference. In any case, once the tires had been replaced, I watched as the truck once again pulled out, turned in the direction of the interstate, and disappeared from view.

I decided not to follow, feeling like I'd seen about all I was going to when it came to the big rig. With traffic continuing to dwindle in the now early hours of the morning, I figured it wasn't worth risking getting seen. It was probably better to consider this evening a win and not push the envelope.

The truck center continued on once the Howard's Haulage rig was gone. A new truck pulled in a few minutes after the last, and again, a couple of the boys rushed over to perform whatever maintenance the new arrival needed. With my job done, I tossed the binoculars back into the glove compartment and made my way back to the interstate before turning in the direction of home.

A couple of miles farther along, I decided to give Linda a call and give her an update on my activities. Truth be told, I was more interested in her meeting with Denise Lord since my mission hadn't exactly yielded us any breakthroughs.

"How was the distribution center?" Linda asked as she answered the phone.

"Nothing of importance," I said as I switched hands on the steering wheel and flicked the rearview mirror up to deflect bright headlights behind me. "Just a normal truck loading routine from the looks of it. I did gain entry and checked out the cargo they're hauling, but it appears above board. How did you do?"

Before she could answer, something substantial suddenly struck me from behind, the impact hard enough for me to lose grip on the wheel.

"Ya-what-the—" was all I had time to yell before something hit me from the side. I had time to look through the passenger side window but only saw the side of a large pickup truck.

"Ben, what is it?" Linda called out, but I couldn't answer her, another pick-up truck behind me hitting the back of my much smaller car a second time.

"Interstate," I called out. "Someone...hitting..." BANG, another impact, this one hard enough to send the Camry lunging sideways. It hit the edge of the road, skittered the final few yards, and struck the metal barrier with a godawful squeal. Sparks exploded as night turned into day before I managed to steer the car away from it.

"Ben, where are—" Linda began, but that was as far as she got. The truck driving alongside me suddenly veered left, the front of it hitting me with a perfect PIT maneuver that sent the Camry first one way and then the other. My tires screamed for grip as I struggled with the steering wheel. I lost complete control as the car began to slide sideways the wrong way along the interstate. Somebody honked, but I was too busy trying to regain control. The last thing I remember is the world suddenly spiraling in front of me as the inside of the car's interior turned into a shrapnel gallery, bits flying in every direction as I felt myself spinning violently like a bottle top. When the steering wheel suddenly jolted hard to one side and the car came to a crashing halt beneath me, the world disappeared in an instant. The last thought that crossed my mind before the darkness took over completely was whether Max would think that I'd abandoned him. It certainly wasn't the ending I had been expecting.

18

For three days, I lay in a coma at St. Clair Hospital, my condition listed as critical for the majority of that time. According to Linda, the doctors didn't know whether I'd ever recover from my injuries with a severe knock to the head the worst of it. If I did wake up, the other concern was my memory, with amnesia the most likely outcome.

When I did eventually wake, not only did I find Linda sleeping on a sofa chair next to my hospital bed but I immediately recognized her, a good sign, according to the first nurse to notice me. The pain didn't feel all that bad, a fact not surprising thanks to the medication, and I managed to sit myself up as Linda began to stir.

The accident itself didn't return immediately. For the immediate hours following my awakening, a dark patch of shadows sat where those specific memories should have been. I remembered following a truck through some backstreets, a forklift passing me in some random aisle between industrial shelving, but not much else.

"You phoned me to say that you'd been to the distribution center," Linda whispered once we were alone again. The nurses gave me little more than thirty minutes between check-ups, and it didn't give Linda and me a lot of time to talk.

"I don't remember us talking at all," I said, closing my eyes and hoping for some of the random flashes of memory to make sense.

Aside from several cuts and abrasions to my hands and face and the head injury, I'd also suffered a compound fracture of my forearm, two cracked ribs, and a fractured toe on my right foot. The cast on my arm would remain with me for some time. Looking at my body as a whole, it had taken one hell of a beating, and I was no closer to knowing how or why other than knowing I had been involved in a car wreck.

When visiting hours officially ended at around eight that night, I tried my hardest to keep Linda with me, but the on-duty nurse insisted I get some much-needed rest.

"Dontcha know that sleep's the best healer of all," she said as she puffed up my pillow.

"I'll be back first thing in the morning," Linda said as we finally gave in and agreed to follow orders. The nurse was right about one thing. Despite having essentially slept for three days straight, I was tired, the fatigue hanging heavy over me. I don't think I lasted much more than ten minutes after Linda waved and left for the night, sleep welcoming me back with ease.

Sleep in a hospital is very different than sleep in your own bed. For one thing, the random noises, regardless of how muted they might appear, provide a constant stream of interruptions. But...they are nothing compared to the constant interruption of nurses doing their rounds for endless check-ups. One came to see me each and every hour, and while the routine may have been nothing more than checking my temperature and blood pressure, it was still enough to bring me back to the land of the living.

I think the most sleep I got that night was between the hours of five and seven during a shift change. When the new nurse woke me with a fresh round of checks and prods, I knew that slumbering had effectively come to an end, not a bad thing when Linda showed up just a half hour later and looked like she had news.

We waited until the nurse left us alone again before Linda pulled out her laptop and sat it on the mobile table next to the remnants of my limited breakfast. She opened the lid, punched a couple of buttons, and brought the screen to life.

"Managed to get my hands on the footage from your crash," Linda said, lowering her voice to ensure the conversation remained between just the two of us. She looked over her shoulder to make sure nobody else was coming into the room and then hit the play button.

The video itself ran for just under a minute and consisted of several camera angles that Linda had stitched together. I watched in disbelief as the Camry first drove almost alone for the first twenty seconds or so before two sizeable pick-up trucks rolled into view. They appeared to be the same make and model, black Toyota Tundras, and both on a mission of death.

I watched as the one in the center lane sped up somewhat, came alongside my car, and matched my speed. The other waited for the first to get into position before the driver hit the gas and drove straight into the rear of me. The truck hit hard, the smaller vehicle momentarily speeding up as it literally bounced off the much larger truck. The second the Camry seemed to regain composure, the second truck closed the distance and pushed me into the guardrail.

From what I could see, it appeared that each of the pick-ups had two occupants with both passengers holding what appeared to be handguns. I shuddered at the thought of those same men coming to finish me off after my eventual crash. How I came to end up in a hospital bed at all must have been a miracle in itself.

A huge shower of sparks exploded from the driver's side of the car as the Camry lurched into the guardrail again, this time helped by the second truck veering directly into the side of its prey. A front view of the scene showed me struggling to regain control before the guardrail suddenly came to an end and the Camry took a slight detour into a ditch.

The real surprise happened when the Camry came to a stop some three complete flips later after losing both its front and rear bumpers in a tangle of broken plastic and lights. The two trucks pulled up on the shoulder of the road, and each of the passengers climbed out. A taxi also stopped just as the two men slowly made their way down the slope but stopped when a second and a third car stopped to render assistance.

Another chill ran through me as I watched several people jump out of their cars and run toward mine. The two from the pick-ups stopped and looked at each other before retreating back to their respective vehicles before making their escape.

"I'd say you were one lucky son of a bitch, my friend," Linda said as the video came to an end. "God knows what would have happened if those other cars didn't stop when they did."

"They saved my life," I said, almost in shock at seeing the truth played out before me. Fate had somehow intervened and given me another chance. That's how I saw it, anyway.

It was a belief I carried with me for the next several days as I went to work healing my body as best I could. There were plenty of visitors, of course, including Grace and Dwight, who also brought with them a ridiculously large bunch of flowers along with a card signed by the entire office.

Speaking of flowers, not all of the ones I received turned out to give my mood a boost. There was one bunch in particular that turned up on the third day, accompanied by a note that immediately brought me back into the moment. It was brought into my room by the delivery guy himself, who had me sign his cell phone screen as confirmation. The bunch looked kind of expensive, although I wasn't exactly an expert on the subject. But it was when I pulled the small envelope sitting in among the flowers out and opened it up that my reality came slamming back down to earth.

Was going to deliver these to your other address but found you weren't there, the note read and beneath it, an address. While the words didn't really register at first, they just about bodyslammed me when I saw what the person had written next. *1416 Riverview Lane, Freeport.*

A sickening feeling birthed somewhere deep in my middle as a ripple of fear washed over me. Limited amnesia or not, that address instantly gut-punched me back to reality, and I immediately grabbed my phone to call Linda.

Somebody knew our secret. As I waited for my investigator to come to the hospital, I sat on the edge of the bed with a thousand thoughts running through my head, each new one more intense than the last. My memories might have been somewhat scrambled, but anything to do with Max Dunning remained intact.

My investigator arrived in record time and immediately checked the delivery, but there was nothing indicating where it might have come from. The note had been printed on a nondescript piece of thin cardboard while the envelope it came in displayed no identifying markers. No company name, no return address, just a plain envelope available for sale at any stationery store.

"You say the delivery guy handed them to you personally?" I nodded my head. "Might be a long shot, but I'll try and get hold of the hospital surveillance. See if I can track them back to their vehicle."

"Linda, they know where we're keeping Max," I whispered with a voice close to panic. "They *know* the address." When she didn't answer me immediately, I pressed the point. "We have to move him someplace else."

"I don't advise that," Linda finally said.

"But they know where he is," I hissed, feeling my world slipping away in a heated mess. "If they tell the authorities, then we're screwed."

"If they were going to tell the authorities, Ben, they would have done so already, and we'd all most likely be in jail by now." She shook her head as I felt my insides coil up. "No, they ain't going to any authorities. They want something from us, that much I know."

"Want what?"

"Who the hell knows? All I know is that if we try and move the kid now, we only risk getting seen by somebody else. And where would we take him anyway? Some random motel out in the middle of nowhere is too risky. Can't take him to any of our houses." She shook her head again. "No, I think it's best we keep him where he is for the moment."

I trusted Linda more than anyone else in my life, but at that moment, I just couldn't understand her call. To me, it felt like a huge risk, hanging our hopes for some unknown threat not to turn us in. I was still trying to think of some way to convince her otherwise when footsteps approached the door and a familiar face walked into the room.

"Gabby? What are you doing here?" I asked as my old neighbor came closer to the bed.

"Heard about your accident and wanted to come and make sure you were OK."

"Linda, you remember my old neighbor, Gabby Chapman?"

"Yes, of course," Linda said, and I watched as the two of them shook hands before my investigator rose from her seat and excused herself. "I'll leave you two alone," she said, giving my shoulder a squeeze. "Got some things to chase up. Catch up later?" She shot me a wink and disappeared out into the day as Gabby took her position on the chair.

"Wow, Ben, you look like shit."

"Thanks," I said with a bemused smile. "You always did have a way with words. How's the podcast going?"

"It's not a podcast," she said almost defensively. "It's a TikTok channel, and it's going great. Building up the subscribers every day."

"That's great," I said although she looked as if she didn't believe me. "No, really. I'm happy for you."

"So what happened? News reports said that you got run off the road."

"Is this an official line of questioning, Ms. Chapman?" She could see I was joking, but I wasn't entirely sure myself that I was.

"Just a concerned friend, I promise."

"I don't remember too much about it, but yes, somebody definitely tried to run me off the road."

"That's so scary," Gabby said, and I could see genuine concern on her face. "Think it's because of who you're defending?"

"That's almost a given," I said.

"How's that going?"

"Not easy, thanks to you," I said, surprising myself at the bluntness. Gabby didn't react, but I did see a hint of color rise in her cheeks.

"I'm sorry for that," she began but immediately changed course. "It wasn't as if I gave up a huge secret, though. I mean everyone else already knew about you. They just hadn't reported it yet."

"And you had to beat them to the punch," I threw in.

"Ben, I'm sorry for that, I really am, but you know the business I'm in. Jesus, you yourself ran to the station as fast as you could to win the client, did you not? Did you not do that to get ahead?"

She was right, of course, and I knew she could see that that was exactly what I was thinking, but I wasn't about to let her off so easily.

"Yes, but I didn't throw anybody under the bus in the process." I saw her reel just a bit, the faint sting of my words just biting her enough to take notice.

"OK, you're right, but I can't do any more than apologize again." I gave her a small smile.

"Forget it," I finally said. "We both have more important things to deal with."

Gabby ended up staying for more than a couple of hours, and we ended up reminiscing about past times. We talked about how much life had changed for the two of us since we'd first met and the people we'd lost along the way. What I couldn't ignore were the feelings I still had for her, feelings I'd conveniently forgotten about over the course of passing years and which now began to resurface. I was attracted to her, yes, but more than that, we had a connection, a commonality we shared involving deep defining moments in our lives. And when Gabby eventually bid me farewell later that afternoon, I knew I wanted more than just one visit from her, but first, there was something I had to do. Before I could pursue anything with my old neighbor, I needed to see my wife.

19

IT WASN'T EXACTLY JUBILATION I FELT THE DAY I FINALLY GOT out of the hospital, but it came pretty close. Grace came and picked me up, along with all of the flowers and get-well balloons that had been accumulating around my bed over the days. We managed to squeeze a lot of them onto my lap thanks to the wheelchair I had to sit in, thanks to hospital policy according to the nurse. I wasn't about to pass up a free ride.

Out in the parking lot, Grace surprised me with a new car that she had hired for me, although this one was a little more substantial. The F-150 looked almost poetic in the morning sunshine, the gray duco glistening with its metallic paint.

"Dwight thought you might need something a little more formidable going forward. Also got you the highest insurance level possible in case you decide to mix it up with strangers again," she told me with a smirk.

"I can't promise I won't," I said, grinning from ear to ear as we loaded my belongings into the backseat.

It felt a little somber in the truck on the way back to the office where I not only dropped Grace off but also headed inside to say hello to let the troops know that I was back on the case. Dwight gave me a heartfelt welcome back when I stuck my head in the door and assured me that the case remained mine and mine alone, a good thing considering my investment in the matter. I wondered what his message would have been if he had known the truth.

Grace insisted on setting up the flowers around the office and reception area. The cards she left on my desk. I didn't spend a lot of time there, and nobody expected me to be there anyway. Dwight almost insisted I take a couple of days to recover at home, and I promised I would, a promise I knew I would break within the first hour of leaving his sight.

The somberness returned the moment I climbed back in the truck and headed out into the morning traffic. If I'm going to be honest with you—and I hope you believe that I have been up to this point—then I need to share every-thing, especially the confused mess I insist on hanging on to about my wife.

When Naomi died, I went through hell, each day feeling like a stretched-out nightmare I was powerless to escape. Worse than that, I believed that I lived it for a reason, perhaps a husband's guilt for not being there to save the love of his life and our unborn child. In a way, I accepted that pain as a kind of responsibility, a requirement I needed to endure if I was going to be allowed to go on with my life. It was during those subsequent months that I learned one massive truth.

For those who've lost someone close to them, I wonder whether you share the same belief as me. The pain felt when grieving...it never quite goes away. It only gets easier to live with, which is why people can get on with their lives. The pain itself, however? When I allow my heart to open, it still feels as raw as the day of her death.

I'd been through all sorts of counseling about the loss, of course, with each new year since the tragedy bringing someone new for me to talk to. While they always insisted I was making progress after a few sessions, I never felt the same and would normally end the appointments after half a dozen or so. That was until I met a man named Tanner Bowden.

Tanner Bowden came to me as a recommendation from a client of mine, one who'd been somewhat of a regular thanks to his taste for the bottle. The first time I met the new counselor, I wasn't sure of how to take him, the man's demeanor more akin to a building site than an office. It was when Bowden shared his own past and the reason he got into counseling in the first place that I immediately found the connection. A drunk driver had run a red light some twelve years earlier and in the process, killed Bowden's wife and two daughters. It was a tragedy that would go on to shape the father's entire future.

After leaving the office, I headed straight to the cemetery where I knew my emotions would really come out. I could already feel them simmering beneath the surface with each passing mile and wasn't surprised to feel my bottom lip quivering when I eventually pulled into the parking lot. Like I said earlier, the pain never disappears completely. A person just learns how to live with it.

I didn't climb out of the truck right away. Being a bright sunny morning, plenty of other folks had the same idea as me to visit their loved ones. I could see plenty of them from my vantage point, and a part of me didn't want to mingle, not when I was already so close to the breaking point.

The good thing is that many of those people felt the same way and knew the unspoken rules. If you don't know what I'm talking about, then I'll make it easy for you. Cemeteries have a certain etiquette. If you see a person with their eyes cast down as they walk, don't go trying to strike up a conversation with them. Downcast eyes mean emotions, and for some, those emotions are the reason they come there in the first place. It's those emotions that bring with them a sense of connection to their loved ones, if that makes sense.

I waited almost ten minutes in the truck, long enough for half the people to reach their destination and the other half to return to their cars. Only when I could see a clear path to Naomi's final resting place did I get out and make my way through the jumble of paths and headstones, the tightness in my chest growing heavier with each step.

Seeing the photo of my wife on the headstone was what brought the first tear rolling. It had been a long time coming, of course, and I knew I'd be powerless once that little traitor broke free.

"Hey, baby," I whispered as I knelt down and kissed the top of the headstone. After another look, I stepped back and took a seat close enough to still make out her beautiful features. "Got into a bit of an accident," I said with a grin as I showed her the cast, grimacing when the ribs reminded me to take it easy.

For a moment, I sat there in silence while listening to the sounds filling the air: the birds in the trees, the faint hum of traffic that never seemed to end, and the slight breeze blowing through the needles of a nearby pine. All were the sounds that I came to recognize as those belonging to Naomi and her final resting place.

Once I was sure the tears had taken a temporary hiatus, I told my wife about the accident and my unfortunate stint in the hospital. I then continued with the case itself, and after looking around to make sure I wasn't about to be exposed by some unseen eavesdropper, I told Naomi about Max. I don't know why, but Max seemed to be the trigger that opened the floodgates, the trigger that turned my waterworks on and left me sitting in silence for almost twenty minutes.

While I might have been talking about Max, it was the underlying thought of Naomi lying with our unborn child just a few feet beneath me, our one chance to be a family stolen away in the blink of an eye. Naomi had been my savior, so to speak. She had saved me from a life I had wanted to escape for years. When she entered my life and showed me just how good this world could be, I really thought I'd found my soul mate. I know people tend to throw that term around like confetti on a spring day, but for me, it felt like the real thing, the one person with whom I was meant to be.

We'd often spoken about one day having a baby, but to me, it was never in a serious planning kind of way. Maybe I just had other things to focus on at the time. My idea was that fate might step in and make it happen. Naomi was too. I think meeting me was one of those events in her life she put down as having been written in the universal plan, the pregnancy confirmation another.

Part of why I struggled so much in the months and years after her death was the inability to accept my grief. In simple terms, I felt as if fate had somehow taken offense to me, that I had somehow offended the universe, and losing Naomi when I did was my punishment. I spent many dark nights alone with those thoughts in my head, and they just about destroyed me. I also shared those same thoughts with numerous counselors who would summarily dismiss them and try to guide my thinking in some alternative direction. That was until Tanner Bowden came along. He not only understood my thoughts but had shared them himself during his own grieving, and that was what eventually helped me come to terms with things.

I wasn't ashamed to cry. Unlike most men who believed emotions were a sign of weakness, Bowden explained to me that crying was nothing more than a release valve for the soul. He told me that emotions needed to be dealt with in order to regain control over life itself. It wasn't a weakness but the exact opposite: the strength needed to release those emotions far superior to what many people assumed.

"I have to protect this child, babe," I finally managed after letting the tears run their course. "I have to make sure that those wanting to silence him are brought to justice. If you have any way of helping me, I could really use your input here."

I didn't expect an answer, of course, the request more of a rhetorical one, but imagine my surprise when a goldfinch suddenly landed on Naomi's headstone. It bobbed about a couple of times before turning to face me, where it suddenly froze into place. At the same time, the sun suddenly reappeared from behind one of the few clouds in the sky, lighting up the bird's bright golden chest that seemed to glow in the sunlight.

The skin on my arms prickled as goosebumps raced across my body, the hairs on the back of my neck standing to attention. The moment felt almost out of this world as I sat perfectly still, the two of us in a kind of stare-off. I expected the bird to dart off as quickly as it had arrived, but instead, it suddenly bobbed closer to the front of the headstone and then half-dropped to the ground, where it landed just a couple of feet in front of me.

"What the—" I muttered under my breath, in awe of the bird as I couldn't help but wonder...just wonder whether it could be possible.

Before I could say anything else, the goldfinch twitched left, then right, before shooting into the air and into the nearest tree, where I finally lost sight of it. Most will tell you it was just a coincidence, and yes, it probably was, but silently believing that *something* might have happened isn't a crime, and I'll take what I can get.

Feeling like my wife had dropped in for a bit, I told her about hearing from Gabby again and how she was now a famous TikTokker. I also hinted that perhaps I needed to allow myself to open up to the possibility of another serious relationship although I couldn't quite commit to the promise. Instead, I left the idea on the proverbial table, promising myself to at least consider the possibility.

All up, I think I sat with Naomi for a couple of hours before I ran out of things to say. Cried out and feeling like I had once again managed to ground myself, I slowly got back to my feet and kissed the top of the headstone just as I always did. It felt good to have opened up again and let out the secrets of my life. Who knew? Maybe there really was an afterlife that allowed for some limited form of intervention, and that goldfinch was just a small sign of that reality.

Heading back to the truck, I could feel the smile on my face stretched to its limits. It felt good although the limp thanks to the toe did put somewhat of a downer on the moment. That and the faint throbbing in my forearm. The nurse had given me some painkillers to take, but I wasn't a fan and knew I would save them for when it became unbearable.

I was almost back to the truck when something made me stop, a new sensation filling my mind. The unmistakable feeling that I was being watched suddenly washed over me, and I began to look around for the source. The parking lot was neither huge nor busy, and I could easily see into most of the vehicles. And yet the sensation persisted.

Looking back over my shoulder into the cemetery, I could see several folks moving around, but none appeared to be interested in me. Most looked to be old, each shuffling with that aged walk of uncomfortableness that normally came from bad knees or a busted hip. One or two couples stood near some markers on the far side, while a caretaker appeared to be busy pruning some of the rose bushes.

I didn't physically shrug but felt like I did as I decided to continue on. No point standing there like a goofball when I had places to be. It was when I turned back to the truck that I finally saw the source of my apprehension. Parked about fifty yards away at the very edge of the parking lot sat a motorcycle, the rider leaning across the gas tank. He had his helmet on but the visor up, and I could see him sitting there just watching me. How did I know he was watching me? Because it wasn't the first time I had seen him.

There was no mistaking the red and black leather jacket with the matching helmet or the camera fixed to the top of it. Also the T-shirt under that jacket, the one I'd noticed when the same person delivered the flowers to me at the hospital, the ones with the message telling me they knew about Max.

"Hey," I called out as I waved my one good hand at him. I couldn't have appeared as much of a threat slowly limping in his direction. Even with the cast resting in the sling, I did my best to wave him over, but the ribs didn't want to play that game. "Talk to me," I called out, continuing to walk toward him while at the same time closing the distance to my truck. My hope was to get close enough where I could rush into it and then have a chance to chase the bike down.

I got to within a dozen yards of the pickup before I heard the bike start up. Perhaps reading my mind, the rider never acknowledged me, simply putting his bike into gear before slowly rolling forward a few feet before doing a U-turn. Another few seconds of idling along gave me a moment to consider my options, but I knew there was zero chance when I heard the bike's throttle suddenly open up. The bike turned into a red streak and two seconds later disappeared from view. I heard the engine continuing to wind up for a few seconds longer, but it too eventually faded out completely. Whatever his intention, he wasn't about to reveal it to me just yet.

20

Mario Perez

AT ROUGHLY THE SAME TIME THAT BEN CARTER WAS IN A potential face-off with a mystery motorcyclist, Perez sat in his cell much like he had for the majority of his time since arriving at Allegheny County Jail. He'd grown accustomed to the noise of the pod to a certain extent but still found it somewhat overwhelming at times, especially when inmates began arguing over the most mundane things imaginable. The most common was the television, of course, but debts, drugs, and sheer boredom were also commonplace.

One way Perez managed to deal with the endless drone of voices was to snooze his way through the day. Not surprisingly, nights were the most peaceful within the unit, and he'd decided early on that flipping his waking hours with his sleeping ones was one way to avoid the majority of it. He was still lucky enough to have a cell all to himself, but he also knew that could change at any given moment. It was a routine that he'd grown accustomed to quite quickly and one he knew he could stick to if only the prison itself remained the same. Snoozing through the day and reading at night worked much better than he imagined. Unfortunately, the universe felt a little different, and all that changed not long after his arrival in prison.

It didn't matter which part of the prison an inmate found himself in with the rules of the jungle still dictating everyday life. Most of the usual sayings define it perfectly, like only the strong survive, wolves and sheep, and of course the strong prey on the weak. Perez wasn't weak by any stretch of the imagination. He stood almost six feet tall with a frame to match. On the night of his admission, he tipped the scales at two hundred forty pounds, although he was fully clothed at the time.

He wasn't the biggest in the pod but far from the smallest, his body size perhaps somewhere in the middle of the population. Confidence was also something he held in reserve, although he wasn't one to go flaunting it the way some of the more flamboyant inmates did. What he remembered most from previous stints in jail was the repetitive way most pod populations seemed to mirror each other.

Every pod has a very similar hierarchy. There was the pod boss, the one whose orders everybody else followed in order to not face the wrath of his immediate foot soldiers. In this particular place, that man was Wilson Manning, a three-hundred-pound beast of a man with a temper to match. Then there was the guy who would sell himself as something of a walking Walmart catalog, the one who would promise to get anything an inmate needed into the unit. Waldo Kibbitz had already tried to turn Perez into a customer twice but with little success. Perez had neither the needs nor the finances to bring them to fruition, and Kibbitz took the hint after the second attempt.

Surprisingly, it was the person Perez expected to bond with the least who ended up breaking down his walls. It just so happened to be that most pods held that one person willing to provide sexual favors. There were, of course, also strict heterosexual men who offered services, but these usually required one of two specific currencies in return...drugs or protection. Vivian Lam didn't demand payment although she did benefit from protection for her unique services.

Perez was surprised to find someone like Vivian within the pod at all. Yes, she was a male as far as the Pennsylvania Correctional System was concerned, but it was obvious from her demeanor and appearance that she embraced her femininity. Living in a protection pod was probably the only real option for a person convicted of first-degree murder.

Vivian came to see Perez on the first morning after his arrival, the first of the pod's population to make contact with him. She was at his door merely seconds after unlock and offered to give him a guided tour of the place, complete with specific instructions on which areas and what people to avoid. Hesitant at first, Perez finally agreed when Vivian promised not to call her army of fans to force him to pay. There was something about her laugh that won him over, and he nervously followed her out into the common area.

Just like he had experienced the previous night, three strides out of his cell was all it took for the multitude of faces to turn in his direction, dozens of beady eyes watching his every move. Perez knew he was on show, that the test had begun to see whether he was one of the wolves or one of the sheep. Even Manning walked out of his cell on the upper tier and leaned onto the guard rail as he watched the new arrival. An inmate stood on either side of him, identical twins, both remaining upright with arms crossed across their chests as if guarding their employer.

Walking with his shoulders back and head high, Perez ignored the wall of faces and followed Vivian on her limited guided tour which included getting introduced to a handful of other inmates. He shook with each of them, looking the men in the face to hide any hesitation. A couple of them recognized him, but nobody indicated that his criminal matters would be an issue.

While he would have faced immediate repercussions for his suspected crimes out in the wider prison population, this wasn't the case in a protection pod. Not when he shared the place with everyone from child killers to child porn producers and beyond. This was the kind of place where the next guy had always done something much worse than the previous guy. It was Vivian who told him that asking about someone's crime was a no-no when they eventually got back to his cell.

"There isn't much off limits in here, if you get what I mean, sugar, but asking what someone did is definitely one of them."

"Why are you helping me?" Perez asked while trying to remain polite. He'd met plenty of people like Vivian during his time inside, and none of them ever did anything for free. She didn't answer him immediately, just kind of studying him.

"I see things in people, and I don't see what people have accused you of." Vivian left without waiting for a reply. Perez stood his ground as her final words echoed faintly in the cell before he sat on the edge of the bed.

That had been his first experience in the pod, and while most of the others seemed to also share a very similar relaxed kind of demeanor, not everybody wanted to play along. This was a prison, after all, and this place had a reputation as perhaps one of the worst in the state, if not the country. ACJ was known as one of the worst cesspools society could produce, and most pods reflected the reputation perfectly.

Perez listened to several fights a day break out over mundane things, usually ending with guards running into the place to break things up. The blood flowed almost as freely as the water did, with some fights causing the entire pod to be locked down for hours at a time.

For those first few days, Perez managed to avoid most of the violence. He only met the pod boss once while waiting in line for morning meds, and the interaction only lasted a few seconds when one of his followers ordered Perez to step aside and make way for Manning. The boss didn't speak himself, although he did flash Perez a look on the way past, one that didn't exactly show any friendly intent.

As the days continued to pass, Perez began to believe that he might actually make it through without incident. He'd gotten used to keeping his head down, staying out of the limelight by remaining mostly in his cell except for meal times and meds. Vivian would drop by for an occasional chat, but those visits never lasted more than a few minutes, and for the rest of the time, he would just sleep.

It was a Thursday afternoon when things changed in a sharp and sudden way, and it really shouldn't have come as much of a surprise. He had felt the tension in the pod growing for a couple of days prior, right after the guards performed the latest search. While the prison staff didn't find *all* of the drugs, they did manage to put a huge dent into the supply, and that meant a lot of people would have to go without. No drugs meant tempers would rise as withdrawal symptoms increased. This led to more violence as people chased what little supply remained, and of course, once that happened, anything goes.

The reason Perez didn't like associating with anybody was for one reason and one alone. He didn't want to build relationships. If he had friends, and those friends were attacked, then he would feel compelled to step in and help. It was the same reason he avoided joining a gang: The affiliation would eventually require him to step up and do something that would risk his future.

An hour after the midday meal finished, Vivian came by his cell to say hi. Perez had asked her to keep visits limited to either side of meal times so he could nap, and she'd agreed. The confrontation began almost the second she turned up. Perez could see that she was upset, and he was about to ask her about it when two other inmates suddenly walked to the door of his cell, inmates Perez recognized immediately.

Paul and Reggie were known as the Oswald Twins as well as Wilson Manning's highest-ranked soldiers. They were the ones who stood beside their leader when looking over the common area, followed his commands, and delivered prison justice wherever necessary. Only one of the twins walked into the cell behind Vivian, the other standing guard by the door. Vivian had time to turn around to see who belonged to the footsteps following her before a punch to the face cut off her question.

The screams began almost immediately from the want-to-be woman as she hit the ground. Not letting her wails distract him, Reggie stepped farther into the cell and landed a couple of blows on top of her head before launching a kick to the stomach.

"Hey," Perez yelled as he tried to roll off the bed, his legs tangled up in the body lurching on the floor beneath him. Reggie took one look at him before launching another kick.

"This don't concern you, killer," he snarled as he reached down and grabbed a handful of wiry hair, which he pulled back before delivering a well-aimed punch. The sound of the nose breaking from the impact filled the cell, eclipsing the cries of the unfortunate victim. Vivian howled in pain as two neat lines of blood flowed from her nostrils. Perez took it as a sign to step in, and he did so with seasoned composure.

He caught one of Reggie's fists in mid-flight before it could deliver another blow, pulled the man off balance, and delivered a single punch to the throat. The twin tried to call out for his brother, but with a partially crushed windpipe, he had much bigger issues. With his eyes widening in horror as he clutched at his throat, Reggie gagged a couple of times, sucking in as much air as possible through the remaining gap. Ignoring the man's issues, Perez called for Paul to come fetch his brother. The second Oswald twin stood in the doorway for a split second as the shock of seeing his brother briefly held him back from following through with his own counterattack.

"Think about it long and hard, kid," Perez warned as he stood to his full height, fists ready to go to work. Behind him, Vivian's cries fell away as she looked on in awe.

"Better watch your back from now on," Paul eventually said as he reached for his brother's hand and pulled him out of the cell.

"I always do," Perez said, fully aware that he had just effectively painted a target on his own back.

Looking down at Vivian, he saw that the flow of blood had turned the front of the white T-shirt into a horror show. He held out a hand, and when she took it, Perez helped her to her feet.

"You might need to get someone to look at that," he said, but before Vivian could answer, a couple of guards suddenly showed up.

After one of the guards took Vivian away to the infirmary for medical treatment, the other guard remained behind to question Perez. With no CCTV cameras in the cells, they had no way of knowing what had actually happened. Of course, the vision from the outside cameras showed the twins coming to the cell shortly after Vivian walked in, but that didn't shed any more light on the incident. The guard asked him several times, but with the prison code of silence well known to both parties, the questioning quickly came to an end.

Once alone again, Perez weighed up the situation and knew he would have to make changes. Sleeping through the day with the cell door open was out of the question, as was walking through the pod unaccompanied. There was no way that Manning would let the attack slide, and in this place, that kind of thinking left bodies in its wake. The thought of Manning marking him for a hit made him nervous.

It was those very nerves Perez ended up taking into the interview room later that afternoon after being escorted from the pod. Just before walking out, he looked up to see the pod boss standing on the top tier with his arms folded across his chest eyeing him. Perez knew the deal. Manning needed payback, and it would come sooner rather than later.

He didn't expect to find his lawyer sitting in the interview room, especially with one arm in a sling and an ugly yellowish bruise running down the length of his face. Perez hadn't heard from Carter in several days and knew the court case was scheduled to begin in just over a week, so his visit didn't come as a complete surprise, but the injuries?

"Good to see you, Mario," Carter said as Perez took a seat. He didn't respond until after the guard left the room, locking the door behind him with a metallic clunk.

"You look like you've been spending time in *here*, counselor," Perez said as he cocked a thumb over his shoulder. "What the hell happened?"

"Got into a car accident," his lawyer said. "How have you been?"

"Better than you by the looks of it," Perez said, doing his best to suppress the grin and figuring it best to get to the point. "What brings you down here?"

For a second, he didn't think Carter was going to answer him. He just kind of looked at him with a blank stare, his eyes almost glazed over. When his lawyer did finally speak, he did so with a much lower voice than he'd started out with.

"Mario, I need to know who else you told about you know who." The face alone was enough to indicate who he was talking about, but the question caught Perez off guard.

"Who else I *told*?" He shook his head in confusion. "You think I'd be dumb enough to tell someone?"

"Look, someone knows."

"Who? And if you know that, then why are you asking me?" Carter was frustrated by the response.

"Mario, someone's been phoning me asking questions without identifying themselves. They also hand-delivered flowers to my hospital room along with this."

Carter pulled something out of his briefcase and pushed the small slip of paper across the desk. Perez picked it up and scanned the writing. He studied the note for much longer than it would have taken him to read it before looking over at his lawyer again.

"You think someone's trying to blackmail you?"

Carter shook his head. "I wish I knew. Figured you might have an idea."

"I wish I could help you," Perez said. "I really do, but there's no way I'd be openly sharing this with anybody."

"What about Matthew Foster?" Perez was surprised at hearing the name but didn't show it.

"You think Foster knows about the kid?"

"No, but I know that you used him for your taxes, did you not?"

"Sure."

"Why? Foster doesn't appear to be your kind of accountant. How did you find him?"

"Got recommended to me."

"By who?"

The questions threw him a bit, but Perez managed to hide his reaction. He wanted his lawyer to know everything, but also knew he couldn't just blurt it out. What he needed was for Carter to connect the dots and shut the operation down, hopefully before any of them met their maker. He decided to throw him a bone.

"Klaus Weber," Perez said. "You know him?"

"Who doesn't? He recommended Foster to you?"

"Not quite. Have you heard of Jimmy Lester?" Carter looked to try and find the name in his memory but came up empty and shook his head. "Lester is Weber's illegitimate son. His father hooked up with a stripper back in the day, and now twenty-something years later, his little rugrat wants in on the action."

"Weber is successful. Not a surprise to have a kid wanting to cash in on the connection."

"Oh, he does more than try and cash in on his father's success. Lester's got his fingers in all sorts of pies."

"Without his father's knowledge?"

That was when Perez looked at his lawyer with an expression that told Carter everything he needed to know.

"You know," the lawyer said, "you could always just come clean and tell me what you know. Save us all a whole lot of time so I can concentrate on getting you out of here."

Perez thought about the ever-growing situation back in the pod but knew he was still better off behind the walls of the prison. Out in the real world, he wouldn't last more than a day without someone finding him and ending his miserable life. Custody was about the only chance he had of ever seeing the outside world again without constantly looking over his back.

"Maybe it's the searching you need to do in order to fully understand what's going on," Perez finally said and before Carter could answer, he called out for his escort. "GUARD." A second later, the men heard approaching footsteps, and when the jangle of keys rattled against the other side of the door, Perez gave Carter one final piece of advice. "Just know that he never deserved any of this. Take care of him, counselor."

21

TIME IS NEVER YOUR FRIEND IN THE LEGAL PROFESSION. IT doesn't matter how much you think you have, it's never enough and eventually will always run out. While Linda and I spent the majority of the following week checking and rechecking leads, nothing could slow the wheels of time enough for us to crack the case before I had to turn my full attention to the legal case. Linda continued as much as she could, of course, but for Grace and me, the time had come to take the matter to court.

When I climbed out of the Uber that Monday morning and made my way to the courthouse steps, the waiting media pack immediately surrounded me, bombarding me with questions. At least a dozen cameras filmed the encounter, and I must have stood there for a good twenty minutes answering as many reporters as I could.

The questions ended up becoming quite repetitive

toward the end with many chasing answers about a certain missing child. I'm not sure whether anybody noticed, but hearing Max's name mentioned hit me harder than expected as my insides just about imploded. The worst part was that the more I tried to remain normal, the more I felt the color rising in my cheeks.

Thankfully it was my legal enemy who finally delivered my reprieve, the mass of reporters suddenly turning their attention to the district attorney when he showed up. Behind him, Xavier Bartell looked more like a student following his headmaster as he remained behind his boss, giving Arthur Clements the limelight. I heard him telling the mass of reporters that the search for Max Dunning had indeed been called off as authorities would turn their attention to the main suspect in the hope of finding answers. Once again, my insides reacted accordingly.

Grace met me inside the courthouse, and we immediately headed to one of the interview rooms to finish the final preparations with Mario Perez. While it might not exactly be a win, per se, him having gone through the process before meant I didn't have to explain every last detail to him. The most important thing for my client to remember was to sit quietly beside me and try to keep his emotions in check. Any sudden outbursts would go against us and make my job that much harder.

Shortly after watching the guard escort Perez back to the holding area, I followed Grace down to the courtroom, where people were already beginning to fill the main gallery. My client's trial had drawn the world's attention, and seats in the courtroom were some of the hottest around. This was going to be a sellout, so to speak, and nobody wanted to miss out on grabbing a seat.

Thankfully, mine wasn't one I had to fight for, and I headed down to the defendant's table listening to several people whisper my name behind hands held to their mouths. I did look at one woman on my way past and saw nothing but contempt in those eyes. It wasn't new to me. People generally needed somebody to focus their anger on. With Perez supposedly presumed innocent, who else could they openly deplore without guilt? It wasn't as if I could do anything about it.

I took it in my stride. Someone much wiser than me had once said that it came as part of the pay packet. In other words, I got paid to put up with it. Everybody deserved an honest defense and a chance to prove their innocence. It may as well be the most qualified person willing to help them. In other words...me.

While this might have been the first day of the trial according to most news networks, Xavier Bartell and I had already spent two days working our way through the jury pool to ensure we had the twelve most qualified people to sit in judgment. Together with Judge Ernest Barber, we'd spent the previous Thursday and Friday carefully working our way through the forty-ish people who'd been drawn to participate.

It took some time to weed out those not suitable, but those who survived the culling turned out to be quite reasonable choices. I only had my doubts about one of the twelve, a retired school principal with an attitude to match. Grace felt that the woman would surprise me, and

I decided to take her advice. If I couldn't trust my assistant then who could I trust, right?

What I did notice as I set my briefcase on the table was how good it felt to be back in a courtroom. My normal routine would see me inside one at least a couple of times a week, more during busy periods, but finding Max Dunning on the side of that country road had changed all that. Taking on his case had brought in so many variables and confusing leads, as well as new responsibilities. This wasn't just an open-and-shut case. I had more than just a client to look after and definitely more than just a verdict to chase.

When the DA and his little sidekick eventually took their places, only Bartell offered me a head nod, doing so while his boss was looking the other way. I returned it without hesitation before focusing on getting myself ready. It was while I was closing the lid of my briefcase again and setting it down beside the desk that the bailiff finally stood and called the room to rise.

Silence rolled over the crowd as everybody rose to their feet, and when Judge Barber walked into the courtroom, the silence somehow multiplied even further. Barber's reputation stretched across state lines, the judge's prolific manner of clearing courtrooms well known. He didn't tolerate any form of chaos and would take action without warning. This wasn't a case people wanted to miss out on, and one could feel the energy in the room turn cold the moment he walked in.

"Morning, folks," Barber said as he took his seat, giving the courtroom a cursory glance over the top of his thin-framed glasses. He didn't actually focus on any one person, turning his attention to the paperwork on his desk almost immediately. The bailiff called for the court to take their seats, and the session officially got underway.

Before the prosecutor and I could begin with our opening statements, the rest of the chess pieces had to assemble. When the guards finally brought the defendant out, a very faint murmur raced through the rows of people behind me. Perez didn't pay them the slightest attention and took his seat beside me.

When Barber called for the jury to be brought out, all eyes turned to the door located beside the nest of empty chairs. Again, the guards followed the judge's cue and opened the door before we watched each of the seven men and five women slowly walk out in single file before taking their seats. Only three of the twelve looked over to seek out the defendant. I noticed things like that. The small matters meant something to me.

To me, the courtroom is like a board game, the individual members making up the pieces. The judge, the prosecutor, the defense lawyer, the defendant, the jury, and even the crowd play a part. As far as I am concerned, a person wanting to win needs to know their opposition, and in this game, that means everybody. A case involving a jury means that those twelve people will ultimately decide a defendant's guilt or innocence.

Only those members would ultimately determine Perez's fate, and it was them I had to convince of his innocence. Neither the judge nor the prosecutor decides a defendant's guilt. The problem with juries is that they are just ordinary people, and ordinary people can be manipulated. Bartell and I both knew that cases come down to more than just evidence or witnesses. The entire process itself could bend the case in a certain direction, right down to how the viewing crowd reacted to certain bits of testimony. I've always seen a court case as theater, with each of the participants an actor needing to play their part, and I was about to take center stage.

Once the jury had taken their seats, Barber addressed the court with his usual spiel, highlighting the need for the crowd to remain quiet throughout the proceedings. He did add his warning to the end, reminding the good folks of the city that he wouldn't hesitate to clear the room if he deemed it necessary. The crowd listened in silence with most not even breathing. When he finished, Barber turned to the jury and gave them a reminder of who they were and why they were there. He highlighted the need for them to remain impartial and listen to the presented evidence with a clear mind.

For me, the judge's speech felt like a warm-up of sorts, a time used by the main actors to prepare to take the spotlight. I could see Bartell already straightening his tie as he glanced over whatever points he'd written into his notebook, the pages splayed out before him. When the judge finally finished his part of the opening sequence, he handed the floor to the prosecutor, officially lighting up the scoreboard and setting the game in motion.

"Thank you, Your Honor," Bartell said as he pushed himself up out of the seat and slowly crossed the floor until he stood just a few paces from the front of the only people who mattered to him. "Good morning, members of the jury," he said as he slowly tried to make eye contact with each person in turn. "I know this isn't going to be an easy case for you to sit through, nor will the defense sit back and allow this matter to be presented the way it should. Any case involving a child is difficult, but what makes this one all the more terrifying is that little Max Dunning remains missing."

He paused to look at the floor as if needing to recenter after speaking Max's name. Like I said, this was theater, and Bartell knew how to act.

"We, the prosecution, will show how Mario Perez not only kidnapped the little boy from his caregiver's home but also murdered two people that morning, both of whom had close ties to the child. We will prove beyond a shadow of a doubt that Mario Perez murdered Harold Dunning in cold blood, executing the man in front of his boy in the most heinous of ways."

Another pause as Bartell took time to meet the gaze of multiple jurors before continuing his opening statement.

"We will prove that Mario Perez kidnapped a frightened young woman, a young woman who'd been tasked with protecting a vulnerable child. We will show how he took this young lady out of her home in the middle of the night before brutally murdering her in cold blood before he disposed of her body like trash."

I watched and listened from a distance, not only taking in the prosecutor's words but also the way the jury reacted to them. I zeroed in on individual members just like Grace was, looking for any hint of a reaction from those sitting in judgment. What we were looking for were those easily controlled, those who could be manipulated with words alone. We were looking for things as subtle as being unable to maintain eye contact or even just fidgeting.

When Bartell finally finished his opening statement and retook his seat, the judge handed the floor to me, and I felt warmth course through my system as my insides lit up. Call it adrenaline if you will, but this is the moment I come alive during any case. It felt like familiar territory, almost like coming home. This was the beginning of what you might consider a form of drug taking, the eventual verdict one of the biggest highs imaginable.

"Thank you, Your Honor," I said as I rose from my seat and made my way to the jury. "Good morning, members of the jury. For perhaps the only time in this case, the prosecutor and I tend to agree on something. He's right when he says that this will be a difficult case for you. He's also correct when he says that any case involving a child is difficult. What sets us apart, however, is the guilt of Mario Perez."

Like the prosecutor before me, I also knew how to play the game, using the stage to my full advantage. The way I liked to keep the members of the jury engaged was by making myself a moving focal point. I slowly walked back and forth as I spoke, randomly shifting my gaze from one member to another and never two sitting side by side. I'd shift my gaze from the front row to the back, from the far left to the far right in an instant. Nobody knew where I would look next, and nobody wanted to get caught not paying attention.

"Fact…this case involves the cold-blooded killing of a devoted father. Nobody can deny that Harold Dunning didn't do everything he could to take care of his son—and somebody shot him." I looked from the principal to the trucker sitting in the back row. "Fact…Hillary Warner was taken out of her home at gunpoint and brutally shot. Nobody is denying her cold-blooded murder."

Another few steps during a moment of silence as I shifted my gaze between another two people before continuing.

"Fact…Max Dunning remains missing to this day with his current whereabouts or condition unknown. But… what we will show is that Mario Perez was nothing more than a pawn in these matters, manipulated and used by those responsible for these multiple tragedies. We will both show and prove how the prosecution will try to turn circumstantial evidence into factual accounts in the hope of convincing you that Mr. Perez was acting alone."

When it was time for me to close my opening statement, I did so by stopping for the first time since starting, giving each of the twelve members another glance.

"You have been assembled in this court to determine the guilt of this man," I continued. "Ladies and gentlemen of the jury, your task is to find Mr. Perez guilty but only if you do so beyond reasonable doubt." I paused before repeating myself. "Beyond reasonable doubt. If that is not something you find, given the evidence we intend to present, then it will be your sworn duty to clear my client's name by finding him innocent. Thank you."

Returning to my seat, I could feel the energy in the room as every set of eyes watched my every step. After retaking my seat, Barber gave the jury another address before finally handing the floor back to the prosecutor. The case had officially begun.

22

I wasn't completely surprised when Bartell called Detective Dan Oakland to the stand to open his side of the argument, a cop who would set the scene, so to speak. Oakland walked into the courtroom with an air of professionalism and only wavered when he gave me a sideways glance on his way past. I ignored him, watching as he took his seat and followed the bailiff's instructions during the swearing-in process.

Once finished, the judge handed the witness over to Bartell, who first thanked the judge and then walked to the middle of the floor before engaging the witness.

"Thank you for coming today, Detective. You were one of the first detectives called to the scene, is that correct?"

"Yes, sir. My partner and I arrived at 4:07 that morning."

"What were your initial conclusions about the scene?"

"Based on the position of the body and the manner of

death, it was obvious that the victim was murdered execution style."

"And what indicated this exactly?"

"Firstly, the victim's hands had been tied behind his back using cable ties. Dunning had also been made to kneel before his killer, who then fired a single shot into his face, killing him. The man tipped forward and remained kneeling as he bled out, which was how we found him."

"What about Hillary Warner?"

"Her body was found more than twenty miles away with a similar injury as Harold Dunning."

"You mean she'd been shot in the face?"

"Yes, sir," Oakland continued. "Although she had been blindfolded at the time."

"So she wouldn't have known she was about to die."

"Exactly," Oakland said. "Once we apprehended the suspect and forensics tested his car, we found traces of blood on the side of the truck as well as in the pickup's tray."

"Any idea how those samples would have ended up there?"

"From initial tests, it appeared as if the victim had been shot next to the truck and then loaded into the back of it to be driven to the spot where we eventually found her."

"Do we know the weapon used for these killings?"

"Yes, sir, we do. Once we apprehended the suspect and conducted a preliminary search, I found the murder weapon under the driver's seat of Mr. Perez's truck. A .38 Smith and Wesson revolver."

"That's an old-school weapon, isn't it?"

"It is."

"And did Mr. Perez give you any reason for him having such a weapon?"

"He said he found it."

"Found it?" Bartell threw in a little theater as he turned to look at the jury with a confused expression on his face. "He just happened to find the murder weapon responsible for the deaths of two people directly linked to his truck? That's one hell of a coincidence, is it not, Detective?"

"It certainly is, sir," Oakland said as he looked over at Perez.

"Was there anything else that you found with the weapon, Detective?"

"When we opened up the cylinder, we found two spent cartridges."

"Two fired shots for two victims, is that correct?"

"Yes."

"But no sign of the boy?"

"None whatsoever, unfortunately. We did try to question the defendant, but he has refused to cooperate with us on the matter."

"Thank you, Detective," Bartell finished before turning to the judge. "No further questions, Your Honor."

"Your witness, Mr. Carter," Barber said, and after thanking the judge, I mimicked Bartell's style by also making my way across the floor toward the witness stand. I liked getting close to the people testifying. It built a kind of connection and also allowed me to look at the jury once in position.

"Detective Oakland, you mentioned that my client refused to cooperate with you when questioned about Max Dunning, is that right?"

"Yes, that's right."

"And yet that's not entirely true, is it?"

"How so?"

"Isn't it in fact true that when questioned, my client repeatedly stated that he didn't know what happened to the child once he left his sight?"

"He did, but we have no evidence that someone else was involved."

"And isn't it also true that given the layout of the crime scene, it would have been near impossible for a single man to carry out both killings as well as keeping a child under control?"

"Not if he had tied everybody up."

"Were Hillary Warner's hands bound when you found her body?"

"No, they were not," Oakland said as he looked down at his hands.

"And did the coroner find any indication that they had been bound before her death?" I asked as I looked across to the jury.

"No, none," Oakland said.

"So it is possible that there could have been somebody else there that morning?" I could see he didn't want to answer, but Oakland knew he couldn't ignore the question. If he did, it would only play into my hands.

"Yes, I guess it could have been possible, but we found—"

"Thank you, Detective," I said as I cut him off and turned to the judge. "Thank you, Your Honor, no further questions."

Heading back to my seat, I looked over to the DA, and the expression on his face was enough to tell me my cross-examination had irritated him. The problem for me was that it wasn't anywhere near what I needed. If I was going to win the case, I would need a little more than possible scenarios that couldn't be proven. If scores had been taken at that moment, the prosecution would have been leading, and I knew I was already falling behind.

"Your next witness, Mr. Bartell," Barber called out once Oakland left the courtroom.

"The prosecution calls Doctor Simon Chang to the stand, Your Honor," Bartell replied, and I immediately turned to watch the coroner enter the room.

Simon Chang wasn't the kind of man to see himself above others. The Malaysian immigrant had held his position for close to two decades after becoming a naturalized American back in the mid-nineties and eventually turning his attention to the coroner's office. He walked with an air of grace few people possessed, smiling at anyone and everyone who crossed his path. The mannerisms of the man screamed warmth, and he came across as one of the most genuine people imaginable.

Chang thanked the bailiff when asked to sit and again

when the swearing-in sequence finished. When he turned and smiled at the judge, Barber gave him a courteous head nod before handing the witness over to the prosecutor.

After crossing the floor again, Bartell began by asking the coroner about his current position, as well as his history within it. Chang answered him with a concerned expression as if needing to show that he understood the seriousness of the question. The moment he finished and waited for the next question, his expression returned to the smile.

Bartell eventually turned the line of questioning to the victims themselves, beginning with the state of the bodies.

"Well, Harold Dunning did show signs that he'd been attacked somewhat. He suffered a laceration to his bottom lip and a bruise on his right cheek, as well as a cracked right rear molar."

"The molar, Dr. Chang. Could you tell when the crack in the tooth happened?"

"Within hours of the man's death," Chang said. "The break was still clean with absolutely no wear around the edges."

"And the bruise itself? Did you happen to find anything significant about the injury?"

Chang never flinched, rolling from one answer to the next like a seasoned pro. "Yes, I just so happened to identify the shape of the bruise as that matching the bottom of a pistol."

"Any specific pistol, Doctor?"

"The very same one found in the defendant's vehicle."

"How can you be so sure?" Bartell gave Perez a bit of a side glance as he asked the question, more theater to direct the jury's attention to my client.

"The revolver in question has a broken grip as shown in your illustration, Mr. Bartell." He pointed to the projector screen showing the photographic evidence. "I used the impression of the bruise and compared it to the weapon and found that the two imprints matched perfectly."

To add to the witness testimony, Bartell highlighted the specific area before returning his attention to the witness.

"Sir, did the bullets used to murder both victims originate from the same weapon?"

"The markings on the bullet retrieved from Ms. Warner certainly did, yes."

"And what about Harold Dunning?"

"Hard to say since the man had a metal plate screwed to the back of his skull. The bullet all but disintegrated upon impact. There wasn't a whole lot for me to test."

"But you can confirm the man died from the same caliber bullet?"

"Without a doubt. Plus given the two victims died from near-matching bullet entry wounds, one can assume them to have been committed by the same weapon."

"Objection, Your Honor," I said, jumping to my feet. "Speculation."

"Sustained," Barber responded almost immediately.

"Just limit your answers to the question asked, Dr. Chang."

"My apologies, Your Honor," Chang said with that same smile before looking back at the prosecutor.

"Dr. Chang, did you find any other injuries on Ms. Warner?"

"No, none. Just a single bullet wound to the face."

"So no other bruising to any parts of her body?"

"Objection, Your Honor," I chimed in. "Asked and answered."

"Overruled, Mr. Carter, but not by a lot. I'll hear what the witness has to say."

"Very well, Your Honor," I said, retaking my seat. Bartell continued.

"Dr. Chang? If you'll answer the question please?"

"I did find subtle damage to one of the victim's fingernails. It appeared to have a fresh break."

"Did you find anything significant with the nail?"

"When I tested some of the material under the nail, I found it to contain human tissue."

"Human tissue? You mean skin?"

"Yes."

"And did you find a match for the skin?"

"I did, yes," Chang said before looking over to Perez. "It matched with the defendant's genetic code."

"Could this particular skin sample have come from an injury like this one?" Bartell continued as he brought a new image up on the screen. It was a picture of a man's upper torso. A dark red line ran across his neck and down to the side of his chest in a neat line.

"That's precisely the type of scratch that would leave a sample under the fingernail, Mr. Bartell."

"Thank you, Dr. Chang. No further questions, Your Honor."

"Your witness, Mr. Carter," Barber called my way. I picked myself up and walked toward the stand.

The thing was, I didn't have any questions to ask him. The man dealt in facts. Other than what he had already shared, there wasn't anything he had that could help my side of the case. Then it came to me.

"Dr. Chang, I'm curious to know if you can determine the time of death for both victims."

"Objection, Your Honor," Bartell said from behind me. "The time of death had already been submitted for both victims." Before Barber had a chance to answer, I cut in.

"Your Honor, I understand the time released by the coroner, but I'm curious as to whether the precise moment can be determined. As in down to the minute." It took Barber a bit, but he eventually began to nod ever so slightly.

"Overruled...for now," he finally said. I took the answer and turned back to the witness.

"Dr. Chang?"

"If I had to narrow it down to as close to the actual time as possible, I'd say at least between five to ten minutes apart." It wasn't the answer I was hoping for.

"Thank you, Doctor," I said and handed the witness back to the judge.

Surprising the court, the judge ended up bringing the session to a premature end, adjourning the case until the following morning. Bartell and I exchanged a curious glance, but that was about the extent of our communication. We both stood when directed by the bailiff, and just like that, the first session of the trial had come to an end.

"Let me know if you need anything," I whispered to Perez just before the court security came to escort him back to the holding area, and although he told me he would, I knew I wouldn't hear from him again until the following morning. He was just that kind of guy, one who didn't go out of his way for help.

Grace and I didn't bother hanging around, and after grabbing my things, we headed out into the foyer to prepare for the inevitable media pack. With the trial now in full swing, I knew the process with the bunch of reporters would remain the same until the final verdict. They would have a thousand questions for me to answer and wouldn't give up until I gave them something worthy.

"Want me to hang around and wait for you?"

I shook my head as we reached the doors. "Nah, it's fine. Grabbing an Uber anyway. Doubt these guys will let me go before the bottom of the hour anyway," I said checking the time. It was just after three, the sun still high in the sky as it blazed the parking lot.

"Sure?"

"Yeah, I'm sure." I thanked Grace and headed out to face the music.

For the first few minutes, the questions came and went just as I had expected. In fact, the entire process followed my predetermined script, that was until I saw Grace standing near the closest edge of the parking lot and watching me. It kind of threw me in a way because it wasn't like her. I could see from the look on her face that something was wrong.

"Thank you, folks, that's all I have for you now," I ended up saying with a hand held up before me in surrender. Of course, the more determined reporters in the crowd refused to give up without a fight and continued throwing the odd question at me as I began to push my way through the middle of them. It took another thank you with a little more conviction for me to finally break through the pack.

"Grace, what is it?" I asked when I got close to where my assistant was standing. She looked around nervously before holding out a slip of paper to me. It had been folded in half, and I took it while trying to understand.

"Found this stuck to my windshield, Ben," she said in a low tone.

Has Ben shared his secret with you yet, Gracy? It's a doozy was what the note read, and I immediately knew the answer to my question. Beneath the question, the sender had printed a phone number and I knew exactly who it would be to answer my call.

"Leave this with me," I said, feeling the color rising in my cheeks, although it had nothing to do with embarrassment.

"You know about this?"

I could have lied again but figured it best to try and give her a bit of an answer, although not one spilling the entire story.

"We have a history, yes," I said. "It's someone trying to get my attention."

"Attention for what, Ben? What are they talking about?"

"It's a stalker, so to speak."

I tried my best to reassure Grace, but something about her demeanor told me she didn't quite believe my explanation.

"I'll deal with it," I finally said, forcing a smile, and told her to go home. Grace hesitated for a few moments before giving in.

I watched my assistant walk back to her car and stood my ground until she disappeared into traffic. Only when I was sure she wouldn't return did I pull my cell phone out and order an Uber home, and once there, I locked myself into my apartment before making contact with the reporter. By that point, my temper had reached just about fever pitch, my face burning with the heat of rage. My fingers were shaking so badly I could barely control the numbers I was pressing, and I had to delete the same one twice before I finally managed to punch in the right sequence.

When the line began ringing, I straightened back up and stood in the middle of my living room as if waiting for mortal combat. I could feel the beating in my chest extend all the way up to my temples, my breaths coming too fast.

"I knew that would get your attention" was how the voice answered the call, and I felt my anger take another step up as I lambasted myself for not hiding the caller ID.

"What the hell do you want from me?"

"An exclusive," the voice said with that same flat tone.

"An...a what?"

"An exclusive," the voice repeated. "You let me share your secret with the world. Let me be the one to tell them all about the little connection you and Perez share."

"You're a reporter?" My insides coiled up in frustration as I lowered my voice to nothing more than a hiss. "Do you have any idea what you're doing? We're talking about the life of a kid here, and you turn out to be nothing more than a bloodsucking leech wanting an exclusive?"

"Yes," the man answered, his voice remaining surprisingly calm. "A bloodsucking leech wanting an exclusive, Ben. And you're going to give it to me."

"What makes you think I would deal with a lowlife like you?"

"Because if you don't, you and I both know your career will end with a single phone call. Not only yours but also that of your pretty little investigator and that child welfare worker friend of yours currently looking after Max. Imagine, Ben, all three of you finished and in prison."

He had me by the balls, and he knew it. There was little I could do but give him what he wanted although I knew I wasn't ready for the world to know. I still needed time, and for that, I needed him to wait.

"Give me a week."

The line filled with laughter, the first emotional response I'd detected in the stranger.

"A week? Do you have any idea how long a week is in the press?"

"Yes, I do, and that's my best offer. I'm not prepared to

risk the kid's life for an exclusive." It wasn't much of a retaliation, I know, but what the man said next sealed the deal.

"All right, Ben" was what he said. "You got seven days."

23

I WANTED TO SCREAM WHEN THE LINE WENT DEAD AGAIN, TO curse the world and everyone in it. The urge to throw my phone across the room and savor the sound of it crashing into the wall also crossed my mind, but I ended up resisting the urge on both counts. Instead, I raised the phone for a second time and called perhaps the only person who not only understood the situation I was in but could also help with fixing things.

"Hey, Ben, how was court today?" Linda said, answering on the second ring.

"Great," I said, doing my best to add a bit of a smile to my tone. It didn't help.

"That's not a happy voice."

"We have a problem," I said as I dropped onto the couch and raised my feet onto the coffee table.

"OK, go on."

"Those flowers delivered to my hospital room?"

"Yes?"

"It's a reporter looking for an exclusive."

"How do you know?"

"Because I've had another couple of run-ins with the guy, most recently via a phone number he left on my assistant's windshield in the courthouse parking lot."

"Oh, shit," Linda whispered, and I felt every inch of her change in mood.

"Yeah, exactly. Anyway, I bought us seven days."

"To do what?"

"To figure this out," I said. "We have seven days before he comes back to claim his reward, and if we don't deliver on time, then he's going to tell the authorities what he knows."

"That's not a long time," Linda said, and I fully agreed.

"Then we'd better pull our fingers out and make things happen."

"Speak for yourself," my investigator snapped back. "I've been busy. Remember Jimmy Lester?"

"Tell me you found something."

"Possibly," Linda said. "He's certainly the mini version of Klaus Weber, that's for sure. Got his fingers in all sorts of shady schemes."

"Anything related to our case?"

"Well, possibly. Have you come across the name Robert Norris? *Detective* Robert Norris?"

"No, " I said after doing my best to search through the memory banks. "I don't think so."

"I'm going to shoot you through an email shortly.

Check it out. It might be nothing, but I'm almost certain there's something worth finding on him."

"All right, I'll check it out," I said and ended the call.

Just as she promised, Linda sent through the email less than five minutes later, giving me just enough time to hit the head, grab a beer from the fridge, and set myself up on the couch with the laptop resting on my thighs. When I downloaded Linda's attachment and opened it, what I found wasn't at all what I was expecting.

Robert Norris's disciplinary record looked about as pumped up as a steroid-popping bodybuilder. Stretching back some thirty years, the detective had faced everything from insubordination to manslaughter charges and everything in between. He'd assaulted colleagues, harassed witnesses, and even threatened a judge over a parking fine.

On the flip side, the man's professional record could have won him Officer of the Decade multiple times, his awards and commendations filling several pages. It took me almost an entire beer to read it, and that was just skimming through the best parts.

To look at the two sides, it appeared to be speaking about two different men entirely, and yet I double-checked. Both records spoke of the same man. He had been honored by the Pittsburgh mayor twice and stood on stage with the state governor for gallantry service. The man was both a hero and a mortal threat, and yet despite all of the negativity, he managed to remain in the same role he'd worked for years.

The thing was, reading about him did nothing for me.

Yes, I could see that he might have been a person of interest and Linda believed he was worth checking out, but it wasn't until I saw a photo of him that the hairs on my neck began to prickle. The file's final page contained several images of the man, in his old patrol uniform as well as wearing a business suit. But it was the image of Norris in regular civilian clothing that piqued my interest, his face partially hidden by a baseball cap. Not just any baseball cap, but a green one featuring the word *Bitter* along the bottom. It was a logo I didn't immediately recognize, although I eventually figured out that probably any Australian would have. After a quick Google search, I found it.

Rather than email her back, I decided to give Linda another quick call, and when she answered, I filled her in on what I had found.

"Perez told me that the person who shot Dunning and Warner wore a baseball cap, remember?"

"Ben, I already told you…half the pop—" but that was as far as she got before I cut her off.

"He also told me it was green and with a specific logo. The word Bitter ran along the bottom of that logo."

"You found the logo?"

"I certainly did. I'm actually surprised I didn't pick up on it earlier."

"What is it?"

"Victoria Bitter, one of the most popular brands of beer in Australia. I'm guessing he must have taken a trip there, but I guess it's not important."

"And you think Norris might be the person who murdered Dunning and Warner?"

"Perez said that both Norris and Cook were there that morning. If they really are working together, then we need to find the connection."

"I'll get to work," Linda said, and before hanging up, she added, "Good luck in court tomorrow.

"Thanks."

I ended up giving Christy a quick call to make sure everything was OK on her end. With us three now compromised and not the only ones aware of Max's whereabouts, I wanted to make sure she hadn't seen anybody suspicious hanging around. I made sure to word it in such a way as to not freak her out. Thankfully she hadn't, and it sounded as if the two of them were having quite the time with Christy teaching Max some cooking skills. It made me smile knowing he was getting cared for by someone qualified for the job.

I slept better that night than I had in some time, either due to exhaustion or simply because the case was making progress. I guess my inner conscience had calmed itself enough for me to get some proper rest. When I woke up the next morning to the sound of my alarm going off next to my head, it felt like the start of a normal day, like some structure had returned to my life.

Breakfast was never my thing during a trial. Grace called it legal fasting, with me relying on just one meal a day, or OMAD. What I did turn to for sustenance was coffee. Black...strong...coffee. I had exactly four cups per day. The first shortly after waking. The second upon arriving at the courthouse where Grace would be waiting for me with a cup in hand. The third during the lunch recess. The final cup I'd sneak in during the afternoon recess but only if one was called.

It was that first sip in the morning that really got me into the swing of things, that bitter streak of warmth stretching all the way down to my toes as the concoction hit my insides. Sometimes, goosebumps accompanied that sensation, giving my body an involuntary spasm as it responded to the caffeine.

After finishing my bathroom needs and slipping into a fresh shirt and suit, I sat and drank the coffee while scanning any new messages in my Inbox before checking the overnight news on the laptop. I'm not OCD in the sense of the condition, but I do find that those structured mornings tend to give me somewhat of a sense of normality. The process takes me almost exactly the same time each morning, and from the first sip to walking out the door took the same twelve to fifteen minutes each time.

The other thing I preferred during a trial was not worrying about a car. Grace had offered to pick me up several times, but she lived on the other side of town, and it would mean driving almost directly past the courthouse and continuing on for another twenty minutes to reach my place. Instead, I opted for an Uber. It didn't encroach on anybody's morning, as it allowed me to sit in the backseat to continue going over my work, and I could mentally prepare for my morning without distraction. It was perfect.

Turning up to court also took on somewhat of a

routine with the same sequence of events happening almost on cue. The Uber dropped me off down on the corner instead of the parking lot and allowed me to walk the short distance to the front of the building. This made me feel a little less like a rockstar turning up to a concert and immediately getting surrounded by hordes of adoring fans. In this case, the fans meant reporters, and they weren't exactly adoring. I was also far from an admired rockstar and so preferred to approach the pack rather than them surrounding my car like a mob.

Getting through the media pack in the mornings was always a little easier as long as I gave them a decent update the night before. With no new information to offer, I made it through the crowd with a couple of standard *We'll see what today brings*, as well an occasional *I'll update you when I find out*. All the while Grace would be standing just inside the front doors, a tray of coffee cups in one hand while watching me juggle the reporters. Like I said...routine.

"How did you do with the stalker?" Grace asked when I managed to push my way into the building. She held out the tray, and I took one of the cups.

"Thank you," I said, first taking a sip before answering her. The effect was the same, my toes almost curling inside my shoes. "Taken care of," I continued as we turned for the common area. The truth is, the question sent a surge of nerves rattling through me. Not a violent one but enough to remind me of the deceit and how close I was to losing those closest to me because of it.

Before heading into the courtroom, Grace and I spent

a few moments going over the day ahead, and once I swallowed the last mouthful of coffee, we headed inside. Just like the previous day, the public gallery was already beginning to fill up as people grabbed their spots for the best show in town. One young woman in particular mumbled something under her breath as I passed by, giving me an added glare along the way. I didn't react. No point. I had more important matters to occupy my mind, and there were plenty of people like that with enough animosity to fill the room.

The routine didn't end with me taking my seat at the defense table. The waiting, the bailiff taking control of the room, and even the judge's shuffle to his bench felt a part of it. The routine didn't essentially end until Bartell called his first witness of the morning, the first real point of difference finally setting the scene for the day.

"The prosecution calls Marlow Wayans, Your Honor," my counterpart said when prompted, and a few moments later, a thin, wiry-looking man walked through the doors before taking his seat on the witness stand. The bailiff swore the forensics expert in before handing him over for questioning.

The problem for me arose when Bartell began asking the witness about the defendant's truck, and Wayans proceeded to explain how he'd had to search for minute samples since it appeared the truck had been cleaned beforehand. I pictured the scene in my mind while the witness explained his method for finding evidence of the murders taking place beside that truck. If Norris had been the one to pull the triggers on both those murders and

Perez had been the one to bring Max and his caregiver to the scene, then perhaps Dunning had also been lured to the place by the two detectives. Perhaps Perez had been given orders to bring the kid so that they could promise Dunning a reunion with his boy. Why else would he bust out of prison and practically walk straight into his own execution?

"Mr. Carter, are you going to cross-examine the witness or not?" Barber suddenly called out, his voice breaking through my thoughts.

"Sorry, Your Honor," I said, only too aware that the entire courtroom was staring at me. "No questions at this time."

Like the coroner before him, the forensics expert spoke facts, certain aspects I could neither prove nor disprove. While I did make sure to cross-examine the subsequent witnesses, it was those initial thoughts I couldn't shake from my mind. As Bartell continued calling his witnesses, I continued working the idea, a plan if you will, to try and lure out the killer the way he had lured a father to his death.

24

I waited until the lunchtime recess to phone my investigator from the parking lot, ensuring that I was far enough away from the crowd. Grace had to pop back to the office for something to do with Dwight, which gave me plenty of time to run my idea past Linda. By that point, I had had quite a decent chance to go through the theory in my head multiple times, hoping that it made sense when I finally had the chance to share it.

"I think what happened is that either Norris or Cook arranged for Dunning to break out of jail and promised to reunite him with Max," I began once we got past the pleasantries. "They arranged for Perez to abduct Hillary Warner and Max and take them to the warehouse."

"Yes, where Norris then shot both Dunning and Warner. But why? What did Dunning have over them that was so dangerous it warranted killing him? And why not finish Max right there and then as well?"

All good questions and ones I had already considered. I might have been distracted from the court case but not the situation we were in.

"Not killing Max I think comes down to the simple fact that both Cook and Norris are family men. I found that Norris even has a couple of grandkids. My guess is killing kids isn't his forte."

"That's why he ordered Perez to take care of it," Linda said.

"And about killing Dunning, do you remember the man he was accused of killing?"

"Michael Lozano, of course." I let the theory continue to evolve as my thoughts ran free in the hope of coming across something substantial.

"What if Cook had been instructed by the cartel to take care of Dunning?"

"Because of his ex-wife? You really think the cartel gave the order?"

"Makes sense, doesn't it?"

Linda didn't answer me right away, and I listened to the silence, picturing her catching up to me. The theory was a stretch, I know, but it was a start, or so I thought.

"So how do we prove it?" she eventually asked.

"Good question," I said, the plan still trying to come together. "Leave it with me for now. I want to have another talk with Perez. I think he's the one to bring this together for us. I just need to approach him in the right way."

"I'll do a little more digging into Robert Norris for now. Maybe I'll get lucky and find something."

"OK, cool. Talk later," I said before ending the call and heading back inside.

I did cut my timing a bit close. The moment I walked through the doors into the courtroom, the bailiff gave me a little stare before bringing the room to order. I barely reached my table before everybody got to their feet and fell silent but not before grabbing the outheld sheet of paper Grace had for me. The judge also gave me a bit of a sideways glance before taking his seat, and I guess they had waited for my return before restarting the trial. My bad. Thankfully the judge didn't mention it verbally and simply ordered the defendant and jury back into the room before handing the floor back to Bartell.

"We call Beryl Wallace to the stand, Your Honor," the prosecutor said as he rose to his feet and began the afternoon session.

Beryl Wallace lived in the house next to Hillary Warner and had since the early days of the JFK administration. Her husband, John, had served in the US Army and fought his way through two tours in Vietnam before buying his ticket during the fall of Saigon. I mention this because it helps to understand the woman's background to get an idea of her demeanor.

Fiercely protective and as sharp as a tack, Beryl Wallace served her neighborhood like a trooper on duty. She had taken Hillary Warner under her wing when the young woman also lost her husband in Afghanistan. To try and deal with her grief, she turned her attention to helping care for children needing a safe place to stay, and Beryl would often help out any way she could.

When the 84-year-old walked into the courtroom, it wasn't the first time I had seen her. She'd already been featured in several newspaper articles as well as a number of news bulletins on television thanks to her neighbor's demise. Beryl had taken it upon herself to spread the word about how incredibly kind and gentle her neighbor had been. Hearing her called as a witness came as no surprise to anybody.

The real surprise for me came when I saw the person sitting on the aisle seat two rows from the back. I had only seen Dwayne Cook a couple of times before. Unlike everyone else, he wasn't watching the latest witness walking into the courtroom; his attention was firmly on me. We held each other's gaze for a few seconds before I yielded, turning my eyes to Beryl Wallace.

The woman walked with remarkable composure although she did give Perez a stare when she crossed the floor to the witness stand. Affirming her oath also came with an added bit of conviction, the nod of the head pumping up and down with a certain amount of aggression. When she turned to face the prosecutor, one could see that she meant business.

"Thank you for coming in today, Mrs. Wallace," Bartell said as he walked closer to the stand.

"Wouldn't have missed it, Mr. Bartell," the old woman replied.

"You've known Hillary Warner for quite some time, haven't you?"

"I have. Seven years this November."

"I'm sure the majority of us have heard you speaking

about your neighbor in the news stories, but how would you describe her? I'd love to hear it in person, and I'm sure everybody else would."

"Hillary was one of the kindest, most gentle souls I have ever met," Wallace began. "When she lost her husband, Mark, it just about shattered her, but I could see the strength in her. She reminded me so much of myself during those similar years, her life almost mirroring my own."

"And you were there when Ms. Warner began taking in children?"

"Oh yes, I was there the night when she first made the decision to go back to school. She figured that changing paths would help with her grief, and so she decided to turn to caring for others."

"If I'm not mistaken, you saw your neighbor on the night of her disappearance, is that correct?"

"I did, yes. She and little Max were playing this video game, racing against each other in these make-believe cars. I remember the two of them laughing so hard..." Her voice faded as the emotions came forth, but she did her best to fend them off. "So sad."

"Yes, quite," Bartell said but lacked any hint of empathy. "And later that night, you saw her again, did you not?"

"Yes, but not until later. First, I saw a truck parked across the street from Hillary's house."

"This truck?" Bartell picked up a photo off his table and walked it back to the witness.

"Yes, that's the one."

"Let it be known that Mrs. Wallace has identified the

truck belonging to the defendant," Bartell continued. "And did you see anybody inside the vehicle?"

"No. I thought it might have belonged to one of the other houses, given it had been there for some time. But then after I saw Hillary and Max leave the house, I saw that the truck was also gone."

"Did you happen to see anybody with your neighbor and the child?"

"Yes, I saw him," the woman snapped and immediately pointed in the direction of Perez.

"You're absolutely sure it was the defendant?"

"Yes, I am. Never been surer."

"Thank you, Mrs. Wallace," Bartell said before ending his questioning.

"Your witness, Mr. Carter," Barber said, and I wasted little time getting to my feet.

"Thank you, Your Honor. Mrs. Wallace, I'm curious to know whether you know the rest of your neighbors as much as you did Ms. Warner?"

"I do, yes."

"Would you say just as well?"

"I guess so."

"Spend time in their homes?"

"Not everybody but some, yes."

"Attend birthdays?"

"Objection, Your Honor, relevance?" Bartell sounded almost protective.

"Your Honor, I'm trying to ascertain whether spying on her neighbors was a regular thing."

"I don't spy," the woman snapped in an instant.

"My apologies, ma'am, I wasn't trying to insult you, I'm just trying to understand how involved you are with your community."

"Overruled," Barber decided. "But get to the point."

"Yes, Your Honor," I said before turning back to the witness. "Mrs. Wallace, I'm curious as to why you didn't just phone one of your neighbors to ask whether the truck belonged to them. Perhaps a visitor or a family member dropping in."

"I didn't think it necessary."

"But you do like to watch over the neighborhood, do you not?"

"I guess so. There's been a bit of crime in the area, and it pays to be vigilant."

"Yes, of course," I said. "Vigilant enough to report your neighbor at Number 26 for appearing to smoke weed on his front porch?"

"I don't know—"

"Or how about reporting your neighbor at Number 24 to child welfare for having multiple men coming to her house at all hours of the night?"

By then, I'd returned to my table and picked up the sheet of paper Grace had handed to me on my way back into the courtroom. I pretended to read it as I made my way back to the witness.

"Seven reports in just the past month alone."

"Objection, Your Honor," Bartell repeated, but thankfully, the judge knew my intention.

"Overruled."

"Isn't it true, Mrs. Wallace, that you like to create

drama for your neighbors? To find issues where there are none?"

"I report things when I have to," Wallace snapped, her face growing redder by the second.

"Yes, but even when there's nothing to report, you like to pretend there is. Would you like me to present to the court the last interaction you had with Officer Patel, who threatened to take you to the station if you didn't stop harassing your neighbors?"

"I saw him," Wallace just about screamed as she pointed at Perez. "I saw him that night."

"No further questions," I said and handed the woman back to the judge.

When I reached the table and looked up to the crowd, Cook was gone, his seat claimed by an old man. Seeing him in the courtroom had taken me by surprise, but it also proved to me that perhaps the theory I'd been working on was right.

The next witness Bartell called to the stand was an Uber driver who saw a blindfolded woman sitting in the passenger seat of the truck while they were parked at a red light. He testified that he tried to give chase but was subsequently run off the road before he could phone the police. By the time they arrived, the truck was long gone.

Bartell continued calling witnesses throughout the afternoon, all the while building his case against my client, but while I did my best to try and keep up with him, I knew I was fighting a losing battle. The problem was that everything the prosecution presented was true.

Perez was guilty of all of it. That was, all of it except the murders.

My concentration continued to betray me as I began trying to work out a way of turning things around. The easy way was just to bring Max to the courtroom and prove that he wasn't dead, but that would put him in harm's way. And it also failed to prove that Perez didn't murder Dunning or Warner. A written confession from my client wouldn't work either, not without some sort of proof linking Cook and Norris to the case. And when Barber finally called an end to the day, that was precisely what I intended to find. If I didn't, then this case would destroy a lot more than just Perez.

25

On a normal day when working a trial, my usual routine was to head back to the office when dismissed early to continue working on whatever trial I was on. Grace would usually either come with me or I would meet her there, and together, we'd proceed however we needed to. That's just how things worked between us. So when I began to stray from the norm, she picked up on it almost immediately.

Grace wasn't one to interfere in anybody's business, not unless she understood the deal and offered some form of help. But when we walked out of the courtroom that afternoon and I declined a ride from her again, she decided to ask the question.

"I hope you don't think me rude, Ben, but you've been acting really weird these past couple of weeks. Is everything OK?"

I wasn't a stranger to being put on the spot and

certainly didn't shy away when placed in such a position, but the truth is, I hated lying to her. Not just her but everybody who had ever been good to me. I wanted to tell her the truth, and she may have even understood enough not to share the secret, but I couldn't take the risk. I also knew that the chances of our secret getting out went up considerably with each extra person who found out about it.

"Just tired, that's all," I said, feeling the lie grit between my teeth like beach sand. "Feeling the pressure of this one, I think."

"I'm almost sorry Dwight agreed for you to take this case on," she said, and it wasn't something I wanted her to think. I took my career seriously, and the notion of me not cutting it when the pressure piled on didn't sit right with me.

"No, please, don't think that. It's just with Max still missing and the media hounding me for answers..."

"And your stalker."

"Yes," I said, cringing ever so slightly. "And my stalker."

"Guess I'll see you back here tomorrow morning?"

"For sure," I said and watched Grace return to her car. She gave me a final wave before pulling onto the road, and just like that, I was alone again.

What I didn't tell Grace was that I needed to go back into the courthouse and try and get to my client before his return to prison. I knew the bus wouldn't come until the very end of the day after all of the courts had shut down, but I couldn't be sure. After taking a final look to make sure she hadn't changed her mind and come back to watch me, I made my way back inside and headed for the holding area.

The security guard manning the counter didn't bat an eyelid when I asked to speak with my client, and I arranged for Perez to be brought to one of the nearby interview rooms. A couple of the other courts were still in session, and so it wasn't anything out of the ordinary.

The surprised look on my client's face when he walked into the room looked almost comical, although neither of us smiled. What I did notice was just how tired he looked, almost appearing the exact way I felt. The guard directed Perez to sit, and once he did, he left us alone to converse.

"You're not busting me out of here, are you, counselor?" That was when I did grin.

"Not today, Mario."

"What's up?"

"It's Detective Robert Norris, isn't it?" I said, keeping my voice low enough to remain in the room. Perez's eyes didn't exactly grow wider, but I did catch a hint of surprise. "He's the one who put you up to kidnapping Hillary Warner and bringing her and the boy to the warehouse." He didn't answer, his eyes studying me as I continued. "He was also the one who arranged Dunning's escape. Dunning had inside help, and I bet if I went searching for it, I'd find Norris connected somehow."

Perez continued studying me, his hands resting on top of each other on the table. He didn't show any sign of speaking, so I decided to reveal my entire theory.

"I also know Dwayne Cook's ex-wife was the sister of Michael Lozano, the same Michael Lozano Dunning robbed for the drugs. My guess is Cook and Norris were hired by the cartel to kill Dunning as retribution for ripping them off. They used Max to lure Dunning to the warehouse."

I leaned slightly back in the chair to signify that I was done. Perez didn't speak for a long time, perhaps even several minutes as we stared at each other across the table. What I'd learned about the man was that he didn't speak until he was absolutely sure he had good reason to.

"Congratulations, counselor," Perez finally said. "You have no idea just how close you are."

"You mean that's not it?" I was genuinely surprised. "Which part do I have wrong?" Perez sighed, but the rest of his expression remained the same.

"The only way we're going to get out of this, Ben, is for you to put me up on the stand."

"Absolutely not," I said, the words rolling out of me before I had a chance to check them. I barely noticed the fact it was the first time he'd ever called me by my first name. "Are you crazy? Do you have any idea how fast Bartell will tear you apart?"

"It's the only way," Perez said. "You know you have to find a way out of this. You and your people need an off-ramp, and I'm it."

"Mario, we'll figure out another way."

"How? Only my testifying will save us, we both know that. If you get me up on the stand and I tell them what I know about Cook and Norris, they will find the evidence, I promise. And only then will Max be safe."

Max. The most important person in the whole damn

mess. It was him we needed to protect, and knowing that the kid was also at the top of Perez's list gave him extra credit in my book. And yet I still couldn't bring myself to throw my client to the wolves. Call it professional apprehension, if you will.

"I can't do it," I finally said. "Whatever happens, we will see this through together, and that means we do it right. I'll find another way."

Before he had a chance to respond, I called out for the guard, and Perez looked almost wounded when the door opened and his escort showed up. Just before he left the room, he called out a final time, maybe hoping I'd reconsider.

"Think about it, Ben. It's the only way."

"Damn it," I mumbled under my breath once the two men left me alone in the room. Frustration didn't even come close to summarizing how I felt. I couldn't believe that I was so close to the truth and yet still wasn't able to bring the killers to justice.

When I walked out of the courthouse for the second time that afternoon, I did so with an added weight on my shoulders. What I should have done was follow my usual routine and just head back to the office with Grace. At least then I wouldn't have to worry about my client doing anything stupid. Imagine if he suddenly decided to just stand up in the middle of the session and start yelling out the truth. How could I stop him? Would I even bother trying?

Instead of summoning an Uber, I decided to walk. Not home as that would mean a good hour of my afternoon spent skirting a couple of busy roads, something I didn't feel like doing. What I did feel like doing was getting a drink, and I knew just the place.

Located just four blocks from the courthouse and set up inside an old fire station was The Hose and Ladder, a place serving up drinks to some of Pittsburgh's finest. Lawyers, cops, paramedics, you name it. The place didn't consider itself to belong to any one field but just kind of grew to offer a quiet place for those working the front lines.

It didn't take me long to reach the place, and once inside, I found just four other patrons scattered around the place cupping their drinks. I ordered a Jack Daniels with no ice and a beer chaser and took both drinks to the darkest booth I could find. I even sat with my back to the room so I didn't have to look at anybody.

The JD barely touched the sides, the amber fluid immediately warming my middle. I held off with the beer as I let the bourbon do its thing, all the while thinking about Perez's last words to me. I did try to push them aside in the hope they'd disappear for good, but they refused.

"Never," I muttered to myself as I took a mouthful of beer, doubling down on my decision not to give in to his request.

I was about to head back to the bar for a bourbon refill, but just as I grabbed the edge of the table to push myself out, someone suddenly slid into the seat opposite. I had time to pause as my mouth tensed to speak but froze when I stared into the face of Dwayne Cook.

"You're not so hard to find after all," he said as he

grinned at me. "A lot easier than that reporter friend of yours."

Gabby. Color rose in my cheeks as visions of him shooting her in the face filled my mind.

"What did you do to her?"

"Her? I'm pretty sure he was a dude," Cook said with a smirk. "But then again, who the hell knows these days, right?"

"A dude? What are you—" I began but that was when it hit me. The reporter. "What did he tell you?"

"Enough for us to know that you have something of ours," Cook said, and that was when I felt the warmth in my middle turn to ice, the chills rolling through me like a freight train.

I had to think quickly. Confusion still dominated my brain, but I felt streaks of clarity trying to poke through. If he knew where Max was, then he wouldn't be sitting in front of me. The biggest question of all, though, was how he knew about the reporter in the first place. As it so happened, Cook had a knack for reading minds.

"You took on the case a little too quickly for our liking, and so we put you under surveillance," he began.

"Who's we?"

"You don't have to ask dumb questions, Benjamin. May I call you Benjamin?" He didn't wait for me to answer. "You know more about us than you think. Surprising, but true. And we know quite a bit about you, which is why I know you'll comply."

"What do you want?"

"The kid. Nothing more. You bring him to us, and you'll never see us again."

"Why?"

Cook grinned again. He was a man used to being asked questions and ignoring them.

"You know, sometimes it pays to just keep out of other people's business. Like having your boss call a certain police chief to hold a potential client until you can get down to the station. Perez was supposed to end up with a public defender, not you."

"And then what? Think a public defender would have gotten him out of there quicker?" And that was when it dawned on me. Cook saw the revelation.

"Oh, would you look at that? The man figures it out."

"That's how you got Dunning out, wasn't it? You had someone sneak him something. A key perhaps?" Cook shrugged his shoulders.

"It certainly would have made things easier for us." That was when another revelation dawned on me.

"You don't know where he is, do you?" Now it was my turn to grin. "And neither did the reporter. He bluffed." I figured that if the reporter didn't tell them but had the address written down somewhere then they might still find it. For all I knew, Norris could have been at the man's home right at that moment searching for it.

"Bring us the boy."

"How much is the cartel paying you to kill him?" Now it was Cook's turn to look confused.

"The cartel?" He shrugged his shoulders, holding his

hands out in a what-if gesture. "What makes you think the cartel is paying us anything?"

"Isn't that why you killed Dunning? Because he ripped the cartel off?"

"Close but no cigar. Anyway, I'm not about to spill our secrets, Benjamin. The kid. Bring him to us." He tilted his head like a confused puppy as he studied me. "We're even willing to give you until three o'clock tomorrow. Nobody has to know. We know you need to make an appearance in court tomorrow. See out the prosecutor's witnesses and then get sick. I don't care if you vomit across the judge, just be convincing. Nobody will be the wiser. Bring him to the warehouse where his father died and this goes away."

"And if I don't?"

"You don't want to find out. That investigator of yours is one pretty lady." He shot me a wink. "Bring the boy or you'll have to find yourself a new colleague."

Before I could respond, Cook slid out of the seat and stood next to me as he looked down.

"Three o'clock, Benjamin."

He gave my shoulder a squeeze before heading for the door, and by the time I looked over my shoulder, the detective was gone. In his wake, he left yet more questions, questions I had no way of answering without help. I ripped the phone from my pocket so fast it almost slipped out of my fingers, and I had to take an extra breath to calm my nerves again. When I finally felt my heart slowing down to a more reasonable pace, I dialed the number of the only person capable of saving Max.

26

Before I could punch in Christy's number, the phone began to ring, the suddenness of the call almost making me drop the thing for a second time. I instantly recognized the number but hesitated to answer before figuring I had no choice.

"Hello?" I expected to hear a male's voice, Norris confirming what his partner had already told me, but to my surprise, it was Linda that spoke.

"Ben, Jesus, I'm glad I got you."

"What's going on?"

"Robert Norris, that is what's going on. He was here."

"Here?"

"My house, Ben. He came to my *house*."

"Did he speak with you?"

"Speak with me? Hell no. The guy had his gun drawn before he reached my door. I only saw him because I was already out. Was just driving up the street when I caught sight of him."

"Where are you now?"

"Sitting in a Walmart parking lot. Wasn't about to hang around and ask questions."

"Was he alone?"

"Yes."

Again, I had to think quickly, not my strong suit when running on a full day of court and a couple of drinks intended to numb my senses. If I asked her to pick me up, the chances of Cook already having surveillance on me and catching us out would almost be a hundred percent.

"Can you get hold of another car?"

"Yes, why?"

"I need you to get Christy and Max and..." I froze, suddenly too aware of Cook's knowledge of my previous conversations. "Do you still have your other phone?"

"Yes?"

"I'll call you right back."

I didn't wait for an answer, instead dropping my cell phone into the half-drunk glass of beer. Next, I headed to the narrow hallway leading to the bathrooms where a single phone hung on the wall. I pulled a couple of coins from my pocket and dialed Linda's number. She answered before it rang.

"What the hell is going on, Ben?"

"I'm at the Hose and Ladder. Cook just bailed me up, and I think he's got eyes on me. Listen, go and get Christy and Max and take them to a hotel. Don't tell me which one, just go. I'll call you tomorrow."

"Ben, what if—"

"Just do it, Linda. We'll speak soon."

I hung up, cutting her words off mid-sentence. Behind me, one of the patrons passed by on his way to the bathroom, and something told me he might not have been as innocent as he tried to appear. Without knowing how many people Cook and Norris had working for them, it was impossible for me to know which direction to take.

Instead of trying to avoid Cook or his men, I figured the best way to move forward was to just play along for now. They already knew where I lived, and so I opted for an Uber and had it take me home. Once there, I changed into more comfortable clothes and finally grabbed a beer to settle down with.

Despite putting on a movie, I barely noticed any of it, the three-hour epic of *Lord of the Rings* playing in its entirety without me paying it the slightest attention. I might have looked up from the beer bottle once or twice during the battles, but other than that, it was the case playing through my mind.

Not surprisingly, sleep almost completely evaded me when I first went to bed. I think I hit the hay a little after ten, and by one, I still found myself tossing and turning trying to get comfortable. It didn't work. I ended up climbing out of bed sometime around two, went back out to the couch, and found an old Audy Murphy movie playing. I left it running with the volume turned all the way down and eventually nodded off from watching the shadows dancing across the wall.

My alarm woke me just four hours later, and at first, I

tried turning the ringing off by slapping my hand down on the bedside. Instead, the tip of my fingers clipped the television remote, sending it spiraling into the air before it landed on the glass top with an almighty crash. My eyes flew open, still feeling disjointed at not finding myself in bed.

My heart sank as the memories of the previous afternoon flooded back and with them the deadline for me to give up Max to the killers. I've always been a glass-half-full kind of guy, so I tried to make light of the situation as best I could.

"At least things will come to an end today," I said under my breath while pushing myself off the couch. "No more need for lies."

I guess, in a way, I was happy that the matter would finally sort itself out. The only question was how. With Norris and Cook no doubt following my every move, I had to tread carefully, which meant heading to court and doing my job until the appropriate time came. I only hoped Linda had done as I asked and managed to get the others out of the house and someplace safe. If she didn't and the two rogue cops found them, then this train ride would come to a hard and sudden halt a lot sooner than expected.

With at least another half a session of court time in the matter, I headed for the bathroom and jumped in the shower. For the first couple of minutes, it was cold water only. It did the trick, my body almost spasming from the shock as goosebumps coursed over it. I held strong, ignoring the discomfort. A moment later, I felt more awake than ever, and after adjusting the faucets just enough to lessen the torture, I went to work with the soap.

When I walked out of my apartment that morning, dressed in my favorite suit and carrying my briefcase, I did so questioning whether I'd return in one piece. These weren't people to mess with, and I knew the chances of my survival and those of my friends depended on how we handled things over the next few hours. With the cops being the ones holding all the cards at that moment, turning to them for help was off the table. As was calling in outside help.

No Uber this morning. And while the temptation to bring the Mustang out into the sunshine did strike me hard, I opted for the pickup truck. If I was going to go down, then I wanted to go down riding something substantial. Who knew? Maybe Cook and Norris would just stand in front of the beast and I could roll right over the top of them.

I grinned at the thought as I climbed in, determined to finally end things. The thought felt too good to ignore, and during the subsequent drive to the courthouse, numerous scenarios played out in my mind. Cook and his partner died a hundred different ways in my mind, with Linda and me standing above them, victorious. It was what I hoped for but knew might not happen, the alternative too painful to consider.

What I didn't expect when I rolled into the courthouse parking lot that morning was for my nemesis to be already there waiting for me. By nemesis, I mean Cook, and by standing there, I mean right by the media pack. A surge of panic squeezed my middle as I met his gaze. What I couldn't see in those eyes was the confirmation that he had Linda.

Once I parked the truck near the back of the lot, I shut off the engine and reached across the seat for my briefcase. A sudden urge to pull out the burner phone flared up. All it would take was one phone call to Linda to confirm the three of them were safe. I looked through the windshield and saw Cook still standing his ground watching me. I had to resist. Faith was a good thing, and I knew I had to keep mine intact. Linda knew what she was doing, and I had to trust her.

As I approached the media pack for what I expected to be the last time, I saw Grace standing just inside the doors of the courthouse holding my morning coffee. I don't know why, but it all felt like a bunch of finals. The last time driving to the courthouse. The last time speaking with the media. Was this my last day on Earth? Was this how it felt to know one's fate had come calling?

I didn't answer as many questions as I normally would have; instead, I kept it to just half a dozen, more than aware of Cook still watching me. He approached me when I answered the last one and pushed my way toward the doors.

"Remember what I told you," he whispered. "Follow the plan and nobody has to get hurt."

He didn't wait for me to reply. He didn't even follow me into the building. When I reached the top of the stairs and looked beside me, Cook was gone. I looked around to try and find him but to no avail.

"You're looking suave this morning," Grace suddenly said from beside me, and I turned to find her standing there holding out the cup tray.

"Thought I'd come dressed to win," I said.

"Well, you look the part, Mr. Carter," she said with a smile, and after thanking her, I followed my assistant into the courtroom.

I don't know how to describe it properly, but for the next thirty minutes or so, my life felt like a movie. Everything I went through felt like I was watching it unfold on a screen. Walking through the foyer, entering the courtroom, taking my seat, greeting Bartell...it could have all been playing out with me watching on from a distance. Maybe some sort of autopilot had taken over, and this was me playing passenger.

The moment I felt like I had returned to my body was when Judge Barber took his seat on the bench and wished the court a good morning. A sharp and sudden pain shot through my middle. It only lasted a second but felt like a blade going through me. What followed felt like an over-abundance of adrenaline hitting my system. My heartbeat increased, beads of sweat formed on my brow, and I thought I was going to pass out. I poured myself a bit of water from the jug and drank, holding the liquid in my mouth. My hands shook so badly that I nearly dropped the glass.

When I turned to look over my shoulder, I found Cook again sitting a couple of rows from the back. He didn't see me looking, his attention fixed on the phone in his hand. Barber began addressing the court, and I returned my focus on the job at hand as Perez was finally brought out. Not surprisingly, he reminded me of his request the moment he sat down. I declined as I watched the jury take their seat.

When Bartell finally called his witness to the stand, it felt like the final opening credits scrolling past, the main feature about to begin. Jennifer Tully proved to be the prosecutor's final attempt to solidify his position and condemn my client to his fate. I had already read the forensics expert's report and knew she would only add to the weight of the case. Bartell looked to be in his element when he eventually rose from his chair and crossed the floor to begin his questioning.

After having the woman state her position and history of the job for the court, he turned the questions immediately to where he knew she would cause the most damage.

"Ms. Tully, could you share with the court the characteristics of the blood samples you found in the defendant's vehicle?"

"Yes, there were two main areas I focused on," she began. "The first was on the side of the vehicle, just above the rear wheel arch. The blood splatter looked significant."

"Could you tell what kind of injury might have caused it?"

"A headshot was the most likely scenario. The pattern was hard to read because of the attempt to clean it, but enough residue remained for me to work with."

"Are you telling this court that Mr. Perez attempted to clean the evidence from his truck?"

"Objection, Your Honor," I snapped as I stood. "There's no proof that my client attempted to clean anything nor that he was with the vehicle at the time someone tampered with the evidence."

"Sustained," Barber said as I retook my seat.

"OK, so somebody attempted to wash the blood off the truck, is that correct?"

"Yes, it is, although they didn't do a very good job. The luminal showed quite a lot of blood residue remaining."

"And you said that was the first area?"

"Yes, I also focused on the vehicle's tray area. It too looked to have held a significant amount of blood before being washed away."

Back and forth the prosecutor went with his client, each of her answers adding yet another nail to the proverbial coffin. When it came time to cross-examine, there wasn't a whole lot I could do, not when the witness, much like a lot of her predecessors, dealt in facts. The blood was on the defendant's vehicle. It matched the victim. Someone had attempted to clean it off. All facts.

I did ask the witness whether she could determine how much blood there might have been, but I knew the answer wasn't going to change the outcome. Hillary Warner was dead, and her blood had been found on the truck belonging to my client. All facts. It was what Bartell said once the witness left the courtroom that sent a new wave of nerves through me.

"The prosecution rests, Your Honor." Bartell looked in my direction. The smirk was enough to tell me he knew he had it in the bag. I'd seen the same on the faces of the jury as well, especially after the final witness. If I was going to win the day, I would have to pull out one hell of a defense.

With the session only an hour old, Barber asked whether I wanted a short recess before proceeding with my side of the case. I felt the attention of the world on me as he awaited my answer, the silence of the room closing in around me. I also felt one particular set of eyes watching from behind, with Cook's stare feeling like a couple of lasers burning into me. I tried to resist but ended up turning to meet his gaze.

It felt like the tipping point, the moment that would decide the fate of every single person involved. Max, Christy, Linda, Grace, Dwight, me, all of our futures riding on what I did next. Cook's instruction had been clear... feign illness and leave the courtroom...

27

If Cook and his partner had done their research on me, they would have found a man who didn't back down from a fight. Not ever. After a final look behind me at the man thinking he was calling the shots, I turned back to the judge and gave him my answer.

"No recess needed, Your Honor. The defense is ready to proceed."

"Very well, Mr. Carter, you may proceed. Call your first witness."

Just before I opened my mouth, I felt a new wave of confidence wash over me, a rush of something I hadn't felt in a long time. After a final look down at the man I had come to defend, I suddenly knew that his fate had been decided long before I ever walked into the courtroom. In a way, Mario Perez had chosen his own path, and there was nothing I could do to steer him off it.

"The defense calls Mario Perez to the stand."

The reaction from the crowd immediately drowned out the echo of my voice, the shock rolling over the room like a tsunami. The people could barely contain their surprise as Barber attempted to regain control. He slammed the gavel down multiple times, calling for order as his voice struggled to be heard. Security called for the same from the mouth of the aisles.

With the judge's reputation well known, I expected him to clear the courtroom, but surprisingly, he didn't. I expected the crowd to go wild but not to the extent they did, and it took the judge and his security detail quite some time to calm the room enough for him to speak again.

"Given the sensitivity of this matter, I will refrain from my usual course of action, which would be to clear this courtroom. But be warned, people," he stated. "Another outbreak like we just witnessed and I will conduct the remainder of these matters behind closed doors."

He didn't look for a response from the gallery. Instead, Barber turned his focus on me and signaled for Perez to take the stand. I looked down at my client and gave him a nod. When Perez stood, he looked at me with what I think was something akin to respect. It only lasted for a microsecond, but I felt every bit of the connection.

While Perez was being sworn in, I watched from behind the table. What I refused to do was turn and look at Cook. His attempt to intimidate me by lying about Linda had failed. His partner's attempt to abduct my investigator had also failed. I didn't know whether she was safe, but what I did know was that she knew her stuff, and that's all I needed to know to retain my faith in her.

When the bailiff finished swearing Perez in and handed the witness over to me, I walked to where I could see both Perez and the jury. I wanted to see their reaction when hearing the evidence, to watch the case finally tip our way. What I didn't expect was for things to turn out the way they did.

"Mr. Perez, how well did you know Harold Dunning?"

"I didn't know him personally, just through work."

"So he was more of a colleague, is that correct?"

"Yes."

He looked calm as he answered my questions, a lot calmer than I was feeling. In the courtroom, you could hear a pin drop, the crowd listening as if holding their collective breath.

"And who was your employer?"

"I did deliveries for Lassiter's Transport."

"Mr. Perez, I'd like to turn our attention to the matter which brings you before this court. Do you deny abducting Max Dunning and Hillary Warner?" Perez actually leaned closer to the microphone to answer.

"No, I abducted them." A collective gasp rose from the gallery but quickly subsided when Barber looked in their direction.

"Do you deny taking them to the warehouse where police would later find the body of Harold Dunning?"

"No, that's where I took them."

"Did you murder Harold Dunning?"

"No, I did not."

"What about Hillary Warner?"

"No, I did not." I took a deep breath and closed my eyes. When I opened them again, I felt a little more centered, centered enough to reveal the truth.

"What about Max? Did you murder him?"

"Definitely not. Detective Robert Norris had ordered me to, but I refused." The crowd responded again, and Perez had to raise his voice to be heard. "He was the one who wanted Max in the warehouse to lure his father there."

"Could you tell us why?"

"Because Dunning knew what he and his partner had been up to."

"His partner?"

Upon hearing the question, Perez looked up into the gallery where he knew Cook to be sitting. I guess he wanted to see his reaction when naming him. I was about to do the same, but the change of expression I saw on my client's face caused me to hesitate. And that was when time seemed to stand still.

Three things happened at almost the same time, each of them clear as daylight, and yet each overshadowed by the others. The first was the transition from glee to horror on Perez's face. The second the screams from the crowd, the first one punctuating the air before others joined in almost immediately. The third, and the one that instantly shook the room to its core, was the gunshot.

I watched as Perez tried to flinch away from something he had no earthly way of avoiding. He raised a hand up in front of his face, but the single bullet passed cleanly underneath it, striking the man at the base of his throat. The bailiff dived to his left, and the judge ducked his head, while those who should have reacted took cover wherever possible. I expected at least one of the security guards to pull their weapons, but none did.

Perez died long before he hit the floor. With a single bullet, the man capable of telling the world the truth was taken out of this world, leaving the rest of us to pick up the pieces. I had time to look over to where the crowd continued scattering and saw Cook with the pistol still aimed in my direction. He fired. The bullet struck the top of the witness stand, sending shards of timber into my face. I flinched, shielding myself from the debris, and when I looked back up to the gallery, the cop had disappeared.

I didn't need confirmation to know my client was gone. Instinct took over, and while I should have stood my ground, I couldn't let Cook get away. Two more gunshots rang out from somewhere down the hallway, and it was enough to get my feet moving. Grace called out to me from where she was hiding behind the divider, but I told her to stay.

Out in the hallway, more people crouched down along the walls. A few were crying, most of them scared. Out in the foyer, more people hid behind whatever cover they could, too panicked to help. Two men in uniform lay on the floor near the front doors, and I could tell by the growing pool of blood beneath each that both had been shot. The shooter was gone.

I continued running, barely slowing for the doors as I pushed my way outside. When I reached the parking lot, I pulled out the burner phone and called Linda. She answered just as I climbed into the truck, and I put her on speaker while firing up the engine.

"All hell just broke loose," I yelled over the sound of the revving engine. "Tell me where you are."

"Comfort Inn on I79 a couple of miles north of Hendersonville, Room 16. Ben, what happened?" She sounded exhausted, no surprise there. My guess was she'd stayed awake all night protecting Christy and Max.

"I'll be there in twenty. Be ready."

"For what? Ben, what *happened*?"

"Perez is dead. Cook shot him when I put him on the stand."

"He shot him in the *courtroom*? But how did Cook..."

"He must have gone in a back entrance or something," I said as I slowed for a red light enough to let the cross traffic know I wasn't about to stop. A couple of them came to a skidding halt as I punched the gas pedal. I barely heard the honking as I continued on. "Perez managed to at least name Norris and Cook before he bought it."

"What about Max?"

"We didn't get to that part."

"Listen," Linda said. "I know someone down at the sheriff's office I can trust. Let me—"

"No, not yet. Cook fled, and I don't know where Norris is. Let me get to you first before we call anybody."

It took a bit of convincing, but Linda eventually gave in and agreed to wait. I dropped my ETA from ten minutes to five as I weaved in and out of traffic, obliterating the speed limit in my desperation. If a police cruiser had seen me, they would have been on my tail in an instant, and that might have alerted the two detectives to my location. I backed off just enough to avoid such a scenario, and thankfully, it gave me the chance to reach my destination undetected.

I pulled into the hotel's parking lot at speed, found the room Linda mentioned, and pulled up in front of it. I was out of the truck in an instant, and she met me in the doorway.

"Is everyone safe?" I asked as I walked into the room. Max sat on the bed with a comic book before him and gave me a wave. "Hey, sport, how's things?"

"Good. Are we going on another trip?"

"Afraid so, kiddo," I said and gave Christy a one-armed hug as I leaned closer to her ear. "How has he been?"

"He's good, really good, Ben. Such a bright boy."

I could see the concern on her face. Unlike Linda, who dealt with this type of thing for a living, Christy was more akin to working with children and planning day trips to malls and cinemas. Rogue cops and potential murderers just weren't her forte.

"We'll be OK," I whispered in her ear, but that was when I felt her tense up.

"You really are stupid, you know that," a new voice said, and when I turned around, both Cook and Norris stood in the doorway with their guns drawn. Linda had already raised her hands, and Cook gestured for me to do the same.

"How did you—"

"Find you?" Cook's smirk was gone as he maintained his distance. "Not hard to put a tracker on a car, you know." He gestured to Linda to hand over her gun. She did. "Get over by your boyfriend, sweetheart." When she didn't move quickly enough, Norris stepped forward and pushed her.

"*Now*, woman."

"What are you going to do?" I asked. "Think you'll just shoot all of us?" I felt something grab my leg and looked down to see Max cowering behind it.

"If we have to," Norris said, stepping forward a bit. "You ruined my retirement plan, you son of a bitch."

"Retirement plan? The cartel didn't pay you enough for Dunning?" The two cops exchanged a glance before Norris turned back to me. "You think the cartel would pay us to rip them off?"

"*You* put Dunning up to stealing the drugs from Lozano," Linda suddenly said. "You weren't acting on the cartel's orders at all."

"That's why you had to kill him," I added, the scheme suddenly becoming clear to me. Perez had been right. I was close but no cigar.

"Lozano wasn't the first time we ripped off cartel drugs," Norris said. "Know how much money uncut gear is worth these days?"

"You murdered Dunning to shut him up but why Hillary?" Linda asked. "And why the boy?"

"Witnesses," Norris said. "Have to clean up loose ends. Who the hell wants a crazy cartel on their ass, right?"

"Perez named you on the stand," I said. "Looks like your retirement plans might be canceled." Norris chuckled as he looked at his partner.

"Nothing a couple of fake passports can't fix, kid." He shook the barrel of his pistol toward the door. "OK, enough talk. Time to go."

"And what if we don't?" I said defiantly. Norris responded by cocking the hammer, the click punctuating the air.

"Your choice."

With no choice but to follow their demands, I led Linda and Christy out of the door. Christy held Max's hand as Cook motioned for us to head to their car parked at the side of the building. We barely made it a few feet when a new voice suddenly called out.

"Sheriff's office, don't move."

Two officers suddenly rounded the corner, one with his pistol trained on the cops while the other aimed a shotgun. I exchanged a quick look with Linda, and she mouthed the word *sorry* to me. She'd made the call to her friend after all. Our group froze, caught between a bunch of weapons all pointed at us. With Norris and Cook behind us and the two deputies in front, we literally stood in the middle of a shitstorm.

"Drop your weapons," the deputy called out as he took a couple of extra steps sideways, effectively increasing the distance from his partner.

"Drop yours," Norris called out as I turned slightly to

see what he would do next. He pulled his badge from his jacket pocket and held it up. "Pittsburgh PD. These are our suspects, and we're taking them in."

The two deputies exchanged a quick look, but neither gave in, their weapons remaining steadfast. Cook and Norris stood their ground as the stand-off continued. With us caught in the middle, I knew there wasn't a thing we could do.

If a firetruck with its sirens wailing didn't pass by at that exact moment, who knows how things might have played out, but it was enough to distract one of the deputies enough for Cook to take a shot. For the fourth time that day, his weapon took the life of an innocent person, the bullet hitting the younger of the two deputies just above the right eye. His head snapped back in an instant as the second deputy unleashed the shotgun.

Christy, Linda, and Max all dropped to the ground in a heartbeat as Cook fired again, but his aim was off, and the bullet went wide. Norris wasn't so lucky. The shotgun blast ended his retirement plan in an instant, the top of his head turned into gore. I shielded the group as best I could as his trigger finger continued squeezing on the way down. It was Linda who wrestled her back-up piece out of her ankle holster and fired at Cook. He dove sideways to try and evade the deputy's next shot but took Linda's bullet in the abdomen.

The fight ended just as fast as it had begun. I was close enough to Cook to lunge at him, and after a brief wrestle, I managed to overpower him enough to grab the gun. He lay on the ground next to my truck breathing heavily while trying to stop the blood pouring through his fingers. Lying in a crumpled heap just a few feet away, Norris had seen better days, his final expression one of surprise. I like to think that it was Max he was thinking of on his way down and how a little kid had ruined his plans.

28

I DON'T KNOW WHETHER EVERY STORY HAS TO HAVE A HAPPY ending, but I was glad to find that this one did. Cook ended up surviving the bullet wound, and after spending a few days down at St. Clair recovering, he was eventually moved into protective custody. He faced multiple charges, and a man in his position wouldn't be seeing the outside of a prison cell for a very long time to come. He knew that, of course, which is why I think he ended up using one of his bed sheets to take his own life in a very private way. Unlike so many of his victims, Dwayne Cook got to choose his own fate, the son of a bitch evading justice for the very last time.

I'm pleased to say that Max also found his forever home shortly after the final pieces of the case were put away. After multiple rounds of paperwork and assessments, Christy chose to take him in, and a few weeks later made it official by adopting him. They make a good family, and wanting a fresh start for the two of them, Christy ended up moving to Silver Creek, where the rest of her family lives. I visit them often.

For me, life went back to normal almost immediately. I say almost because I did get summoned into Dwight's office on my first day back in the office after all the fanfare died down. Talk about a circus. Linda and I spent days doing the network rounds. Max and Christy joined us for a couple, and together, we shared our story with the world. We even ended up on *Good Morning, America*, coming on right after George Clooney.

Dwight looked pissed and for very good reason. I honestly thought he was going to fire me, and I think the move would have been justified. He didn't. Much to my amazement, he forgave me for lying to him and Grace.

"Something we've strived hard to achieve with this business, Ben, is to make people feel a part of our family," Dwight said as we sat opposite each other across the desk. "The one thing I've always demanded is honesty. I don't care what you've done, I don't care what mistakes you make, just be honest. One lie is enough to break trust."

"I know," I began, but he held a hand up.

"Having said that, I fully understand why you did it, and if I was in your shoes, I probably would have done the same." Instead of firing me, he stood up from his chair, walked around to my side of the desk, and held out a hand. When I rose up and shook with him, Dwight said, "Never again, Ben. No secrets."

"No secrets," I repeated, and just like that, the matter was over.

Like I said, life returned pretty much to normal after that. I went back to working regular cases, and Grace helped me along the way. Linda also remained my investigator, and together, we fought for our clients. Days turned into weeks and weeks into months, and before we knew it, the whole mess with the Dunnings had finally subsided into the backs of everyone's minds.

About three months into the new year, Gabby made the move and bought herself a new house out near Oakmont. She loved the rural setting and bought herself a horse and a couple of goats. A week after moving in, she invited me over for a kind of housewarming party for two. Gabby had never been much of a party girl, and the thought of having multiple people walking through her home mortified her.

Instead, she opted for a beer and pizza night, just the two of us hanging around talking about anything except work. The pizza was good, the beer better, and to break in her new 85-inch TV, she introduced me to a show called *Better Call Saul*. I wasn't much of a TV guy, but a couple of episodes in, I was hooked. We ended up turning that one night into a weekly event, and during the course of a pizza and a couple of ales, we'd also watch an episode or two.

Little did I know that Gabby's decision to share one of her favorite shows with me would lead us to close one of the final pieces still left dangling from the Mario Perez case. The moment came on a Thursday night while watching the ninth episode of the second season. Gabby always sat in her recliner, leaving me with either the other one or the sofa. The romance between us still hadn't really sparked at that point. On this particular night, I opted for the latter. On those nights when I did fall asleep, Gabby would toss a blanket over me and head to bed, leaving me to spend the night in relative comfort.

That particular night, I was already tired and almost called her to postpone, but wanting to see what happened next with the show, I pushed through my fatigue and went. The pizza was great as usual, but that episode turned out to be a game changer. We'd reached the part where Mike had stretched his homemade spike strip across the road, and once the delivery truck lost its tires by driving over them, he went to work looking for the money. And that's when it happened.

They say the effects of amnesia can last for years, even decades. Sometimes all it needs is a simple trigger to bring back memories long thought forgotten. I sat up in an instant the moment I saw Mike hit paydirt, something in my brain exploding in a shower of sparks and familiarity.

"Ben?" I kept watching the screen, the saw blade cutting into each of the truck's tires in turn. "Ben, what is it?" That was when I knew.

"Can you give me a bit? I have to call Linda." Looking confused, Gabby agreed, and I punched the call button on my cell while still sitting dazed on the couch. She answered almost immediately, and I skipped past the pleasantries.

"Do you still talk to that sheriff's deputy?"

"Ben? Is that you?" She sounded half asleep.

"Yes, do you?" I'd forgotten his name.

"Who, Jack?"

"Yes, him."

"Sometimes, why?"

It was just a hunch, but as I'd learned plenty of times before, sometimes a hunch is all you need. I told Linda about what I had remembered from the night of my car accident, the one that left me in a coma for three days. She listened intently, and when I finished, she phoned the deputy just as I had asked.

Not two hours after Mike Ehrmantraut unlocked some repressed memory of mine, Linda and I found ourselves following several sheriff's deputies along I70 heading west to Claysville, the three cruisers looking almost like a convoy. We weren't there to watch the truck pull into the distribution center, nor did we see him pull into the repair center. According to the deputy's colleagues, both those events happened. What we wanted to see was the final stage of the operation. Five miles outside Washington, Pennsylvania, the deputy finally lit up his lights and pulled the truck over.

It's funny how things play out sometimes. When I found little Max Dunning cowering on the side of a lonely Pennsylvania country road, the last thing I expected was for that event to change the lives of so many people. I also didn't think that the final chapter of that story would play out almost six months later on the side of another Pennsylvania road.

The four deputies took just a couple of minutes after pulling the truck over to start searching for the drugs inside the spare tires. Imagine my surprise when they turned up barely enough to warrant the effort. Little did I know that my instincts weren't going to be completely dismissed. With a bit more persistence, the officers ended up finding a small compartment located between the spare tire cages and running a few feet down the middle of the trailer. Inside the compartment, they found an original Picasso listed as missing since 2010, the painting known as "Le pigeon aux petits pois."

While the eventual investigation took another week to fully begin assessing each of the clues, that night set the wheels in motion for uncovering one of the most sophisticated stolen art rings in the world. The drugs had been planted simply as a decoy to keep prying eyes away from the real prize. When two of the officers escorted the driver to one of their cruisers, the man began to wail, promising to tell all if they would just let him go. Only the slamming of the door finally shut out his cries but only until they sat him down a couple of hours later with notepads and pens ready to go.

While we could have been there to witness the arrest of Matthew Foster for ourselves, Linda and I decided to continue with our day. We'd had enough of the case by then and figured we'd played our part in the matter. Linda's friend told us later that Foster broke down almost as much as the driver did, wailing about him not knowing a thing about the drugs. That turned out not to be entirely true, and it was through his subsequent confession that officers were able to shut down Lassiter's Transport as well, but that's a story better left for another day.

Don't miss TRIAL BY MURDER. The riveting sequel in the Ben Carter Legal Thriller series.

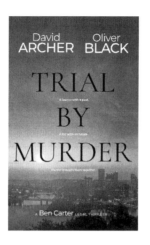

A lawyer with a past. A kid with no future. Murder brought them together.

What should have been nothing more than a harmless burglary turns into a full-blown nightmare for Katherine Wright when she's accused of a cold-blooded double murder by Pittsburgh PD. A high school dropout with a history on the streets, this isn't the first time she's picked up, and it's not long before her problems begin to spiral out of control as an angry community calls for the death sentence.

After hearing about the girl's plight, Ben Carter agrees to take on the case but immediately finds himself drawn into unfamiliar territory. With connections to the mob, the murdered couple's family seeks more than just legal justice, and with a sizable contract out, revenge is the order of the day. Can Ben prove his client's innocence before the hitmen deliver or will his own name be added to an ever-growing list of victims?

Purchase at: www.righthouse.com/trial-by-murder
(Or scan the QR code below.)

NOTE: flip to the very end to read an exclusive sneak peak...

DON'T MISS ANYTHING!

If you want to stay up to date on all new releases in this series, with these authors, or with any of our new deals, you can do so by joining our newsletters below.

In addition, you will immediately gain access to our entire *Right House VIP Library,* which currently includes six original novels!

righthouse.com/email

(Easy to unsubscribe. No spam. Ever.)

ALSO BY DAVID ARCHER

Up to date books can be found at:
www.righthouse.com/david-archer

ROGUE THRILLERS
Gates of Hell (Book 1)
Hell's Fury (Book 2)

JACOB HUNTER THRILLERS
The Kyiv File (Book 1)
The Bogota File (Book 2)
The Havana File (Book 3)

PETER BLACK THRILLERS
Burden of the Assassin (Book 1)
The Man Without A Face (Book 2)
Unpunished Deeds (Book 3)
Hunter Killer (Book 4)
Silent Shadows (Book 5)
The Last Run (Book 6)
Dark Corners (Book 7)
Ghost Operative (Book 8)
A Fire Burning (Book 9)

ALEX MASON THRILLERS
Odin (Book 1)
Ice Cold Spy (Book 2)

Mason's Law (Book 3)

Assets and Liabilities (Book 4)

Russian Roulette (Book 5)

Executive Order (Book 6)

Dead Man Talking (Book 7)

All The King's Men (Book 8)

Flashpoint (Book 9)

Brotherhood of the Goat (Book 10)

Dead Hot (Book 11)

Blood on Megiddo (Book 12)

Son of Hell (Book 13)

Merchant of Death (Book 14)

NOAH WOLF THRILLERS

Code Name Camelot (Book 1)

Lone Wolf (Book 2)

In Sheep's Clothing (Book 3)

Hit for Hire (Book 4)

The Wolf's Bite (Book 5)

Black Sheep (Book 6)

Balance of Power (Book 7)

Time to Hunt (Book 8)

Red Square (Book 9)

Highest Order (Book 10)

Edge of Anarchy (Book 11)

Unknown Evil (Book 12)

Black Harvest (Book 13)

World Order (Book 14)

Caged Animal (Book 15)

Deep Allegiance (Book 16)

Pack Leader (Book 17)

High Treason (Book 18)

A Wolf Among Men (Book 19)

Rogue Intelligence (Book 20)

Alpha (Book 21)

Rogue Wolf (Book 22)

Shadows of Allegiance (Book 23)

In the Grip of Darkness (Book 24)

Wolves in the Dark (Book 25)

SAM PRICHARD MYSTERIES

The Grave Man (Book 1)

Death Sung Softly (Book 2)

Love and War (Book 3)

Framed (Book 4)

The Kill List (Book 5)

Drifter: Part One (Book 6)

Drifter: Part Two (Book 7)

Drifter: Part Three (Book 8)

The Last Song (Book 9)

Ghost (Book 10)

Hidden Agenda (Book 11)

SAM AND INDIE MYSTERIES

Aces and Eights (Book 1)

Fact or Fiction (Book 2)

Close to Home (Book 3)

Brave New World (Book 4)

Innocent Conspiracy (Book 5)

Unfinished Business (Book 6)

Live Bait (Book 7)

Alter Ego (Book 8)

More Than It Seems (Book 9)

Moving On (Book 10)

Worst Nightmare (Book 11)

Chasing Ghosts (Book 12)

Serial Superstition (Book 13)

CHANCE REDDICK THRILLERS

Innocent Injustice (Book 1)

Angel of Justice (Book 2)

High Stakes Hunting (Book 3)

Personal Asset (Book 4)

CASSIE MCGRAW MYSTERIES

What Lies Beneath (Book 1)

Can't Fight Fate (Book 2)

One Last Game (Book 3)

Never Really Gone (Book 4)

ABOUT US

Right House is an independent publisher created by authors for readers. We specialize in Action, Thriller, Mystery, and Crime novels.

If you enjoyed this novel, then there is a good chance you will like what else we have to offer! Please stay up to date by using any of the links below.

Join our mailing lists to stay up to date -->
righthouse.com/email
Visit our website --> righthouse.com
Contact us --> contact@righthouse.com

facebook.com/righthousebooks
x.com/righthousebooks
instagram.com/righthousebooks

EXCLUSIVE SNEAK PEAK OF...

TRIAL BY MURDER

.

CHAPTER ONE

Something about the innocence in the girl's eyes was what first drew my attention to Katherine Wright, a girl who would end up changing the course of countless lives. She had already lived a hard life herself, the stone-faced expression conveying experiences far beyond her years. At just eighteen, this was a girl who had cut her teeth for life on the streets, finding safety within the shadows others cowered away from.

Her life could have taken many alternative routes, all of them better than the one she ended up on. Reading through the file, I couldn't help but wonder what tragedies her childhood must have consisted of for her to believe that she'd be safer alone out on the streets. From what I had read, her home didn't appear to be anything out of the ordinary. Her parents were still together, and looking at the photos of them, they were still very much in love.

A murder charge was what brought the Wright girl's file onto my desk. Actually, it was *two* murder charges that she faced, one for Amadore Costa and one for his wife, Ersilia. The newlyweds were Italian immigrants who came to the US in the early '80s with hopes of starting a new life and raising a family. The couple ended up doing both, only to end up brutally gunned down in their own home some forty years later.

While some random couple's names contained in a case file shouldn't have stirred up further emotions, seeing the Costas' did, and not in a good way. It wasn't so much the names Amadore or Ersilia that triggered me but their connection to another Costa, their son Riccardo. Pick up any recent newspaper containing crime-related incidents within the greater Pittsburgh area, and chances are you'll read some sort of reference to Riccardo Costa.

The city of Pittsburgh and the local Italian Mafia shared a history stretching all the way back to the late nineteenth century, and Riccardo Costa served as just the latest in a long line of wannabe gangsters. He began young, growing his own empire over the course of a decade to rise up as one of the city's heavy hitters, and if there was one thing I knew from the beginning, it was that the killing of his parents wouldn't go unanswered. Was this a case I really wanted to get involved in?

After spending time going through the file, I'd made up my mind, dropped it into my briefcase, grabbed the keys to my Mustang, and headed out of my office. Challenges were what I thrived on, and aside from the whole

Harold and Max Dunning thing from the previous year, I hadn't had a meaty case in quite some time.

"I'm off to the jail," I told Grace Tanner, my associate, on the way past her desk. She looked up at me from her computer screen with a smile.

"Want me to come along?"

"Not for the first meeting," I said and checked my watch. "I should make it back afterward, though, if you want to help me go through the case in more detail."

"Of course," Grace said and returned her attention to the file she'd been working on.

The one thing I'd learned about meeting new clients was that without a certain sense of trust, defending them in court became far more difficult. It only took me about a year's worth of cases to figure out that the serious ones, like murders, required a certain approach in order for a connection to grow. In short, I needed them to open up to me, and if they didn't, then the chances of me helping them beat their charges vastly diminished.

Twenty minutes later, I pulled into the Allegheny County Jail parking lot, found a space some four rows back, and grabbed my briefcase. When I climbed out, I took a moment to look at the buildings before me, the tall red brick façade with its recessed windows a foreboding sight. I'd walked into the place to meet with clients plenty of times before, but there'd never been any as young as Katherine Wright facing murder charges. The closest in age to her I'd defended was a twenty-year-old named Emelia Hendrickson, a woman who fought back against an abusive boyfriend and accidentally killed him during a fight. It was a case I lost after she broke down on the stand and confessed.

The thought of a girl as young as Katherine being held in such a place didn't sit well with me, not when knowing the kinds of things that went on in a jail like the one before me. I'd also heard plenty of stories from clients about the horrors beyond the walls and was thinking about one in particular when a voice pulled me from my thoughts.

"Ben Carter, right?"

I looked around to see two men approaching me, one walking slightly behind the other and looking every bit as threatening as a bodyguard should. I knew when I saw the names of his parents in the file that Riccardo Costa would eventually make himself known to me, but I had no idea it would happen so fast, especially since I'd only taken on the case within the past hour.

"Yes, it is," I said as I tried to picture who in the office would have made the call to the underworld boss. I had my suspicions.

Costa stopped a few feet in front of me, and instead of holding a hand out to shake, he instead clasped his hands together in front of his groin as if guarding his manhood. For a second, he just stood there staring at me, his eyes hidden behind dark sunglasses. The two men looked almost identical, both in appearance and stature, but it was obvious who the man in charge was. Costa carried himself with a lot more confidence, and there was just an extra shine to the suit he wore, a shine that conveyed value.

He took a deep breath and sighed loudly for what I could only assume was dramatic effect. From what I knew of him, he loved to employ intimidation tactics on his adversaries, and I was probably enemy number one.

"I hear you're representing the killer of my parents" was what he finally said to me.

"Now why would you think that?" I asked, trying hard to sound jovial.

He tilted his head just enough to indicate that he'd heard me but didn't immediately answer. It was another one of his intimidation tactics, something I was more than used to. Sometimes, defending people drew the attention of those who might suffer because of an unwanted outcome. Costa wasn't the first big-name opponent of a client of mine.

"Don't play games with me, Mr. Carter," he finally said.

"Yes, I am, if you must know," I said, refusing to let his intimidation work on me. "Everyone deserves a good lawyer."

"Is that what you are, Mr. Carter? A good lawyer?"

"I can hold my own, I guess."

Not happy with my response, Costa took a step forward while his hands remained in the same position. The bodyguard stood his ground, but I could see the muscles underneath the material tense just a little, preparing to unleash at the first hint of retaliation. A bullet to the head wasn't something I particularly wanted that afternoon, and I made a mental note not to make any sudden moves. Costa lowered his voice to try and intimi-date me even more.

"I want you to deliver a message for me. I want you to tell your client that she doesn't stand a chance of seeing another sunrise, Mr. Carter. I want you to tell her that." As if needing to amplify his words, he took another step forward, slowly peeled his sunglasses off, and stared me directly in the eyes. "You tell her that for me, Ben Carter."

There's something about a man grieving the death of his parents. It's not anything specific that can be pointed out, and yet I could tell he was hurting, all of his feelings tensed up into a tight ball inside him. His eyes didn't look bloodshot from endless crying, and I doubt he would have shed a tear anyway, especially within view of anybody else. No, this was the kind of man who swallowed his pain and held it within the confines of his soul. It would simmer there until he was ready to unleash it on whoever was unfortunate enough to be in the line of fire.

I could have responded in another way, of course, but with the tension between us balanced on a knife's edge, I didn't want to push my luck. I don't think Costa would have reacted rationally, given what I already knew of the man. Throw in his recent loss, and you had the makings of someone prepared to kill at the drop of a hat...or a wayward comment.

"Innocent until proven guilty, Mr. Costa," I said, refusing to back down completely as he leaned even closer toward me to listen. He turned his ear slightly toward me to show how closely he was listening—yet another attempt to intimidate.

"We know she did it, and that's good enough for me," he hissed through clenched teeth. "You tell her for me. You make sure she gets my message."

He didn't bother waiting for me to respond and turned his back after sliding the sunglasses back onto his face. The bodyguard held his position until his boss was a good number of yards beyond him before he, too, backed away. I watched until they climbed back into their BMW, where the driver sat waiting for them. Just as I knew they would, the car slowly rolled past me, and the window was already down so Costa could eyeball me.

I waited until the car left the parking lot and disappeared from view before I turned back to the jail, considering my next move. If I knew one thing for certain, it was that his threat was real. If he intended to have Katherine Wright killed for the murder of his parents, then it would definitely happen and sooner rather than later. This wasn't a man who held back revenge, not when the fragility of his family had been exposed.

Weakness wasn't something a mobster displayed. It opened up all manner of issues, and the death of his parents showed others that their family was vulnerable. I'd read about gangs descending into years of conflict for such incidents, turning city streets into war zones while fighting for both honor and turf. If Costa felt the slightest hint of someone seeing the death of his parents as a sign of weakness, then he would waste little time to hit back, and that spelled certain doom for my client, a client I still hadn't met.

Bail was my only option to save her. I couldn't leave

the girl in a place where she would be a sitting duck, not after such a direct threat. Men like Riccardo Costa paid big money to be able to extend their reach into inaccessible places like county jails. I had no doubt that a few lowly-paid prison officers would also be on the gang's payroll, not to mention those among their own ranks already serving time inside.

Speaking of time, I knew I'd be pushing it, given the hour of the day, but after hearing the threat firsthand, it was a chance I had to take. I took out my cell phone and sent Grace a message asking her to get me an urgent bail hearing down at the courthouse for that afternoon. I made sure to capitalize URGENT so she understood... well, the urgency of the matter. If I was going to have a chance at saving a young girl from the wrath of a Mafia mobster, then I would first need to get her out of a place bursting at the seams with potential hitmen.

Purchase to keep reading:
www.righthouse.com/trial-by-murder